HIGHLAND LEGACY

B.J. SCOTT

SOUL MATE PUBLISHING

New York

HIGHLAND LEGACY
Copyright©2011
B.J. SCOTT

Cover Design by Rae Monet, Inc.

This book is a work of fiction. The names, characters, places, and incidents are the products of the author's imagination or are used fictitiously. Any resemblance to actual events, business establishments, locales, or persons, living or dead, is entirely coincidental.

All rights reserved. No part of this publication may be reproduced, stored in a retrieval system, or transmitted in any form or by any means (electronic, mechanical, photocopying, recording, or otherwise) without the priority written permission of both the copyright owner and the publisher. The only exception is brief quotations in printed reviews.

The scanning, uploading, and distribution of this book via the Internet or via any other means without the permission of the publisher is illegal and punishable by law. Please purchase only authorized electronic editions, and do not participate in or encourage electronic piracy of copyrighted materials. Your support of the author's rights is appreciated.

Published in the United States of America by
Soul Mate Publishing
P.O. Box 24
Macedon, New York, 14502

ISBN-13: 978-1-61935-101-1

www.SoulMatePublishing.com
The publisher does not have any control over and does not assume any responsibility for author or third-party Web sites or their content.

*In Memory of my stepdaughter, Lisa Babbage.
Taken too soon. Forever in my heart.*

*This book is dedicated to my wonderful husband
and soul mate, Steve.
Without your love, support, and encouragement,
I would never have realized my dreams.*

*To my father, who was always there for me
and inspired me to reach for my goals.
He taught me that anything is possible
if you are willing to work for it.
I love you and miss you more than words can say.*

*To my mom, for her endless love and support —
here is a new book for your collection
of romance novels.*

Acknowledgements

With so many people to thank, it is hard to know where to begin. So I will start with the beginning and thank my parents, family, children, and my husband, Steve, for their never-ending love and support.

I would like to thank Michelle, known to the romance community as Eliza Knight and Michelle Brandon, for taking me under her wing and sharing her knowledge and love for writing. Without your friendship, encouragement, and talent for editing, this book would not be possible.

I want to thank my friends Linda and Kimm for listening to my stories and encouraging me to reach for my dream.

I also want to thank the staff of Soul Mate Publishing and Senior Editor Debby Gilbert for all their work and for giving me this opportunity to share my book.

Finally, I want to thank the romance readers and fellow writers. Without you, there would be no books.

Chapter 1

Dunkeld Scotland, 1306.

Duncan Macmillan's nostrils flared, and his piercing blue eyes narrowed with anger. Judging by the rigidity of his stance, the bulge of his neck veins, and scowl of utter contempt, Cailin had pushed her father beyond his limits. Again.

They'd quarreled often, and each time, he cursed her wild spirit, and temerity, swore fairies stole his real child at birth and left a changeling in her place. An unyielding man, he ruled Clan Macmillan with an iron fist, and made no exceptions. Cailin experienced the force of his wrath on more than one occasion, and bore the physical and emotional scars.

He paced his chamber like a restless animal ready to pounce on its prey. "Laird MacMurray arrives on the morrow and expects to find a cheerful, willing bride. You'll not embarrass me with your obstinacy!"

"Banish me, beat me, or throw me into the pit if you wish, but I will not marry a man I dinna love. Especially a vile, contemptible swine who is almost three times my age." As the rebellious words left her lips, memories of past punishments flooded her mind, but she refused to concede to her father's demands, regardless of the consequences.

"This alliance is important to the clan, and I've given my word." He balled his fist and took a step in her direction.

Cailin crossed her arms over her chest and glared up at him in defiance. "The alliance does not interest you as much as the cattle, land, and chest of gold he has offered for my hand." She took a slow, deep breath for courage, and continued. "My happiness is of no importance to you. Not as long as you can pad your coffers, and increase your holdings. I am nothing more to you than a pawn, property for sale to the highest bidder."

His face flushed red as he stomped toward her with a hand raised in preparation to strike. "Insolent, ungrateful lass, I'll teach you to speak to me with such disrespect. When I'm finished, you'll rue the day you were born."

"I have, for eighteen summers," she snapped back in retaliation. The stinging backhand she received brought her to her knees.

"Husband, please." Before he could deliver another blow, his wife, Catherine, stepped between them, and placed her hand on Duncan's raised arm. "She's your daughter, and you must show more compassion and understanding. I am sure once she has time to get accustomed to the idea, she will do your bidding. Won't you?" She glanced over her shoulder, and gave Cailin a pleading look.

Duncan glared down at his wife. "She's been a wee devil since birth, and it is about time she learned her place. Step out of my way, or you'll learn your place as well." He grasped Catherine by the shoulders, and briskly moved her aside.

Cailin slowly climbed to her feet and wiped the trickle of blood from her lower lip with the back of her hand. "Dinna fash yourself, Catherine, it is a private matter to be settled between my father and me. Not one so easily resolved. Mayhap you should go and rest."

Only two years her senior, Catherine carried in her belly what Cailin prayed would be the son her father had always wanted. If he finally had a male heir, she'd be freed from the burden of blame, guilt, and obligation that had plagued her entire life.

Duncan's body shook as he pointed his finger in his daughter's direction. "Do you see what I mean? Even when someone tries to help her, she shows no appreciation. Not a day goes by I have not wished she had—"

"Go ahead, Father. Admit you wish me dead instead of my twin brother and that you blame me for my mother's death." Toe to toe, she stood in front of him. She swallowed hard past the lump in her throat and fought back tears. "No matter what I accomplish, my efforts will never be good enough. If I could bring my mother back from the dead, I would gladly trade my life for hers. I wish I had been born a lad, and not a lass, but—"

"Aye, instead of a son, I've been cursed with a headstrong daughter who is the bane of my existence. I am surprised any man would ask to marry the likes of you. But on the morrow, you will wed Laird MacMurray."

His cruel words cut straight to the core, but she'd not give him the satisfaction of knowing he'd wounded her again. "He marries because he needs a mother for his nine unruly bairns, and someone to bear him more. They say he killed his last wife when he found out she could no longer breed." The thought of bedding Graham MacMurray made her skin crawl. "Mayhap he lusts after the land and wealth I shall inherit should anything happen to you. As your heir, I will be a wealthy woman in the event of your death."

Would she ever know if a man wanted to marry her for love, or would she always wonder if greed motivated her suitors? Then again, if all men were like her father, prayed for sons, cared only for wealth and power, she'd rather take the vows and spend the rest of her life at a convent. She'd not be like her mother and marry out of obligation or duty to her clan. Nor would she risk bringing a daughter into this world, only to have her shunned by her father and bartered for with less regard than a hog or a steer. No, she'd not take Laird MacMurray as her husband. Mayhap, she'd never marry.

"Excuse me, my lord." The door opened and a servant stepped into Duncan's chamber.

Duncan spun around and scowled at the young man. "Ian, what is the meaning of this interruption?"

"For—forgive me, my lord, but a messenger comes from the Clan MacMurray. He bears a gift for lady Cailin." With his head bowed and his eyes fixed on the floor, Ian moved in her direction and held out a small wooden box. "His laird has been unavoidably detained, and will not arrive for a week or more."

"Nay!" Cailin threw her hands up in protest, shook her head, and backed away. "Tell him I dinna want his gift."

Duncan snatched the box and opened the hinged lid. From a bed of lamb's wool, he plucked a ruby and emerald encrusted brooch with the MacMurray Clan crest. After he'd carefully examined the pin, he thrust his hand forward. "You'll not insult your betrothed by refusing his fine gift. This must be worth a fortune."

"I dinna care if he is insulted. There will be no wedding. When I marry, it will be to a man I love." She turned to face Ian. "Send the brooch back, and have the messenger inform his laird I'll not be bought."

Duncan pinched the bridge of his nose and shook his head. "Love has nothing to do with marriage. The sooner you put aside these foolish notions the better." He took a step closer, his hands fisted at his sides. "You will do as I say."

"What should I tell the messenger?" Ian shrugged and glanced from Cailin to Duncan.

"Tell him my daughter thanks his laird for the fine gift and anxiously awaits his arrival. And while you're below, tell Cook to send a tray to my solar. I'll not be down to break my fast this morning."

Using her father's momentary distraction as an

opportunity to put an end to their futile discussion, Cailin inched toward the door, turned on her heels, and fled his chambers.

"Damnation lass! We're not finished with this matter. You'll do as you're told, or I'll—" Duncan called after her, but she slammed the large oak door, muffling the rest of his tirade.

She raced down the long hallway. Surprised, and relieved, that he did not give chase, she paused at the top of the stairs. The daughter of one of Scotland's most powerful lairds, she knew a day would come when he'd demand she marry, but she'd never believed he'd choose a man she found appalling in every way. Despite her lot in life, she'd always fantasized of a marriage based on passion, and mutual respect. She prayed nightly for a man who would adore her and rescue her from a life of servitude and duty.

Devastatingly handsome, in a rugged sort of way, he'd have the finely honed body of a Norse god, the strength and bravado of a warrior, yet the kindness and gentle heart of a bard. "Be he rich or poor, warrior or poet, I will marry a man I love, or I'll not wed at all. With that oath on her lips, she bolted down the stone steps.

Despite the whispers and wayward glances of the servants, Cailin didn't stop running until she'd reached the bailey. Her only option was to run away. The thought of leaving her home and all she held dear, of venturing out into the world alone, frightened her, but she had no choice. Her father would never yield on this matter, and neither would she.

The messenger's arrival provided the perfect opportunity to escape her father's ire, but to get beyond the castle walls unchallenged could prove more difficult. If Duncan got wind of her intent, he'd lock her in her chamber until the dreadful day her betrothed arrived, but she had to try.

With Scotland in a state of constant turmoil and the

high risk of running into thieves, scoundrels, or worse, English soldiers, she seldom left the castle without her nurse and an armed escort. Guilt tugged at her heart when she thought about Eildth, the only mother she'd ever known. She hated the idea of leaving her behind, and she would miss her nursemaid terribly. But marriage to Laird MacMurray would be a fate far worse than death. Once she'd settled in her new home, she'd send word and let her nurse know she was safe.

The sound of metal clanging against metal and men shouting brought her back to the task at hand. Most of her father's men were busy training in the lists, leaving only a few to safeguard the parapets. The servants and crofters milling about the bailey tended to their business and paid her no mind. Her heart pounded like a battering ram against her chest, but she remained focused on her destination. With her head held high, she sauntered across the inner courtyard as if she didn't have a care in the world—a feat much easier said than done. As she neared the postern gate, freedom, she realized her worst fear. A guard rounded the corner of the castle, heading in her direction.

"Good day, m'lady."

"It is a lovely day, Miles." *Can he hear my heart pounding? Can he sense I am up to something?* She fisted her hands in her skirt to keep them from trembling and stepped aside so he could pass.

With a curt nod, he continued on his way and, to her great relief, did not look back. As soon as he was out of sight, she slipped through the gate.

There was no time to waste. She might be free, but to tarry so close to the castle would not be prudent. The question was where to go and how to get there. She had no time to plan beyond the present moment. The future was fraught with danger and uncertainty.

Her lady's maid lived in a small croft at the edge of the village. In public, the girl showed the proper respect to her mistress. But behind closed doors, and despite the difference in their social status, they shared their hopes, and dreams. They were friends—creating yet another bone of contention between her and her father. In his opinion, the daughter of the laird did not fraternize with the servants. But Cailin never let that stop her, and she cherished the time they spent together. Surely if she explained why she had to leave Dunkeld, Myrna would help her gather the supplies she needed for the arduous journey ahead. She thought about asking her friend to accompany her, but she would not do anything that might put her in danger.

Myrna would not be home until dusk, so Cailin opted to wait in her secret place, a small, secluded cove, where the River Tay joined the loch. She made her way along the familiar forest trails, allowing the earthy scent of pine, spring blossoms, moss, and leaves to fill her senses. A raven called in the distance, and the comforting sound of water rushing over rocks grew louder with each step. She quickened her pace.

Certain she was alone, Cailin stepped free of the forest's protective cover, and paused, committing the scenery to memory. She smiled when she spied a red doe and her fawn grazing on tender shoots of grass. A hawk circled overhead before it swooped down to pluck a mouse from the field. Fragrant heather, and assorted wildflowers, covered the moors as far as the eye could see. She'd miss the beauty and tranquility the riverbank offered.

Cailin removed her slippers, then dipped her toes into the water. She shivered, and drew her foot away. The spring air might be mild, but the river still held winter's chill. Squatting down, she used her hand to scoop up the sparkling liquid, and took a drink. She closed her eyes, savoring the cool, fresh taste passing over her tongue. Her stomach growled. She hadn't eaten in over twelve hours, and wished she had helped herself to some cheese and bread before going to see her father. A few feet from where she stood, a bush bursting with ripe berries beckoned. They would suffice until she could meet with Myrna, and ask her to gather some supplies from the castle stores. She plucked a handful of crimson morsels, and popped one into her mouth.

"Well, what have we here?"

The gruff English accent sent a shiver of trepidation slithering down her spine. Her eyes darted in all directions as she searched for the source of the comment, and a subsequent means of escape. She turned to run, but bumped into an English Officer, his mouth drawn into a sinister grin.

Could this day get any worse?

The vile man grabbed the crotch of his trews, pumped his hips in a lewd manner, and laughed. "You appear to have lost your way, my pretty little wench. Perhaps I can be of assistance." He tipped the clay jug he carried to his lips, and after taking a long, slow drink, he tossed it aside, then closed the gap between them. "Come here and give me a kiss."

Show no fear.

She squared her shoulders, and tried to appear calm, and in control—a far cry from the panic squeezing her chest and causing her stomach to churn. "You are drunk, and out of line. My father is the Macmillan, and he will see you—"

"Enough talk. My ballocks are aching, and I know the cure. I haven't had a Scottish whore in at least a week." He lunged forward, caught her around the waist, and pulled her against his chest. "What say you and I have a little bit of fun? When I've had my fill of you, my friend Thomas can have a turn." He shot a glance in the direction of the woods.

When a second scoundrel stepped into the clearing, she was certain all color had drained from her face. She might have a chance against one man, albeit a slim one, but two men narrowed her odds of escape to nil. Yet she refused to surrender her innocence without a fight.

"You're forgetting the wench you had a few days ago,

when we raided the crofter's cabin near Glasgow." Thomas stood a few feet away with his hands on his hips. "Pity you had to slit her throat before I got a chance to have her."

"The ugly wench was old enough to be my mum. Besides, she would not stop screaming. This one is more to my liking." Her captor tightened his grip, and slid his hand along the swell of her breasts. "Once I'm finished with her, I promise to let you have a go."

"Why do you always get to go first?"

"Because I outrank you," the first man replied as he dipped his head and nipped her neck. When she clawed at his face and tried to break free, he grabbed her wrist, twisting her arm behind her back.

"She's a wild one, Harry. You've got your hands full." Thomas laughed. "Maybe having you take some of the fight out of her isn't such a bad idea."

"Defy me again, and I'll slit your throat. It makes no difference to me if you are dead or alive when I breed you." Harry shoved her to the ground, trapped her wrists above her head with one hand, and hiked up her skirt with the other. "Lovely," he groaned as he slid his hand up her inner thigh, then cupped her most intimate place. "I'm going to enjoy every inch of you." Wasting no time, he tugged at the laces of his trews and quickly covered her with his body.

She gasped for air. She couldn't breathe or move. He had to outweigh her by at least one hundred pounds. The proof of his arousal dug into her hip while his groping hands roamed her breasts. The sound of fabric tearing was followed by a rush of cold air on her shoulder.

"Let me go—"

His mouth crashed down on hers, smothering her protest. She gagged when he tried to pry her lips apart with his tongue, and cringed at his harsh, brutal kiss. He took without asking, and ravaged without mercy. His touch made her skin crawl, and the smell of ale, tobacco, unwashed flesh, and rotting teeth sickened her stomach. Her only desire was to escape from the vile man, and to scrub her body clean of his stench. In an effort to fight back, she bit down on his lower lip. When he reared back, crying out in pain, she brought up her knee and caught him square in the groin. But the blow didn't have the force she'd hoped for, only serving to rile him more.

"Bitch! I'll teach you to flaunt yourself like a wicked siren, and then deny me."

A balled fist connected with her jaw, followed by another. She saw stars, and nausea twisted her belly.

"You'll not be teaching anyone a lesson, if I have anything to say about the matter."

Someone grabbed her assailant by the shoulders and dragged him to his feet. No longer pinned to the ground by his crushing weight, Cailin scrambled to her feet, and started running toward the forest. She heard the men shouting and the sound of their swords connecting, but didn't pause to look back.

She raced along the path, ignoring the small branches as they swiped her cheeks, and ducked beneath the larger ones. Rocks and forest debris bit into the tender flesh of her bare feet, but she did not slow her pace. Cailin choked back a painful sob, summoned her last dregs of courage, and forged ahead. Deprived of oxygen, her lungs burned as if on fire. Her muscles cramped and her legs grew heavier with every step, but as long as there was a breath left in her body, as long as there was a chance of escape, she refused to give up.

The crunch of leaves beneath a thunderous footfall alerted her to the fact that the English soldiers who had tried to rape her were only a few paces behind, and closing in fast.

Don't think. Run!

When she believed she could go no farther, the sight of the watchtower, and belfry of the village kirk brought a glimmer of hope. The familiar smell of cook fires burning lifted her spirits, the rhythmic din of the smithy's hammer like music to her ears. If she could go a few more yards and climb a small embankment, she'd be safe. But her foot caught in a tangle of roots, and before she could steady herself, she lay sprawled in the dirt, the air forced from her lungs when her chest hit the ground.

The deafening roar of her pounding heart drowned out all other sounds. She clawed at a tree stump, tried to stand, but she'd run out of time. A large hand clamped down on her shoulder, holding her in place. Another hand covered her mouth and stifled her cry for help. She struck out wildly, trying to fight back, but her fists collided with a solid wall of unyielding muscle.

"Dinna fight me, lass, I mean you no harm. I'll remove my hand, and let you up if you promise not to scream. Do you give me your word?" When she stopped struggling and nodded, his hand slid from her mouth, allowing her to draw in a gulp of air. In one swift move, he flipped her to her back and squatted beside her. "You scurry like a rabbit, and running you to ground was a most difficult task."

Her eyes widened, searching those of the man hovering above her. At least six-foot-two, his honed-to-perfection body, a solid wall of muscle beneath a taut saffron shirt, was an obvious testament to years of training, discipline, and hard work. With a straight aristocratic nose, high prominent cheekbones, full lips, and a strong square chin—covered with a day's worth of dark stubble—his features left her awestruck. Brown eyes, as dark as night, fierce, yet filled with mystery and passion, held her gaze. A thick mane, the color of a raven's wing, hung loose about his shoulders.

She gave her head a shake. This stranger could be her savior—the man who'd intervened on the riverbank, and had helped to facilitate her escape—or he could be another bastard, waiting his turn to ravage her body. The attack had happened so fast, and she didn't get a good look at the man who had come to her aid. The rich Scottish burr in his voice indicated he was not an Englishman like her attackers, but she didn't plan to find out if he was with them.

The sun filtered through the trees and caught a glint of steel. Her attention drawn to the dirk hanging at his side, she swallowed hard past the lump in her throat, uncertain if she could slay a man in cold blood. Did she have the strength, and courage, to plunge the blade into his heart? She'd have one chance, and if she failed, he'd no doubt use the same weapon to slit her throat.

The choice was clear. If she didn't try, she'd be at his mercy. Her fingers wrapped around the leather-bound hilt, and before he guessed her intent, she slid the dagger from its sheath. Bent on survival, she asked God's forgiveness, and struck out with all the force she could muster.

Chapter 2

He easily dodged the ill-placed blow, grasped her arm mid-air, and twisted her wrist sharply to the right. "Saint's teeth, are you daft, or do you have a death wish? I mean you no harm."

She winced in pain, but refused to cry out. No match for his strength, her fingers unfurled, and she dropped the dagger in the dirt. She struggled, but her attempt to wrench free of his grasp resulted in a tighter grip. "Let me go, you blackguard! My father will see you drawn and quartered if you harm me. If you so much as—"

"Calm yourself. Unless you wish to wait for another rutting English bastard who is looking to dip his rod into a Scottish honey pot, I intend to help you up and see you home safely."

"How dare you speak to me in such a bawdy manner? You are obviously not a man of class or breeding. A gentleman would not speak to a lady of such things."

"I only mean to impress upon you how close you came to losing your innocence, mayhap your life. You're lucky I rode by when I did." A cocky grin tugged at his lips. "Besides, I never claimed to be a gentleman. Now, if you're finished acting like a woman possessed, let me help you up." Before she could reply, he pulled her into a sitting position and released her arm. "You denied an English officer's advances. The arrogant bastards have been known to hang a Scottish lass for a lot less."

She rubbed her aching wrist and narrowed her eyes in anger. "I was doing fine on my own and dinna need your assistance."

"I must admit, you did seem to have everything under control when I arrived." He rocked back on his heels and chuckled. "You actually had the buggers shaking in their boots."

She raised her chin, and glared up at him. "A few more minutes, and I would have taught the scoundrel a lesson and made my escape."

"Believe what you will, but if I dinna hear you cry out, there is no telling what might have happened. Once they'd had their fill, I have no doubt they'd have slit your throat." His smile faded, and a serious look crossed his face. "A dead woman tells no tales."

Her eyes flashed in the direction of the river. "We may have escaped, but the English are not known to give up so easily. They could come along at any time."

"The men who attacked you will not give chase." He patted the sword at his side.

Blood stained the polished metal. Her mouth went dry, and an irrepressible tremor laced her voice when she spoke. "You killed them?" She did not condone violence, yet found some measure of comfort in the belief her assailants might be dead. She quickly crossed herself and silently begged the Almighty's forgiveness.

"One of the fools refused to surrender his weapon and charged at me like a wild boar. We battled, and the blade found its mark. He lies on yonder bank." He pointed in the direction of the river. "Once I'd dealt with one rogue, the other attacked me from behind. He proved easier to subdue, and I tied him to a tree. He lives, but I'm afraid he'll have a nasty headache once he awakens."

Her own head started to pound. She rubbed her temples. "When the English find out what has happened, you'll be hanged."

"The man dinna see my face, and even if he did, I

fear not for myself. Once you're safe at the keep with your family, I'll take my leave. With any luck, I'll be long gone before they find them, and no one will link me to the deed."

Returning to the keep was the last thing she wanted to do. Her father would be furious and punish her when he found out she'd left without his permission. She could hear the horrible crack of the whip, and could feel the familiar sting of welts on her back. Determined to force down the bile that rose in her throat, she swallowed hard and stiffened her spine. *Physical wounds will heal, but marriage to Graham MacMurray would be far worse torture.*

After what she'd been through this day, it was blatantly clear a woman traveling alone was an easy target for rogues and scoundrels. Cailin drew her knees up to her chest, encircled them with her arms, and lowered her head. She closed her eyes and rocked back and forth. *This cannot be happening. Please let me wake and put an end to this nightmare."* When she opened her eyes, he hovered over her, an expression of concern on his face.

"Are you all right, lass?" He stroked her cheek.

She shied from his touch. "I'm fine." She nibbled on her lower lip, tasting blood. Judging by the pain in her right cheek and jaw, she'd have bruises where the soldier struck her about the face. She clutched at the tattered gown, torn at the shoulder during the scuffle. She drew the edges closed in an attempt to cover the exposed swell of her breast. As if suddenly encased in ice, her teeth began to chatter and her body trembled.

"You're not a good liar. Despite what you claim, you're pale and trembling." He uncapped the wineskin at his side, brought it to her lips, and demanded she drink.

She sputtered, then shoved his hand away. The amber liquid spilled from her mouth and ran down her chin. "What foul poison do you give me?"

"*Uisge-beatha.*"

"Whisky? I have no taste for spirits." She shook her head, pursing her lips when he tried to offer her more.

"What you like does not interest me. What's good for you does." Despite her protest, he held her steady and brought the wineskin to her lips again.

The whisky stung the cut on her lip, burning her throat, yet warming her belly.

"That's a good lass, drink," he crooned. After lowering the wineskin, he raised her chin. With a gentle sweep of his thumb, he wiped away the mix of blood and whisky from her lower lip. "Does the cut hurt?"

"Not overmuch." His concern appeared genuine, but when she tried to look away, his grip held firm.

"Did the rogue harm you anywhere else?" Dark eyes narrowed as his scrutiny shifted to her cheek, where she no doubt sported bruises, then back to the shoulder of her torn gown.

"Nay." She shook her head.

"Then we must be grateful for wee miracles. These are dangerous times. Why were you beyond the castle walls without an escort?"

"On a bonny day, I like to take walks along the River Tay. When the weather is warm, I swim in the loch. The spot is very private, and no one has ever bothered me before today." She wasn't about to tell him of her plans to run away.

His brow furrowed. "Do you make a habit of wandering about the woods unescorted? I cannot believe your father permits such a thing."

"He does not know I go alone. My nur-" Not wanting to appear a child, she quickly corrected herself. "My maid usually accompanies me. However, Eilidh wasn't feeling well today, and I dinna want to drag her away from the keep. I only planned to be gone for a short while," she lied.

He listened without comment, but as she recounted the details of the attack, the glower on his face relayed his disapproval of her actions. Despite her effort to hold them back, tears slid down her cheek.

With a gentle brush of his hand, he wiped away the tears. This time, she didn't pull away. His voice mellowed. "I'm glad I came along when I did. What's your name?"

"Cailin Macmillan."

His expression hardened, and a frown creased his brow. "*Cailean?*" he muttered her name aloud in Gaelic. "Your parents gave you a name that means bairn or lad?"

She squared her shoulders, raised her chin, and looked him in the eye. "It is a serviceable name and not a common one to be sure."

Most men preferred their women demure and complacent, but Connor found women with sass and tenacity more appealing. "There is nothing common about you, Lady Cailin." The words slipped out before he could stop them.

Huge jade eyes, brimming with unshed tears, triggered an unwelcome tightness in his chest, and a sudden need to pull her into his arms, to offer comfort. Drawn by a force he found difficult to ignore, Connor fought the urge to dip his head, and taste her pouty lips.

He cursed beneath his breath. This was not the time or place to lose his head over a woman. He had no room in his life for anyone or anything but the cause. In an effort to regain his composure, he cleared his throat and redirected the conversation. "You were never close to your father?"

"Nay. He wishes I had died, and not my twin brother. He has never forgiven me for being born first."

Stunned by her blunt words, he didn't know how to respond. He'd idolized his own father, and couldn't imagine a man not cherishing his child, be the wee one a daughter or a son.

"My father thinks me obstinate, willful, and headstrong." A winsome smile tugged at the corner of her lips. "Mayhap he is right to some extent."

She had a smile that could melt a man's heart, and make him jump through fire just to see it. A surge of lust and desire fired his blood—the last thing he expected or needed. He had no room in his life for a woman. A fierce warrior and champion of the Scottish bid for independence, he led his men into battle with his emotions held tightly in check. Prepared to die for the cause, he'd vowed never to fall in love, never to leave behind a wife and children to mourn him.

Not that he denied himself the pleasures of the flesh. He'd been known to bed many a lass, and none complained about his skill beneath the blankets. However, they knew love and commitment would never enter into the picture. In his opinion, love was a useless emotion, a myth. Love made men weak, and only led to heartbreak, anger, and sorrow. He had no use for love, and pledged never to allow himself to fall victim to Cupid's arrow.

"I have not seen you in the village before today." She hesitated. "I'm afraid, sir, you have me at a disadvantage. You know who I am, but I dinna know your name."

"Connor Fraser. My castle is in Beauly, a wee town near Inverness."

"You are far from home. Your wife and children must miss you very much."

"I'm not married. I have no desire to take a wife, and have no room in my life for a family." He answered more abruptly than he'd planned, but given the way his groin stirred, he wanted to make things clear from the start—for both their sakes.

"What brought you to Dunkeld?"

"I had business in Perth on behalf of Robert the Bruce. I was riding home when I heard you call for help."

"So, you're a Highlander, and a patriot."

"Aye, the Frasers have long fought for—" A noise in the bushes caught his attention, and his head snapped around in the direction of the commotion. He studied the area and seeing no one, held out his hand in her direction. "Let me help you to stand. We've wasted enough time on idle chatter and dare not tarry any longer. While the two men who attacked you pose no threat, there is an English garrison camped not far from here, and a patrol could come along at any moment. I'll escort you home, where they can tend to your needs, and then take my leave. I was supposed to meet someone at the Dunkeld Inn this morning, and am already late."

"Nay!" She shook her head and scooted back, widening the gap between them. She glanced down at her torn clothing. "I cannot go home like this. What will my father say?"

"With English soldiers milling about, the Macmillan must be daft to let you out of his sight unescorted. If you were my daughter and had left the keep alone, I'd take you over my knee and paddle your arse."

A*nd a lovely arse you have.* He struggled to squelch his lascivious thoughts, but a man would have to be blind, or a eunuch, not to notice her luscious figure and captivating beauty.

Her posture stiffened and she glared up at him. "I am not a bairn, and dinna need someone to tell me when, and where, I can go. I celebrated my saint's day a fortnight ago. I've seen eight and ten summers, and am more than auld enough to marry and to make my own decisions," she replied proudly.

True, she'd already reached an age when most young women were married and heavy with child, but compared to his six and twenty summers, she was still a bairn, or so he tried to tell himself. Despite his effort to subdue his lustful thoughts, the defiant look in her eyes and proud jut of her chin made him smile.

Cailin spoke the truth. She was not a child. Even at the tender age of eighteen, she had the body of a goddess. Soft wine colored wool clung to her body like a second skin. Cut low at the bodice, her simple formfitting gown accentuated a slender figure, high round breasts, and womanly curves that would drive any man wild with desire. Like fine porcelain, her skin was flawless—aside, from the sprinkling of freckles dusting her high, elegant cheekbones to the bridge of her delicately upturned nose.

She wore her waist-length auburn hair—the color of an autumn sunset—tightly plaited and wrapped with thin strips of leather. Several stray strands bounced about her shoulders, while a few wavy locks framed her heart-shaped face. Freed, he was certain her tresses would flow like a river of silk down the center of her back.

He plucked a dry leaf from her hair, and then another. He longed to run his fingers through her glorious mane. *Does the soft nest of curls at the apex of her thighs match the splendor of that on her head?* He grew hard, the ache in his groin intensifying to the point of pain. The thought of tasting her luscious lips, sampling her ripe round breasts, and discovering the color of the hair that guarded her nether region spurred a frenzy of lust and desire unlike anything he had ever known.

He bit back a curse and tried to banish the vision of her soft supple body moving restlessly beneath him, his aching shaft buried to the hilt in the velvet warmth of her hot moist sheath, of her moaning with pleasure as he took her in long, slow strokes. He cursed again. If he did not stop this woolgathering, he would lose control and take her there, and now. *You're a grown man and not a randy lad. Robert awaits your return. All of Scotland is counting on you.*

"To wander the woods unprotected is dangerous folly. You should be more careful."

"I am a woman grown and dinna need your advice."

"That remains to be seen." Before she could refuse him again, he grasped her hand, stunned when a strong jolt of energy surged between them. Judging by her sharp intake of breath, and the look of surprise on her face, she felt it, too. He quickly collected himself and helped her to her feet. "Come, I will see you home before someone finds the soldiers." The sooner he returned her to her father's keep and put temptation behind him, the better.

"I cannot go home."

Ignoring her protest, he brought his fingers to his lips and whistled. A massive black destrier burst through the trees and halted in the middle of the path. With his head raised and nostrils flared, the warhorse pawed at the ground. Connor whistled again, and the stallion obediently trotted over and nudged his arm.

"A friend of yours?" she asked drolly.

"I've owned Thor since he was a yearling." He reached into the canvas sack on the back of his saddle, pulled out a length of plaid, and draped the woolen fabric about her head and shoulders. "Your hair is beautiful, and I'm sure the envy of every lass in the village. While it is a shame to cover it, we must do what we can to hide your identity. Keep your head down and hopefully no one will recognize you." From a pouch on his belt, he tugged out her slippers, and handed them to her. "Best you put these on and make haste."

"Where did you find them?"

"They were on the riverbank, and I thought you might have need of them."

Cailin quickly slid her feet into the slippers. "Thank you."

"Best we leave. A patrol could come along at any minute." He didn't give her time to argue. His hands slid around her waist and lifted her onto Thor's back. Once she was seated, he mounted behind her.

Her head whipped around so she faced him. "It is

scandalous for a maiden to ride this close to a man if he is not her husband."

He didn't reply—he couldn't speak. Instead, he shifted in the saddle behind her and stifled a groan. Given the way his body reacted to the softness of her bottom pressed against his aching groin, the tantalizing fragrance of her hair—a subtle mix of heather, lavender soap, and sunshine—this was going to be a long ride. A sharp kick of his boot prompted Thor to lunge forward.

They traveled the short distance in silence. When they came to a halt in a small copse of trees near the postern gate of *Mhaolain Castle,* Cailin turned to face him. "Mayhap, I should go the rest of the way alone. I know my way about the bailey and when the guards make their rounds. To have you with me would surely attract attention."

"You're probably right. Your father might not understand why we are alone together, and I dinna want to damage your reputation. Once you're safely inside, I'll take my leave." He slid from the horse and offered her his hand.

She couldn't bring herself to move. With her head bowed, and eyes downcast, she toyed with the corner of the plaid he'd wrapped around her shoulders. A strange ache gnawed at the pit of her stomach, and an insidious sadness crept over her. This was madness, she didn't even know the man, but she wanted him to stay. Better yet, she wished he would take her with him. She silently prayed he would carry her away from Dunkeld forever.

"Are you certain you will be all right?" He wrapped his hands around her waist and lifted her from the saddle.

His touch sizzled, slicing through her like a bolt of lightning, igniting her very core. Erotic sparks erupted from within and flew in every direction. When her feet touched the ground, she slowly raised her eyes, and her gaze locked with his. "Aye. I will never forget your kindness."

Connor leaned closer. "Cailin," he muttered her name on a shuddering breath, and his mouth captured hers.

The way her name rolled off his tongue gave her gooseflesh. At first, the kiss was tender, almost chaste. Languorously, his tongue teased the seam of her lips, willing her to open to his sweet invasion. To give in to desire was wrong, yet she offered no resistance when his arms enveloped her, and he pulled her into his embrace.

Her fingers splayed across the broad span of his chest, and she felt his heart quicken beneath her touch. Her mouth softened, and her lips parted. Timidly, allowing the tip of her tongue to sample his, she tasted his passion and desire. When he engulfed her in his arms and kissed her senseless, she found herself wanting more—more of this—more of him.

Foreign, wanton thoughts, for which she would surely burn in Hell, flooded her mind. Yet, an inner voice told her these newly awakened feelings were the most natural thing in the world. She had been raised to believe it disgraceful, and evil, for a lady to crave a man's touch. But they couldn't possibly mean this. How could such a glorious thing be sinful, yet feel so amazing?

Huddled securely in his arms, she closed her eyes and let his wild, woodsy masculine fragrance fill her senses. Like an aphrodisiac, it caused her blood to heat and every nerve in her body to tighten, awakening sensations she never knew existed.

Connor deepened the kiss, and his tongue swept past her teeth to plunder her mouth. Like a starving man, he feasted on her lips. His kiss hungry, greedy, yet surprisingly gentle. He swallowed her tiny whimpers of pleasure, and tightened his embrace. With one hand anchored at the nape of her neck, he held her lips against his own, while the other hand explored the dip of her waist, and then settled on her bottom. When he pulled her into the hollow of his thighs, his rock hard shaft pressed against her belly. Pliant in his arms, they fit perfectly—as if he had been born to hold her like this. She let her head fall back, and his mouth slid from hers, leaving a hot trail of kisses along her neck.

"You taste like heaven." A low groan escaped his lips when he dropped his hands to his sides and took a step back. "Forgive me for taking such liberties."

She sucked in a sharp breath, and then exhaled slowly. To continue on this path would be a mistake. A proper lady would never behave in such a willful way, but the loss of physical contact caused her heart to clench.

She stumbled backward until her spine rested against the curtain wall. Speechless, she brought her finger to her mouth, gently tracing where his lips had been. Today had been one of revelations and metamorphosis. She had gone from a child to a woman in the space of a few hours. Two men had pressed their lips to hers, yet the same act had drawn two completely different reactions.

The soldier's revolting kiss and lewd intent had made her skin crawl, while Connor's kisses fueled her passion and desire. Freshened with mint and fennel, his breath was sweet, hot, and moist against her lips. He kissed her gently, reverently, and when it became possessive, and all consuming, she had no wish to pull away, or to fight the swell of emotion rising from her very core. While his strong hands caressed, his sensual mouth explored and enticed. She wanted to fall to her knees and pray the moment would never end.

Still bewildered by the power of his kiss, Cailin stood motionless, staring into Connor's heavy-lidded, passion-filled eyes. She blinked several times, then lowered her gaze. "Thank you for your help, m'lord, but you should be on your way."

He nodded, and moved aside, but as she stepped forward, she swayed toward him. When he grasped her waist to hold her steady, she braced her hands on his chest. His heart thundered beneath her fingertips, as if clawing to get out. Yet she dare not look up at him, lest she swoon again. "It appears I'm once more in your debt. You can release me now."

His hands fell to his sides, and he gave her room to pass. When she reached the gate, she turned and smiled. "I am grateful for all your help. I'll never forget you or your..." She hesitated, again bringing her fingers to her lips. Unable to continue, she slipped inside.

Chapter 3

Cloaked by the shadows of the curtain wall, Cailin crouched behind some bushes and waited for the sentry to pass. She'd memorized the routes used to patrol the castle grounds and when the guards made their rounds...or so she thought. He was early. Something was amiss.

Her breath caught when he stopped and stared in the direction of the postern gate. Afraid to move a muscle, lest she be discovered, she nibbled on her lower lip and willed him to leave. Her heart raced, and beads of perspiration collected on her brow and in the valley between her breasts. While only a few feet away, the keep's tower seemed like miles. Minutes felt like an eternity. When he finally moved on, she blew out a ragged sigh and offered up a silent prayer of thanks.

With the coast now cleared, she gathered up her skirts, made a dash for the rear of the castle, and entered a large storage room. Relieved to be alone, she wasted no time and moved to the opposite side of the room. She opened the door a crack and peered into the kitchen across the hall. There, servants bustled about, preparing for the noonday meal, far too busy to pay her any mind.

What now? Should I risk going to my solar on the above floor to change, or would I be wiser to slip into the chapel at the end of the hall? If they find me there, I'll tell them I have spent the morning in prayer. Heaven only knows I need to pray. To pray my father does not find out I left the castle unattended, that the English do not link Connor or I to the soldier's death. I still must leave before Laird MacMurray arrives, but first, I will need a better plan. A woman traveling alone is an easy target.

She glanced down at her disheveled appearance and soiled gown. The garment had seen better days and the plaid she wore about her shoulders belonged to another clan. Someone would surely notice. Left with no choice but to go to her chamber to change her clothes, she took a deep breath for courage and prepared to step into the hall. She eased the door open, but quickly closed it again when she heard the voices of her nurse Eilidh and her father's steward, Drummond, coming toward her. The louder their voices got, the faster her heart pounded.

"Where has the lass gotten to? The laird was furious when he demanded I bring her to him, and I told him she was not in her chamber. I wish she'd not antagonize him. As his steward, I must listen to him rant. As her nurse, you need to offer counsel on her unacceptable behavior."

A crotchety old man of at least three score, Drummond always sided with her father. Cailin could picture him waving his bony finger in front of Eilidh's nose. If her nurse had been alone, she might have revealed herself, asked for her advice and help. But Drummond would take great pleasure in presenting her to her father for punishment.

"True, she has always been a spirited lass, but like her mother, she has a good heart. Sadly, she is no longer a bairn and has a mind of her own." Eilidh clucked her tongue the way she did when Cailin had done something she did not approve of. "However, it is not like her to wander beyond the castle walls without an escort. You cannot possibly believe she is capable of murder?"

"The decision is not mine to make. The English commander claims to have a witness to the deed and has vowed to leave no stone unturned until he finds the lass. He means to see justice served and does not strike me as the kind of man who gives up easily," Drummond answered.

"Have you searched everywhere? The longer it takes for us to find her, the harder it will be to prove her innocence."

"Aye, we have scoured every inch of the castle from top to bottom."

"We must keep looking. This place is crawling with the Saxon buggers. If what they claim is true, I fear not even her father will be able to help her." Concern resonated in Eilidh's voice.

How had the English found out her identity so quickly? The attack flashed before her mind's eye. *My father is the Macmillan and laird of this land.* She had her answer, and her father's prophecy was about to come true. Her wild spirit and temerity would prove to be her demise. In her attempt to appear brave, and to stave off the attack, she'd foolishly told her assailants who she was.

She could not stay in the castle and risk being caught. Nor would she betray Connor to absolve herself. She had to sneak out again, but how? To escape when English soldiers swarmed the keep would be nearly impossible. With her ear pressed against the door, she listened as Eildth and Drummond continued on their way. When she no longer heard their retreating footsteps, she opened the door wide enough to see into the hall.

Myrna stood near the door of the kitchen. Cailin softly cleared her throat. When the maid glanced in her direction, she brought a finger to her lips and motioned with a wave of her hand for the girl to come to her. She closed the door and stepped into the shadows. When it opened with a creak, she held her breath in anticipation.

An expression of concern crossed Myra's face as she stepped into the storage room and quickly closed the door. "Och, m'lady, you are in great danger and must flee. If the English find you, they'll arrest you and see you hanged for murder. The commander of the garrison, Lord Borden, claims you killed his brother."

Cailin gasped and clutched a shaky hand to her throat. "Lord Borden, are you certain?"

"Aye, I was in the great hall when he arrived and was announced to your father. Do you know him?"

An icy shiver ran down Cailin's spine. She knew the man all too well, and had hoped never to see him again. "He visited the keep a few years ago, on king's business. When no one was around to witness, he made improper advances. He held me against my will, kissed me, and told me it was his right as an English lord to be my first lover."

Myrna's eyes widened and her mouth dropped open. "What did you do?"

"I fought him, scratched his face, and then ran as fast as my legs would carry me. He left that same day, and I prayed I would never lay eyes on him again."

"You dinna mentioned this to anyone?"

"I had just turned five and ten summers. My father hardly acknowledged my existence, and I am sure Lord Borden would have called me a liar." She shifted her weight from one foot to the other. It had been three summers, but it seemed like yesterday. "He never told my father what happened, but vowed I would someday pay for my defiance." She wrung her hands and began to pace. "Now he accuses me of murdering his brother. I fear he has finally found his means of revenge."

Myrna threw her arms around her mistress's shoulders, pulled her into a tight embrace, and then held her at arm's length. "Tell me you dinna kill his brother," she pleaded. "I could not bear to think of you at the mercy of those Saxon swine. Surely if you tell your father what happened in the past, he will not stand for this."

Cailin pressed two fingers to her friend's lips. "Myrna, please, if you prattle on, someone will overhear. I dinna kill anyone, but Lord Borden would never believe me. The fact that the soldiers meant to rape and murder me will not matter. He'll be more interested in retribution for the past than the truth."

"Did they harm you? Your gown is torn and your cheek is bruised. Why were you beyond the castle walls without an escort, and however did you manage to escape? Tell me they dinna force you to do unspeakable things." An excitable girl, Myrna asked the questions in rapid succession.

"This morning, my father and I quarreled about his plan to see me marry Laird MacMurray. He would not listen to reason, and my only option was to leave Dunkeld. I'd have left sooner, but I needed your help to gather some supplies. Besides, you've been like a sister to me, the only friend I've ever known. I could not leave without saying good-bye. I even thought to ask you to come along, but decided it was too dangerous. It was while I waited, the soldiers attacked me."

Myrna's voice trembled with emotion when she spoke. "You must have been terrified."

"Aye, but I did my best to hide my fear. When the first man grabbed me, I fought back, but he was too strong. Even if I had gotten away from him, I was no match for two men. I was about to give up hope when a man came to my assistance. A scuffle ensued, and in the confusion, I ran into the woods. I dinna look back."

"Do you know the man who came to your aid?"

"Nay. I was lucky to get away unscathed, and dinna get a good look at his face. I'm sure he is long gone by now," Cailin lied. The less her dear friend knew, the better.

"Once Lord Borden learns another was present, and likely the one guilty of the crime, you will surely be exonerated. You must try to speak with him."

Cailin shook her head. "Nay, Myrna, you must keep what I've told you in the strictest of confidence. Do you promise? Swear?"

The maid nodded and crossed her heart. "I promise to

keep your secret. Even if I dinna understand why you choose to remain silent. What else can I do to help you?"

Cailin took both of Myrna's hands in her own and gave them a squeeze. "First, I'll need some supplies for my journey. If you could bring me some bread, cheese, and a wineskin in which I can carry water, I'd be grateful. I'll also need some clothing. Mayhap a disguise, so I won't be noticed." She laid her finger along the side of her nose and, after taking a minute to think, she smiled. "Liam, the new squire, is about my size. I'm certain he keeps some spare clothing and boots in the stable. Fetch those as well, and bring them to me."

"Why would you need the lad's clothes? I could go to your chamber, get some of your fine gowns and a warm cloak."

"Disguised as a lad, I will draw less attention."

"Och, you mustn't, m'lady. It is far too dangerous." Myrna wrung her hands in worry. "Are you sure there is no other way? Mayhap if you speak to your father, he will protect you."

"He'd hand me over and see me hanged, rather than risk the wrath of the English King. Nay, I must do this on my own. Will you get the things I've asked for?"

Myrna nodded. "Of course I will." She threw her arms around Cailin's shoulders and gave her a hug. "I will miss you. Promise you'll be careful."

Fighting back tears, Cailin eased away. "I promise to take care, but we must hurry."

Myrna dragged the back of her hand across her tear-stained cheek, turned on her heels, and left to do her mistress' bidding.

Cailin hoped the lad's clothing would be enough to hide her identity. Her nerves got the better of her and she began to pace. Unable to forget Connor's comments about her hair being the envy of all the women in the village, she stopped abruptly at a rack of utensils hanging on the wall. Without hesitation, she selected a dirk and fingered the heavy, thick braid hanging over her shoulder. She sucked in a quick, sharp breath, raised the blade, and in one swift motion, cut off her prized possession.

She wrapped the braid in the Fraser plaid and hid them both behind a barrel of oats. She ran her fingers through short, bluntly cropped hair that hung in a riot of curls just below the nape of her neck. Now, if she donned the squire's clothes, no one would guess she was a lass.

After what seemed like an eternity, Myrna returned. She carried a bundle of clothes under her arm and a haversack in her hand. "Saints alive! You've cut your beautiful hair." She dropped what she carried and covered her mouth with both hands.

"My hair will grow back." Cailin made light of her actions. "If I am stopped along the way, there is less chance of my true identity being revealed." While she explained her plan, she slipped out of her own clothing and picked up the stable boy's trews. She curled up her nose and turned her head away. "Does he sleep in the stall with the horses? These filthy garments smell of sweat, horse, and manure."

"The dirt and unpleasant odor will aid in your disguise." Myrna chuckled.

"I suppose you're right. If I look like a lad, and smell like a lad..." Holding her breath, Cailin slid her legs into the trews and laced them up at the waist. She stood very still as her friend wrapped a length of linen around her upper torso to bind her breasts. Once completed, she slipped an equally grimy tunic over her head. She placed her feet into a pair of well-worn boots, and tucked the dirk into a sheath that hung at her side. "How do I look?" Cailin asked as she turned in a full circle.

Without a word, Myrna moved toward the large stone hearth, scooped up a handful of ash, and smudged the soot on

Cailin's cheeks. "This will complete your disguise and cover the bruises." She took a step back and handed her mistress a tattered woolen cap. "If you tuck your hair beneath the hat, no one will ever guess you are a lass, let alone the daughter of a laird."

Cailin did as her friend suggested, and asked again, "How do I look?"

"Like you just crawled out from a pile of manure and are in desperate need of a bath." She laughed, and smudged a little more ash on Cailin's face. "When you walk, hunch your shoulders and shuffle your feet. Lads never stand up straight, and they dinna walk in a dainty manner."

Her physical disguise complete, Cailin mentally prepared herself for the task at hand. "You best see to your chores. Someone might miss you and begin to wonder what you are about." She took the sack of food from Myrna. "Thank you for your help, and your friendship. I will never forget you." Raising her chin and squaring her shoulders, Cailin headed for the door. Myna sobbed as she departed, but Cailin refused to look back. Leaving her home and those she loved was hard enough. A long tearful goodbye would only make her departure more painful.

Before leaving the safety of the storeroom, she opened the door and scanned the bailey. The coast was clear. Despite her effort to keep it at bay, fear tugged at her gut as she stepped out into the sunshine and headed toward the postern gate. With her head lowered and her eyes trailing the ground, she moved quickly. She'd thought about taking her palfrey as a means of transport, but everyone in the village knew the dapple-grey mare. Instead, she'd decided to head out on foot. Once a safe distance from the keep, she'd borrow a horse from one of the crofter's fields. When she reached her destination and found work, she'd send sufficient coin to pay for the animal, and then some.

A few more feet and she'd be at the gate. Freedom

beckoned, and she quickened her pace.

"You there! Boy! Halt!" a man shouted across the bailey, stopping her in her tracks. For three years, she'd heard that voice in her nightmares. By the time she'd turned around, Lord Borden was only a few paces behind her.

He hadn't changed. Standing at least six-foot-two, the dashing man in his early forties exuded a distinct air of arrogance and authority. He still wore his dark blond hair neatly cropped and swept back from his face, displaying his icy grey eyes and rugged masculine features.

A scarlet tunic, embossed with a golden eagle across the chest, covered his imposing form. A wealthy man, several thick gold chains graced his neck. On his right hand, he sported a large ornate ruby and emerald ring. A heavily jeweled sword hung at his side. The hauberk and chausses of chain mail he wore for protection added to his menacing appearance.

She fought the urge to turn and run. A fool's errand, since she'd get but a few yards before he tackled her and dragged her to the ground. She prayed he would not recognize her.

"Fetch my horse from the stable, and don't keep me waiting."

"Y—your horse, m'lord?" Relief seeped into her bones. He thought she was a lad. "I'll find him and bring him to you." She lowered the cadence of her voice, keeping her response short.

"Find him?" A frown furrowed his brow. "Are you too daft to remember what happened a few hours ago? He's the big bay gelding with the white blaze and four white socks. The same horse you put in the stable when I arrived."

She didn't answer him. Her mouth went dry and panic twisted her stomach into a knot when she caught sight of her father, heading in their direction. Her disguise might have fooled Borden, but could she deceive her father as well? If Duncan Macmillan recognized her, he'd surely turn her over without a second thought.

"Well, speak up, boy. Are you daft?"

"N—no, m'lord. I'll fetch the horse right away." She turned and ran toward the stable. Once inside, she searched the stalls, relieved to find the only horse matching Borden's description was already saddled. She grasped the reins and led the destrier out of the stall. But when she reached the door, she hesitated, peered through a knothole, and listened to the conversation between Borden and her father.

"I have instructed my men to continue the search. Once your daughter is found, she will be taken back to England to stand trial. It is about time you Scottish rabble learned your place. King Edward will no longer tolerate any deviance, and those who do not obey his laws will be punished. As you know, I have a personal stake in this matter. My brother was murdered, and I will not rest until justice has been served."

"Come, Lord Borden, we are both reasonable men. You cannot believe my daughter is capable of such a heinous crime."

"She is capable of a lot more than you know."

"Mayhap we could come to some sort of agreement."

"Agreement?"

Despite her father's attempt to lower his voice, she heard every word. "My daughter is a lass of great beauty, and a virgin. Were you to bed her, I have no doubt you'd find her very pleasing between the blankets. Should you take a fancy to her, she could bear you many fine sons."

Cailin could not believe her ears. Had her father actually offered her to this horrible Englishman? Death would be a more welcomed fate. She wanted to burst from the stable and protest, but she had to hold her tongue. Going off in a fit of rage would serve no purpose other than to reveal her identity and get her arrested.

"Are you suggesting I marry your daughter? That I dishonor the memory of my brother and betray my king?"

Borden asked with a hint of distain in his voice.

"Aye—I mean no. I am suggesting you consider your options and what you stand to gain. Her dowry would rival that of a princess, and her body will more than satisfy your carnal needs. If you dinna wish to wed the lass, take her as your leman, and use her as long as you see fit."

Borden threw back his head and laughed. "I am well aware of your daughter's beauty. But, tell me, why I should barter for something I can take for free? She may be a fetching wench, but no woman is worth risking my wealth, my title, and the favor of my king. I will not return to England without the person responsible for Harold's murder." The arrogance in Borden's voice was unmistakable. "Your daughter stands accused of murder and treason, crimes punishable by execution. Edward will not tolerate any excuses, and you can mark my words, he will see her reprimanded to the fullest extent of the law."

"Have I not shown my loyalty these many years? I signed the Ragman Roll after the Battle of Berwick upon Tweed, and I have not raised arms against England."

"King Edward merely tolerates your kind. To exterminate each and every bootlicking Scot would be too much trouble. But try his patience, and I am sure he will make an exception and see you executed for treason as well. Best you remember that. Hopefully, your daughter's death will serve as a stark reminder to all. Disobeying King Edward's decrees will not be tolerated."

"She deserves a fair trial!" Duncan blurted out.

"Edward I of Plantagenet, the King of England and Scotland, and his chief justicair, Sir William Ormsby, will see she stands trial, and I can assure you the punishment will fit the crimes." Borden moved toward the stable. "Now if you are done wasting my time, I'll be on my way. Where is that simple-minded boy with my horse?"

Cailin lead the destrier from the stable. In an attempt to

remain out of her father's line of vision, she stayed close to the stallion's side, her eyes trailing the ground. "Here he is m'lord. I trust you will find him well fed and cared for." She held out the reins.

"It's about time. In another minute, I'd have come looking for you and tanned your arse. Maybe I still will." He pulled the leather-bound crop from behind his saddle and waved it above her head.

She raised her eyes and prepared to accept her punishment. Despite her gut-wrenching fear, she refused to cower before him.

"I dinna think it will be necessary to beat the lad."

Duncan stepped between her and Borden, a move that had Cailin wondering if he had seen through her disguise. Normally, he'd have agreed with Borden and encouraged a thorough thrashing. Her father had no patience for servants that dawdled or did not attend to his needs promptly.

The two men stared down at her, causing the hairs on the back of her neck to stand on end. If the look on Duncan's face and the quick intake of breath were any indicator, he'd recognized her. If so, why didn't he say something?

"I dinna believe in sparing the rod, but the lad is new to the stable, and I am sure he has learned a valuable lesson this day." Duncan grabbed her by the ear, twisting it until she yelped. "Have you learned to mind?"

She nodded, but did not reply. Lest she cry out again, or worse, give them both a piece of her mind. She hated the way her father treated the servants, and being forced to grovel before him made her blood boil. Too proud to take orders from Borden, Duncan would wait for him to leave the castle. Once the blackguard left the keep, her father would likely reconsider his leniency, and deliver the punishment tenfold. He paid little attention to the servants, and would be hard-pressed to know one from the other. She prayed Liam would not bear the brunt of his retaliation in her stead.

"I think if your laird took a strip of flesh off your hide, he could be certain you'd move much faster in the future. You Scots are too soft." Borden snatched the reins from her hand, mounted his horse with ease, and turned to one of his officers. "I will be at the camp. Do not stop searching. Once the girl is found, bring her to me at once."

"Yes, sir." The young man snapped to attention and saluted.

"If you are finished with me, m'lord, I have chores to attend to," Cailin said to her father.

Duncan hesitated before he answered. "Be off with you, and see I dinna regret my decision to spare your backside."

"Yes, m'lord. Thank you, m'lord." She bowed and backed away, the words of submission leaving a nasty taste in her mouth. As she ran toward the stable, she swore an oath beneath her breath. "I will never grovel to my father or any man again."

She raced through the stable, knocking over several buckets of water in her haste, and exited through the rear door. The postern gate was only a few feet away, and there were no English soldiers in sight. Thinking it best to wait until Borden had left the castle grounds before making her move, she watched from behind a rain barrel as the guards raised the portcullis.

"Arrogant, self-aggrandizing bastard," she mumbled under her breath. "I wish I could have told you exactly what I think of you. Better yet, I should have thrust my dagger into your heart." Instead, she held her tongue, and her breath, as Borden and two of his soldiers rode through the raised iron gate.

She exhaled slowly, her shoulders sagging, and she rested her head against the rim of the barrel. While her disguise had fooled Borden, and mayhap her father, she wasn't sure she could outrun or outsmart them for long. If only she'd asked Connor to take her with him.

"Connor." She closed her eyes, and touched her lips. For a moment, she forgot about the argument with her father, the attack on the riverbank, the pain of the soldier's fist, the pompous English Lord. Instead, she remembered the sweet press of Connor's mouth against her own, the rapid flutter of her heart, and the wondrous sensations that tugged at her belly and beyond. Despite the dire circumstances under which they'd met, he left a lasting impression. If she survived this ordeal and lived to be one hundred, she'd never forget the earth-shattering taste of his lips.

Already, she missed his smile, the rich timber of his voice and gentleness of his touch. The thought of never seeing him again left her feeling empty, and alone. Like a whirlwind, he'd come into her life, rescued her from danger, swept her off her feet, and was gone again before she had a chance to catch her breath. He'd awakened the woman in her, opening a Pandora's Box of emotion and sensuality she had no desire to close.

Cailin gave her head a shake. She didn't need a man to protect her. Besides, men like Connor had no room in their lives for love, and she would not settle for less. On a mission for the cause, he'd have said no if she had asked to accompany him. But it didn't change the fact that she had to flee Dunkeld and was a woman traveling alone. If she ran into trouble, having an ally close by would be an advantage.

Connor told me he had to meet someone at the Inn before leaving town. Mayhap, he will still be there. If I follow him and stay out of sight until it is too late for him to turn me away, he'll have no choice but to take me with him to the Bruce's camp. I can then ask the Scottish King for sanctuary.

A horse would make the journey to the inn much quicker, and she knew where to find one. The crofter at the edge of the village had several fine animals and seldom had anyone keeping watch. Intent on putting as much distance between her and the castle as possible, she took off running, only pausing long enough to take a bay mare from Robbie Kerr's field.

Chapter 4

Accused of murdering John Comyn, Robert the Bruce found himself faced with an important decision—lay claim to the Scottish throne, or spend the rest of his life a fugitive. After meeting with his friend, William Lambert, several noblemen, and the Bishop of Glasgow, he traveled to Scone Abbey. On March 25, 1306, before these witnesses, he declared himself King Robert I of Scotland.

However, not everyone was pleased with this development or acknowledged his claim to the throne. Bent on revenge, and with the support of the English King, Comyn's brother-in-law, Aymer de Valence secured the area around Perth. The future Earl of Pembroke planned to challenge Robert the Bruce and put an end to the Scottish rebellion.

When he reached the Dunkeld Inn, Connor reined in his horse and slid from the saddle. The sooner he met with Travis MacLean and exchanged information concerning English activities in Perth, the sooner he could head north and rejoin the Bruce. After the events of the day, the more distance he put between him and Cailin, the better. The mere thought of the feisty lass ignited a fire in his groin. He cursed beneath his breath. She was the type of woman a man wanted to bear his children and to cherish for life, not the kind you bedded and left behind.

"Can I tend to your horse, m'lord?" A lanky boy, about ten and two, bolted from the stable and stumbled to a halt.

"Aye. We have a long journey ahead of us, so give him a good rubdown and an extra helping of oats." He tousled the boy's scruffy blond hair, then handed over the reins and a piece of silver.

The boy clenched his fist around the coin. "I'll take good care of him, m'lord."

Connor climbed the steps of the inn two at a time, pushed opened the large oak door, and stepped inside—his senses assaulted by the scent of peat smoke, stale ale, and sweat. With narrowed eyes, he scanned the dimly lit room, but saw no sign of Travis. Instead, he recognized two men sitting at a table beside the hearth. The last people he'd ever expected to see in Dunkeld.

The younger of the two men stared in his direction. He tilted back his chair, balancing it on only two legs and spoke loud enough for everyone in the room to hear. "Would you look at the slimy thing that just crawled in?"

"Aye, have you ever seen anything so revolting?" The other man added his comments and laughed.

Connor's hand closed over the hilt of his sword, and he strode with purpose toward their table. Before the two men knew his intentions, he kicked the leg of the tilted chair, and sent it crashing to the floor, along with its occupant. The man shouted a curse when his head struck the hearth with a loud thud.

When the larger man doubled over in a belly laugh, mocking his friend's misfortunate tumble, Connor closed in from behind. His fingers fisted in thick red hair, he snapped the man's head back and pressed the blade of his sword to the man's throat. "Not so cock-sure now, are you?"

"I'll have no bloodshed in my inn!" A portly man stepped out from behind a long wooden bar. He wiped his hands on a rag, and then tossed the scrap of cloth into the corner. "You can finish this ruckus outside." He pointed toward the door.

Ignoring the innkeeper's demands, Connor's attention returned to his opponent. "What have you to say now, you sairy heap of cow dung? Will we take this outside or finish here?" He released the man's hair, lowered his sword, and stepped aside—giving him time to respond to the challenge.

The large man lumbered to his feet and slowly turned around. He dragged his hand across his unkempt beard, spat on the floor, and then drew his sword. "I say we finish this here, and may the better man win."

A six-foot-six solid wall of muscle towered over Connor, but he refused to back down. Prepared to do battle, he took a fighting stance and raised his sword, but the sight of the younger man climbing to his feet distracted him.

"You need to keep both eyes on your enemy." The large man lunged forward with surprising agility. But instead of using his sword to answer the challenge, he wrapped his massive arms around Connor's waist, trapped his arms against his sides, and then lifted him from the ground as if he weighed no more than a feather.

"Put me down, you big ox," Connor hissed through clenched teeth. "You'll give these men the wrong impression. They'll be thinking you want to tup me, not fight me."

They had captured the attention of every man in the room. Some eyed them with concern, a few called out bawdy comments, while others snickered behind their hand. The innkeeper moved to the center of the room, and two buxom serving wenches watched the events unfold from behind the bar.

A boisterous laugh echoed in the room as the large man let Connor drop to the floor, grasped his forearm, and slapped him on the back. "About time you arrived. We've been waiting since early this morn and were beginning to wonder what happened." He turned toward the innkeeper. "Bring my brother a tankard of ale to quench his thirst, and another for Bryce and me. When you get a minute, have one of those pretty lassies fetch us some roasted lamb and potatoes. I'm starving."

"The man is always thinking about his stomach." Bryce gingerly rubbed his hand across the back of his head and moved toward his brothers. "I dinna know if I should hug you or punch you in the mouth, Connor. I've a lump the size of an egg."

"You always had a hard head," Connor said in jest.

Bryce fisted his hands at his sides, but instead of striking, he threw his arms around his brother's shoulders, and pulled him into a tight embrace. "I am pleased to see you well. However, if you pull a daft stunt like that again, I may not be as amiable."

"You'll have to gain a few stones if you hope to best me. Besides, if the rumors I've heard bandied about the countryside are true, you're a lover, not a fighter." Connor laughed.

At six-foot-two, Bryce, the youngest of the three Fraser brothers, equaled Connor's height, but had a slimmer build. Shoulder length chestnut braids framed his rugged features. From the time they were young, people commented on how much they resembled each other, and their mother's side of the family. On the other hand, Alasdair, the oldest, with his sky-blue eyes, locks of fire, and burly stature, took after their father. While all three were fierce warriors, Bryce's reputation as a lady's man and charmer had fathers clamoring to lock up their daughters.

After returning his disgruntled little brother's embrace, Connor scanned the room. "What are you and Alasdair doing here? Have you seen Travis MacLean?"

"Robert received word that Travis was wounded in a skirmish with the English three days ago. He had no way to contact you, so sent us to meet you in his stead." Alasdair stepped forward and lowered his voice. "The area around Perth has been a hotbed of late, and he wanted to make sure you got through without any trouble from those Saxon buggers. I think Simon had a hand in this as well."

Connor nodded. "You may be right. I know how our cousin worries like a mother hen if we are out of sight for too long."

He held a great deal of respect for Sir Simon Fraser and for his contribution to the cause. Like William Wallace and Andrew Moray, he fought valiantly for Scotland's independence, refusing to bow to Longshanks's tyranny.

The innkeeper crossed the room, balancing three tankards of ale on a narrow wooden tray. "Here you go, lads. My daughter will bring out your food in a few minutes." He placed the drinks on the table. "I would never have taken the lot of you for brothers."

"I'm the smart one, and they're the pretty ones." Alasdair laughed and slapped Bryce on the back.

Bryce sneered at his oldest brother. "That is a matter of opinion."

Connor offered the innkeeper his thanks and tossed some coins on his tray. Facing his brothers, he raised a tankard in the air and offered a toast before taking a sip. "*Slainte!*"

Alasdair lifted his mug in response. "*Slainte mhath.*" After downing his ale in one gulp, he gave a loud belch, and then wiped his mouth on the sleeve of his tunic.

Connor shook his head. "I can see his manners have not improved since last I saw him."

"Nay, he's brazen, ill-tempered, and as slovenly as ever."

"I'll show you manners—" Alasdair began, but his rebuttal ended abruptly when a young woman placed three trenchers, a loaf of bread, and a steaming platter of food on the table in front of him. He closed his eyes and inhaled the aroma.

"Some things never change. All an enemy need do is

to dangle a leg of mutton in front of him and he'd offer no resistance." Bryce reached for a tankard of ale.

Alasdair snorted, filled his trencher, and began shoveling food into his mouth. "Help yourselves, lads, this is the best food I've tasted in months."

The fragrant aroma of spices and roasted meat caused Connor's stomach to growl. He handed a trencher to Bryce, and then grabbed one for himself. "Best you get some before Alasdair eats everything."

"Have you heard?" A boy shouted as he burst through the door. Winded from running, he bent over at the waist, his hands on his knees, and gasped for air.

Connor stood, his eyes fixed on the lad.

"Catch your breath, Brian, and then tell us what all the *palver* is about." The innkeeper placed his hand on the boy's shoulder.

"T—they're here. The English are here." The boy accepted a mug of water offered by one of the serving wenches and drank greedily.

"In Dunkeld?" the innkeeper asked. "Mayhap they are just passing through the area."

The boy lowered the mug and spoke. "Nay, they've set up camp along the river." He took another gulp of water before he continued. "They arrived at the castle just prior the noonday meal. The commander said his brother was murdered on the riverbank this morn and demanded the laird turn over the person responsible. He said he'd see the castle and village turned upside-down until he found the murderer."

A tall, burly man in his late twenties sprang to his feet, grabbed the boy by his shoulders, and spun him around. "How many English, and did they say who they were looking for?"

Another man sitting at the same table stood, grasping the arm of the first man. "Calm down, Hagan. Once he catches his breath, he'll tell us. Won't you, laddie?" He glanced at the boy.

Brian nodded. "I dinna know who they seek. I slipped out of the castle and raced to the village to spread the word that they were here."

Angus patted the boy on the back. "You've done the right thing, Brian. Tell me, how many men did you see?"

"I counted at least twenty-five soldiers with heavy horses, mayhap more."

"Damnation!" Hagan shouted. "I'll not sit here and let those English bastards trudge into our village and push their weight around without a fight. It is time we teach them a lesson they'll not soon forget and send them crawling home on their bellies with their tails between their legs. We have more than enough men to run them off."

The other man nodded. "I agree. The Macmillan forces are feared by most. I'm surprised the laird dinna laugh in their faces and send the English on their way."

"Mayhap, he doesn't want to anger Longshanks and risk the full weight of his wrath," another man at the table commented. "If they get what they've come for, mayhap they'll leave peaceably."

"They dinna know the meaning of the word. I say we stand up to the buggers, show them we'll not bow to English tyranny. Who's with me?" Hagan raised his fist in the air and shouted the clan war cry. "A Macmillan!" The room erupted with the sound of men pledging their support.

Connor cursed and took a step forward, but Alasdair clamped his hand around his wrist. "What are you doing? This doesn't concern you." He slammed his tankard down on the table, sloshing ale everywhere. "Once we have finished our meal, we need to be on our way."

"I must try and stop them." Connor twisted his arm and broke free of his brother's grasp.

"You cannot be serious." Alasdair lowered his voice so only his brothers could hear. "The Scottish army depends on the missives you carry. Let the Macmillan's handle their affairs." He dragged the back of his hand across his mouth and reached for his tankard of ale.

"You'll not be giving me orders. In case you have forgotten, when we returned to Beauly to assume responsibility for Clan Fraser and our father's castle, you declined the elders' request to assume your rightful position as laird. A duty I found myself forced to accept in your stead." Connor glared down at his older brother.

"Keith was the oldest son, not me." Alasdair lowered his eyes and shook his head. "I never wanted to be laird."

"That may be so, but Keith is dead, and you were next in line. I have no issue with your decision to pass the responsibility to me, but you cannot have it both ways. I am laird, and I make the decisions."

"I am aware of that, but what goes on here is none of your concern," Alasdair reiterated sharply. "Laird or not, you are still my younger brother, and if you dinna sit down now, I'll tie you up, toss you over my horse's arse, and carry you back to Robert in fine fashion."

"These men have no idea what they would be getting themselves into. If they push the English, they will push back. Longshanks will leap at the chance to use their defiance as just cause to enforce his laws and invade Scotland. He will not hesitate to send an army into Dunkeld and trample anyone who gets in his way." Connor faced Bryce. "What have you to say?"

"The Macmillan has one of the largest army's in Scotland. Alasdair is right. Let them handle their own affairs." Bryce picked up his tankard and finished his ale.

"They might be strong enough to squash a small garrison, but not the entire English army. I must try to talk some sense into them. They need to bide their time and wait until Robert is ready to take a stand against Aymer de Valence."

"We cannot tell them about the Bruce's plans, nor can we get involved in every disagreement along the way. Not when there is a major battle brewing in Perth, one that could mean the turning point in the war," Bryce said, offering just cause to refrain from getting involved.

"Why are you ready to risk your neck and shirk your duty?" Alasdair clenched his teeth and raked his hand through his hair. "The English are determined to take over Scotland again, and we must pick our battles wisely. We cannot get involved every time they show their ugly faces. We will be of more use if we get the news to Robert and let these people take care of this matter themselves. Once they've found the person responsible for the murder, they'll most likely be on their way."

For once, what his brothers said made sense. Connor paused to consider the ramifications of his interference. To react without thinking, without a solid plan of action, would solve nothing. Did the threat to the people of Dunkeld cause his recklessness, or did his concern for Cailin get the better of him? If the English had been to the castle and had questioned the Macmillan and were still looking for the person responsible for killing the soldier, she was safe. While he wanted to stay and help the villagers, if he or his brothers were captured, they'd be letting Robert down and putting all of Scotland in jeopardy.

Rather than intervene, Connor watched as the Macmillan clan members left the inn.

"I am glad you came to your senses. Now, sit down and finish your meal." Alasdair tugged on Connor's wrist with one hand and pulled out his chair with the other. "This is Macmillan business, and none of your affair."

"You're wrong." In a hushed voice, Connor explained to his brothers what had happened on the riverbank.

Spewing a string of ribald curses, Alasdair climbed to his feet so fast, his chair toppled over and hit the floor with a crash. "Why didn't you say something sooner? Best we leave now. It won't be long before the English come poking their noses around the village. Someone might recognize you." He looked longingly at the remainder of their meal. With a sigh, he grabbed a piece of lamb, popped the morsel into his mouth, then licked the juices from his fingers before heading for the door.

Cailin crouched behind a bail of straw as several of her clansmen rushed past. Led by Hagan and Angus, they raised their swords, shouting the Macmillan war cry. She fought the urge to stop her cousins and ask what caused their anger. But after getting this far and going to such extremes to mask her identity, to reveal herself now would be foolish.

Her cousins would never betray her to her father or the English. But if they discovered her plan, they would do their best to persuade her to stay, or worse, they might try to intervene on her behalf. She'd never forgive herself if anything happened to either of them.

She nibbled on her lower lip and waited for Connor to emerge from the inn. When he'd left her at the castle, he informed her of his plan to leave for the Highlands once he completed his business in Dunkeld. What if he'd changed his mind, decided to spend the night, or was occupied by one of the innkeeper's voluptuous daughters? After all, a man had to sate his needs, or so she'd been told. A twinge of jealousy tugged at her stomach when she thought of him bedding another woman.

She gave her head a shake. How could she be jealous? He owed her no loyalty. In fact, she hardly knew the man, and she meant nothing more to him than a brief encounter.

When the door burst open and Connor stepped out of the inn, her heart skipped a beat. While the two men who accompanied him were dashing, they couldn't hold a candle to Connor's raw masculinity and animal magnetism. Her breath caught when he paused and glanced in her direction. Did he know she watched?

"Is something amiss?" the red-haired man asked.

Connor hesitated, narrowed his eyes for a moment, and then turned to face the man. "Nay, but we best make haste. There's no telling when the English will arrive." With that, he headed for the stable, his two companions close on his heels.

Chapter 5

The village of Dunkeld lay nestled at the base of Ben Lawer, one of the most impressive mountains in Scotland. Beyond the valley lay the treacherous terrain through the lawers of Perthshire—a route best traveled in daylight.

The Fraser brothers made the trek through dense forest, up steep slopes, and along rocky crags in silence. But as the sun set and evening approached, Connor stopped his horse in a clearing and surveyed the area.

"We've ridden hard and the horses are spent." Connor peered up at the cloudless sky. "The night will be clear. This is a good spot to make our camp."

"Do you think it wise to tarry?" Alasdair glanced over his shoulder in the direction from which they'd come. "If the Saxon buggers are following us, mayhap we should continue on."

"I would wager they had their hands full with the Clan Macmillan. If they are following us, we have a good start on them." Connor slid from the saddle and stretched.

"All the more reason to keep going." Bryce dismounted and moved toward his brother. "We've traveled these paths many times. If we continue through the night, we can put many more miles between us. The sooner we deliver the missives to Robert, the sooner he can plan his attack."

Connor shook his head. "The horses need to rest. If we run them into the ground, where will we be? Kildrummy Castle is a three day ride, and a very long way to walk without a mount. We will camp here, get a good night's rest, and get a fresh start before sunrise."

Bryce nodded. "I'll go down to the stream and fetch

some water. Mayhap the fish are biting." He handed his reins to Alasdair. Before heading off, he took three empty wineskins and a small sack from behind his saddle.

"I'll see the horses fed and watered." Alasdair took Thor's reins from Connor and led their mounts to pasture.

In his brothers' absence, Connor gathered wood for the fire. But he kept his head on a swivel, ready to respond to a threat in the blink of an eye. He bent to pick up some twigs and hesitated, certain he'd heard a noise in the bushes. Hairs prickled on the back of his neck and the icy chill of impending danger crept up his spine. He narrowed his eyes and scanned the woods surrounding the clearing, watching and listening for the sound of anything out of the ordinary. Aside from the rustling of leaves in the breeze, the hoot of an owl, and the melodious din of crickets, the woods were silent. But he could not shake the uneasy feeling they were being watched.

Connor shrugged, dismissing his concerns. He stacked the wood, then added some branches and dried leaves for kindling before setting the pile ablaze. Within seconds, the amber flames licked at the logs, ravenously consuming the dry tinder. As he stared into the flames, his mind wandered back to the battle with the soldiers on the riverbank...to Cailin. When he closed his eyes, he could see her image, could smell the subtle mix of heather and lavender, could almost taste her pouty lips.

What sounded like a muffled sneeze broke his concentration. Out of reflex, his hand slid over the hilt of his sword. Heart pounding and adrenalin pumping, he crept toward the edge of the clearing. A tree branch snapped behind him. With lightning speed, he drew his weapon, spun around in the direction of the noise, and took a defensive stance.

"Go easy, brother." Bryce held both hands in the air and halted in his tracks. "Best you put the blade away before you hurt someone."

"Never sneak up on a man, lest you wish him to run you through." Connor slid his sword into its sheath, then raked his fingers through his hair. "When next you approach, announce yourself."

"As you can see, I've snagged an eel and two fat catfish." Bryce lowered his hands and moved into the clearing.

"Did someone say catfish?" Alasdair asked as he approached from the other direction. He grinned, patted his belly, and licked his lips. "I'm starving."

Bryce laughed. "You're a fine pair. One of you thinks with his stomach, the other is as jumpy as a nervous cat."

Ignoring the comment, Connor turned toward Alasdair. "Did you feed the horses? On the morrow, we have a long ride ahead of us, and I want to get an early start."

"Aye. After they drank their fill at the stream, I gave them oats and left them enough rope, so they could graze on the grass. After we've eaten, I'll secure them for the night. That is if Bryce ever decides to cook those fish."

Bryce slid a sharpened stick through the eel and hung it over the fire. "I thought you'd just bite their heads off and eat them raw. If not, you can clean them." He tossed the fish to Alasdair, then snickered when his oldest brother grabbed his dirk and stomped away, grumbling under his breath. "Mayhap he'll appreciate my cooking if he has to work for his supper."

Once the fish were cleaned and gutted, Alasdair sprawled out on the ground and took a nap while Bryce finished preparing their meal. Connor walked the perimeter of the clearing, unable to shake the mounting disquiet, the gut feeling that someone was out there.

The rustle of bushes caught his eye, confirming his suspicions. He nonchalantly returned to the fire, crouched down beside Bryce, and stirred the coals with a stick. "We're being watched."

"What do you mean?" Alasdair sat with a start and

reached for his sword. "Are you certain?" He went to stand up, but stopped when Connor placed a hand on his arm.

With his eyes fixed on the glowing embers, Connor answered. "Dinna make any sudden moves. For the last few hours I've had the feeling someone followed us. Now I'm certain. They hide in the bracken about a hundred paces to the east."

"Thieves?" Bryce whispered. "Or mayhap the English are closer than we thought."

Alasdair leaned in closer. "What do you plan to do?"

"Surprise him and find out what he wants. Kill him, if need be." Connor rose and stretched as if nothing was amiss. He twisted from side to side, working out the kinks in his back, and then casually strode toward the horses.

Cailin watched him disappear behind a grove of trees on the opposite side of the clearing. In her attempt to stifle a sneeze, her elbow rustled a branch. When she moved into the bracken, she bumped into a hawthorn bush. Sharp barbs poked at her backside, and she covered her mouth to stifle a squeal. Tears welled in her eyes, but she didn't make a sound. When Connor moved in her direction, with his eyes narrow and his nostrils flared, she thought he'd seen her. She expected him to charge at her with his sword drawn. Instead, he wandered off in the other direction. His two companions remained by the fire. If Connor sensed her presence, he'd obviously not made it known to them.

She cursed under her breath and slowly backed away from the clearing. She knew better than to get so close. But the aroma of cooked fish lured her in, caused her empty stomach to twist and growl. What she wouldn't give for one savory bite or a sip of cool water to quench her thirst. While she'd waited for Connor to emerge from the Dunkeld

Inn, she'd placed her wineskin and sack of provisions on the ground beside her. In her haste to follow, she'd left the supplies behind. By the time she'd realized her mistake, they were too far from Dunkeld to turn back.

"Hold fast, or I'll slit your throat."

She hadn't heard him approach. Strong arms wrapped around her waist, the weight and momentum of his body propelling her forward. Stunned by the force of the blow, the air rushed from her lungs when her chest hit the ground. She sputtered in an attempt to clear the dirt and leaves from her mouth.

Pinned to the ground, she couldn't budge. Nor could she see the face of the man who attacked her. How could this happen twice in one day? Had someone followed her? Or had a thief stumbled upon her hiding place? Her mind raced with possibilities. Her heart hammered against her ribs and fear tugged at her belly, but the instinct for survival proved greater. She'd stood her ground against the soldiers on the riverbank, and if necessary, she'd fight this man to the bitter end.

He trapped her arms at her sides, but she could still move her hands. Her fingers curled around the hilt of her dirk, and she fumbled to slide it from its sheath. When he rolled to the right, taking her with him, she struck out with all her strength.

The blade connected. Fabric tore, and flesh gave way. Something warm and sticky splashed on her cheek. He howled in pain and let out a string of curses. But he was standing before she could make another move. He grabbed the collar of her tunic, dragging her to her feet. One hand clamped around her upper arm with bruising force, and he raised the other balled fist in the air.

When she saw Connor's face, she couldn't speak. She closed her eyes, and waited for a blow that never came. Instead she heard his sharp intake of breath and felt his finger slide down her soot-covered cheek.

"Damnation! What are you doing here?" Holding her at arm's length, he shook her until she opened her eyes. "Foolish lass, have you lost what is left of your senses? Why are you following me, and why are you dressed like this?" He fired off the questions in rapid succession, leaving her no time to answer. He pulled the cap from her head and groaned aloud. "Saint's teeth, what have you done to your hair?"

She refused to fall apart or to throw herself into his arms and weep. "If I choose to cut my hair and dress as a lad, it is none of your concern."

"None of my concern?" His fingers tightened around her upper arms. "Twice you have pulled a dirk on me today, and this is the second time you might have been killed for doing so. I left you at your father's keep. What are you doing here?" He released his hold on her and took a step back.

Her heart pounded in her chest, the sound of it resonating in her ears. She cleared her throat to speak. "The English were at the castle to arrest me for murder when I arrived. I recognized the lord in charge. The soldier who attacked me on the riverbank was his brother."

"You know this man?"

"A few years ago Lord Borden visited *Mhaolain*. He tried to have his way with me, but I refused to give in to his demands. He vowed I would pay for my insolence."

Connor's hands fisted at his sides, and his face contorted with anger.

"Now, he has even more reason to seek revenge. He demanded my father turn me over, so he could take me back to England to stand trial, to see me executed."

"Surely your father would not surrender you so easily."

"You dinna know my father. Och, aye, he tried to make a deal. Rather than arrest me, he suggested the commander take me to his bed, told him to use me as he saw fit, and then to discard me when he finished." Tears rolled down her cheek. She quickly wiped them away with the back of her hand. "I had to run away."

His voice softened. "If I had known you were in danger, I would not have left Dunkeld. I'd have done everything in my power to help you." He took a step closer and held out his hand.

She countered his move and took a step back. "I dinna need your help. I dinna need anyone's help."

"You're far too independent and cynical."

"I learned to trust no one and to fend for myself at a very young age. Besides, if I had asked you to take me with you, you would have said no. If I'd have come to you in Dunkeld, you would have taken me back to my father's keep."

"When did you plan to announce your presence?"

She shook her head. "I did not. It was my plan to do this on my own. I thought only to follow you to the camp of Robert the Bruce and once there, to ask him for sanctuary."

In one swift move, he wrapped his arm around her waist and pulled her against his chest. "I won't turn my back on you, lass. I killed the soldier, not you. Had I known they blamed you for the deed, I'd have moved Heaven and Earth to see you safe."

"I told you that I dinna want your help. I—"

She struggled to break free of his grasp, but he tightened his hold and stifled her protest by claiming her lips.

"Saint's teeth, man, what are you doing?" Alasdair stumbled up from behind. "Kissing a lad? Have you gone daft?"

"You have to admit, this does not look good." Bryce joined them. "You said you were going to kill the bugger, not kiss him." He raised a brow, scanning Cailin from top to bottom.

Connor released her and stepped away. "It's not what you think."

"Not what we think? First, you tell us we are being

watched and not to make any sudden moves. You asked us to let you handle things and disappeared into the bushes. Now, we find you kissing a lad." Alasdair's rebuttal was harsh and to the point. "You're bleeding. Did this filthy, scrawny scoundrel cut you?"

Cailin stepped out from behind Connor with her hands planted on her hips. "Who are you calling scrawny? You are a rude, ill-mannered ox." After the words slipped from her lips, she covered her mouth and lowered her eyes. She didn't know these men, or if they posed her any danger. She looked to Connor for answers and noticed a large bloodstain on his tunic.

"I'm so sorry, Connor. When I struck out with my dirk, I only meant to defend myself. I dinna know it was you."

"Dinna fash yourself." Connor raised his hand to cover his wound. "I'll be fine."

"You know this sniveling little varmint?" Alasdair grabbed the collar of her tunic.

Connor yanked his brother's hand away. "Touch her again, and I'll break your arm."

"Her?" Alasdair's mouth gaped open.

Connor placed his hand on the small of her back and nudged her forward. "I present the Lady Cailin Macmillan. M'lady, these two buffoons are my brothers, Alasdair and Bryce."

"L-Lady? Are you telling us this is a lass dressed as a lad?" Bryce rubbed his head in confusion.

"They're not usually this dense." Connor leered at his brothers. "They have obviously forgotten their manners as well."

"Forgive me m'lady." Bryce bowed. "What is she doing here? Why is she dressed like a lad?" he whispered to Connor.

"She did this to escape the English. She'll be traveling with us to Kildrummy."

"To hell with manners! A woman will only slow us down." Alasdair shook his head and clucked his tongue. "This is not the time or place to lose your head over a lass. She can stay the night, but must return to Dunkeld in the morning."

"I've not lost my head or my senses. She needs our help and if she wishes to accompany us, she will have to keep up the pace. Once we arrive at Kildrummy Castle, I'll turn her over to Robert and that will be the end of it."

"It is you who will have to keep up with me. I can out ride any man, can handle a cross bow, wield a sword, and fight like a warrior." Cailin stepped forward, standing toe to toe with Connor's older brother. "I refuse to go back to Dunkeld. If you won't help me, I'll make it to Kildrummy Castle on my own. I'll not be intimidated." She stared at Connor. "By anyone."

Alasdair raised a hairy brow and laughed. "She's a feisty one, I'll give her that. But we have a long, grueling journey ahead of us, and I say it is no place for a lass."

Connor held his hands out in question. "Tell me, brother, would you see her arrested and hanged for a murder she dinna commit? Or mayhap, you would rather see her left behind to be raped and tortured by those lecherous English bastards?"

"She'll be more trouble than it's worth," Alasdair grumbled.

"If you dinna wish to travel with a woman, you can continue the journey alone." Connor finished what he had to say, then waited for an answer.

"A Fraser stands by his brothers. Where one goes, we all go," Alasdair conceded. "Where is her horse? I'll put it with the others."

Cailin pointed to her palfrey tethered to a tree. "She might be small, but she is a mare with a lot of heart."

"A lot like her rider." Connor smiled.

"Have you noticed her limping? She's not putting full weight on her left front foot." Bryce approached the mare with his hand outstretched.

"She faltered from time to time, but managed to keep going all day."

Concerned she may have caused the horse undo pain, she stood behind Bryce while he examined the mare's foot.

"She's picked up a stone and bruised the coffin bone in her hoof. If you continue to ride her, it will only get worse." He slid the bridle over the mare's head. "We'll let her go free."

"How will I get to Kildrummy Castle without a horse?"

"You'll ride with me." Connor reached for her hand. "Come, we'll go back to camp."

"What about my mare?" She dug in her heels, refusing to move. "We cannot just leave her to be killed by wild animals."

Connor pinched the bridge of his nose and blew out a sigh. "We'll take the horse along and leave her with the first crofter we come to." He grasped Cailin's hand and tugged. "Come, we'll eat, and then get some rest. We need to be up and away before sunrise."

Cailin closed her fingers around his palm and nodded. "I'm very sorry about wounding you. Will you let me take a look at it when we get to camp? It likely needs stitching."

"I'm fine. You did what was necessary given the circumstances. I must admit, you handle yourself very well in a crisis." He brushed the soot from her cheek with a sweep of his thumb. "After we've eaten, I think a dip in the stream would benefit you immensely."

Cailin wolfed down her third oatcake, and reached for another portion of fish.

"For a wee lass, she has a hardy appetite." Alasdair picked up the last morsel of eel, popped it in his mouth, and licked his fingers.

"Now, that is a case of the pot calling the kettle black." Bryce chuckled.

"I have not eaten since yesterday and find myself quite famished." She dabbed her lips with a small square of linen.

"How could anyone set out on a journey without proper supplies?" Alasdair stood and brushed the crumbs from his tunic, belched loudly, and started to walk away. "Typical for a woman."

Cailin sprang to her feet and spoke to his retreating form. "On the contrary, sir. I had sufficient provisions, enough to last me several days. However, in my haste to follow you, I left them behind."

"She'll be a pain in the arse. You can mark my words." With a low growl, Alasdair lay down on a palette of leaves and plaid, and turned his back to her.

As Connor watched the interaction between Cailin and his brother, he couldn't help wondering what he had gotten himself into. He smiled at the way she stood her ground and stuck out her tongue when Alasdair wasn't looking. But at the same time, he cursed the temerity and spirit that fired his blood and made him want her more than any other woman he'd ever known. He couldn't send her back to face the English alone, but taking her with them could prove the biggest challenge of his life.

"I'll take the first watch, but before I do, let me have a look at your wound." Bryce approached, carrying a small leather pouch.

"I'm fine." Connor brought a hand to his injured shoulder. "You fuss like a mother hen. Leave me be."

Bryce threw up his hands in surrender, sauntered across the clearing, and sat on a large boulder. "I'll wake the bear to relieve me in a few hours." He pointed at their snoring older brother.

"Where shall I sleep?" Cailin asked.

"I've a palette right here." Connor pointed at a pile of plaid on the ground before him, and kneeled down.

She pressed her hand to her throat and let out a sharp gasp. "Surely, you dinna mean for me to share your palette?"

"It is large enough for two. Unless you have a mind to sleep on the cold ground, I'd suggest you lay down now. We have a long ride ahead of us tomorrow. " Connor sprawled out and patted the spot beside him.

"I'll not share your palette." She crossed her arms over her chest and stomped her foot.

"Suit yourself." While pretending to close his eyes, he watched her through slightly raised lashes. She stood for a few minutes, and then slowly lowered herself to the ground. Keeping to her word, she lay just beyond the edge of his plaid.

Stubborn wench.

He woke with a start a few hours later to the tickle of hair beneath his nose, the warmth of her body snuggled at his side. Her small hand rested on his chest, her breathing slow and even. His body stirred in response to her nearness. Heaven help him, he wanted this woman. This was going to be a very long night.

Chapter 6

They rose at dawn and covered many miles before the sun peeked above the trees. Bryce rode up beside Connor. "How fares your shoulder? I could carry the lass with me for a while."

"She rides with me." Connor shifted Cailin in his arms, being careful not to wake her.

"You were never a good liar. The way your face contorts when you move and the beads of sweat on your brow tell me otherwise. Best you let me have another look."

Unable to sleep with Cailin so near, Connor had taken both the second and third watches. When he relieved Bryce, he reluctantly allowed his brother to dress his wound.

"We dinna have time to stop."

"You're a *thrawn* man, Connor. If the wound festers and you become fevered, you'll slow us down. Besides, the horses are spent, and I'm sure the lass could use something to eat and drink."

"Did someone mention food?" Alasdair's head shot up and a broad grin crossed his face. "I'm so hungry, I could eat a bear."

"Oatcakes and ale will have to do. That is, if we can convince our pig-headed brother to stop long enough to break our fast." Bryce shot a quick glance in Connor's direction. "You know how ornery Alasdair gets when he's not been fed."

"If we stopped to eat every time Alasdair's stomach growled, we'd be stopping every few miles."

"I pity the lass he marries. The poor thing will spend her days and nights chained in the kitchen, too tired for anything else." Bryce laughed.

"The way the three of you squabble makes me glad to be an only child." Cailin stifled a yawn with the back of her hand and languorously stretched like a well-stroked cat.

Their eyes locked, but Connor quickly turned his head. To gaze upon such beauty and not touch was the purest form of torture. Despite her dirt-smudged cheeks and cropped hair, she was the most alluring woman he'd ever met. He'd struggled throughout the night to quiet the fire in his loins, to suppress the overwhelming urge to make her his own. Now, her winsome smile challenged what little remained of his reserve.

He remembered the sweet taste of their first kiss and the plumpness of her lips as he slid his tongue along the seam, willing them to open. He closed his eyes and stifled the urge to moan aloud. The desire to possess a woman had never been so strong, yet he knew it could never go beyond a dream.

Each time she shifted in his lap, the burning ache in his groin intensified. Could she feel the burgeoning proof of his arousal? The soft sighs she'd made as she slept stirred his curiosity. Would she make those same contented mewls when he buried himself within her most intimate place and drove her to the edge of ecstasy? Suddenly filled with lust, and hovering on the edge of reason, Connor reined in his horse.

"If you two buffoons promise to quit your grumbling, we'll stop long enough to rest the horses and break our fast. By yonder stream will do." Connor pointed to a small grove of trees on the bank of a swift-moving river. He slid from his saddle, but kept his hips pressed against Thor's belly, hoping no one had noticed the way his trews tented like those of a randy lad.

When he reached up and placed his hands around Cailin's waist, a firestorm of lust and urgent need erupted from deep within his soul. He released her as soon as her feet touched the ground. Cursing, he stepped to the left, rested his head on Thor's neck, and began counting beneath his breath.

"Are you all right? Does your wound cause you pain?" Cailin asked with concern.

"Nay," he answered abruptly, and stormed away in the direction of the stream. *Mayhap a dunk in icy water will cool my desire.* "Alasdair, see the horses are fed and watered. Bryce, prepare the rations for our meal." Connor glanced over his shoulder when he spoke, but kept walking.

Cailin scurried behind him. "Please let me tend to your wound."

He stopped dead in his tracks and spun around to face her. "Not now! Dinna make me regret the decision to bring you along."

"Of all the cruel, arrogant things to say. Why, I—"

"Best you tend to your needs and stretch your legs while you have the chance." Connor cut her off, and took a menacing step in her direction. Despite the crestfallen look on her face, and the sudden urge to gather her into his arms and apologize, he turned, and resumed his trek toward the river. Alone.

After a string of ribald curses only he could hear, Connor swore an oath to end his infatuation with Cailin here, and now. While he hated to treat her so abruptly, he'd decided the best way to discourage her was to act as if her presence annoyed him. If she hated him, she'd keep her distance. If she kept her distance, he'd be able to control the lust, and desire, that caused his blood to boil and his heart to race like a runaway horse.

"Your brother is an irritating, infuriating, insufferable beast. Not only is he stubborn, he's a fool to boot." Cailin stomped in their direction. "He'd keel over and faint dead away before he'd admit he needed help. If his wound is not tended properly, it will fester and he'll die. If that's what he wants, so be it. I wash my hands of him."

"The lass is definitely smitten with our brother." Alasdair snickered.

Cailin stopped her tirade and glared at him. "I beg your pardon?"

"He said it looks like rain." When Cailin shaded her eyes and glanced up at the sun, Bryce cuffed Alasdair across the back of his head and quickly stepped out of his reach.

"Rain?" Cailin sounded confused, and understandably so, since there wasn't a cloud in the sky.

Bryce handed her an oatcake and a wedge of cheese. "Come and break your fast. You must be famished." He pointed to a fallen tree. "Sit down and I'll get you some ale."

Cailin settled on the log and nibbled on her oatcake. "I would prefer water if you have it."

"Water?" Alasdair huffed and grabbed another oatcake. "Why would anyone that's right in the head want water when they can have ale, or better yet, whisky?" He brought the wineskin to his lips, took a large gulp, and then belched loudly.

Cailin glanced in the direction Connor had headed. "Will he be all right?" she asked Bryce when he sat on the log beside her. He offered her a horn filled with water, which she took with a nod of thanks. "His wound is bleeding, and I can tell by the grimace on his face that it pains him greatly."

"Connor has seen far worse. Best you dinna push him on it," Bryce cautioned.

"He's a very confusing man. One minute he's gentle, kind, and brave, and the next he acts like an angry ogre who can not stand the sight of me."

"Connor is a man torn between duty and his heart."

"I dinna understand."

"He has always put needs of others before his own. Be patient. He'll come around. Beneath that gruff exterior, my brother is a good man."

"He carries so much pain, not only from his wound. I can see it in his eyes. Grief and sadness torture his soul."

"Aye, Connor tends to brood, and to take the strife of the world upon his shoulders."

"Has he always been this way?"

"He brooded as a child, but it became more intense after the death of our father and oldest brother."

"What happened?"

"They died in the bloody massacre at Berwick upon the Tweed. Da made the journey every spring to fetch supplies. This time, the Scottish lairds who had refused to swear fealty to England arranged a secret meeting to discuss their course of action. Somehow, Longshanks got wind of the gathering and attacked the village in retaliation for the defiance and acts of rebellion. The villagers believed the town invincible, until the English breeched the earthwork defenses and overran the battlements, causing fear and panic." Bryce paused, and took a swallow of ale before he continued.

"The bastards slaughtered anyone who got in their path. By the time it was over, they had put nearly eight-thousand men, women, and children to sword."

Cailin's eyes widened and she clutched her hand to her throat. "How is it that your father and brother died, yet the three of you survived?"

"Da gave us each a piece of silver and told us to visit the peddler's, while he and Keith attended the cattle auction. When the attack began, we were on the far side of the village. We made our way through the commotion, but by the time we got to the cattle barn, they were dead."

"How horrible," Cailin gasped. "I cannot imagine being so young and seeing such a terrible thing."

"That day is one that none of us will forget. Alasdair

had seen ten and six summers, Connor ten and four, and I'd seen ten and one. I remember every detail as if it were yesterday."

"What of your poor mother? How did she cope with the loss of her husband and son?"

Bryce crossed himself and lowered his head. "Mother, and our youngest brother, Evan, died one year earlier in a raid on our village. He had only seen seven summers."

"I'm sorry." Her heart clenched and tears burned her eyes. "Who cared for you after the death of your parents?"

"Our father's cousin, Simon Fraser."

"The patriot Sir Simon Fraser?"

"Aye. You've heard of him?"

"Everyone in Scotland has heard of Sir Simon Fraser's contributions to the cause."

"He is one of the bravest men I've ever known and one of the most wanted men in Scotland. After the capture and execution of William Wallace, Simon refused to swear fealty to England. Those who know him say it will take the entire English army to capture him. Now that Robert the Bruce has laid claim to the throne of Scotland, Longshanks is more determined than ever to put an end the resistance. Simon has been as good to us as any father. We lived with him in the lowlands until we were old enough to return to our beloved Highlands and claim our father's land and title. Alasdair had no desire to be laird. The clan elders agreed and the responsibility fell on Connor's shoulders."

"Your father would be proud of the men you've become." Cailin slid her hand over his forearm and gave it a comforting squeeze. "After what happened to your parents, I can understand why Connor is dedicated to the cause."

"He's dedicated to the point of obsession. He swore an oath of revenge on our father's grave, vowed to see Scotland free of English tyranny—or to die trying."

"For a man to carry such a heavy burden is not healthy."

She glanced in the direction of the stream. "Do you think he'll ever let go of the grief and allow himself to feel, to love? Does he not long for a home and heirs to carry on your family's brave legacy?"

"Connor claims to have no use for love and says he wants no woman in his life. I think he is afraid to risk his heart. Then again, mayhap he has never met the right lass. Carrying such a burden may not be healthy, but try telling him that." Bryce snorted, and then finished his ale.

"I will." Cailin smiled and climbed to her feet. "Have you some clean strips of linen, a needle, and twine? Mayhap some whisky would be useful to clean the wound and dull the pain."

Nodding, he rose to his feet. After retrieving the requested items from his saddlebag, he handed them to Cailin. "Tread lightly, lass. Connor can be like a cornered boar when riled."

"I'll keep that in mind," she replied, and headed off toward the stream.

Connor lay on the riverbank with his eyes closed, his forearm resting across his brow. He'd removed his shirt. The dressing covering his wound was soaked in blood and a fine sheen of perspiration misted his body. When he shifted his position, a grimace of pain shot across his face, triggering a rush of guilt and remorse. She'd never have cut him, had she known he was her assailant. But when he jumped her from behind, she thought only to protect herself. He told her he'd have done the same thing were the tables turned, but it didn't ease her mind.

"M'lord."

Connor's eyes flew open and he jerked into a sitting position. A low feral groan escaped his lips. Instead of springing to his feet with his sword drawn—as would be a warrior's normal reaction to an intruder—he lay back on the bed of moss and closed his eyes. "Why do you bother me, when all I want is a few minutes peace?"

"You have not eaten and your wound has gone unattended far too long."

"I'm not hungry, and I'd like to be left alone."

Ignoring his remarks, Cailin knelt beside the stream. She dunked a strip of linen in the water, and then went to his side.

He held his hand up in protest, but she pushed it aside, and reached for the soiled bandage. To keep him from rising, she placed a hand on his uninjured shoulder and tugged the soiled dressing free, revealing a jagged wound.

Her stomach sank. "The gash will take several stitches to close it. I brought some spirits. Would you like a drink to dull the pain before I clean it?"

"Nay, just do it. I'll have no peace until you get your way." He turned his head to the side, biting down on his lower lip when she poured the whisky over the wound.

She picked up the needle between two trembling fingers and held her breath. When the sharp point pierced his flesh, a small trickle of blood ran down his chest, settling amidst soft black curls. The needle slid through his skin like a warmed knife in butter. After piercing the other side, she pulled the twine taught, tied the ends, repeating the process until the wound was closed. Throughout the ordeal, he remained silent and didn't move a muscle.

"I am finished." She blew out a sigh of relief, wiped the sweat from her brow, and rocked back on her heels. "With any luck, the wound will heal without infection. I wish I had some comphrey and willow bark to make a poultice." Guilt ridden, she watched as he struggled to sit up. Had she not acted in such haste, this would not have happened.

Connor brought his fingers to her lips. "The wound will

heal. You have a gentle touch, m'lady. Thank you." After rising to his feet, he offered her his hand. "Come, we must be on our way."

She accepted his assistance, then moved toward him. "I need to place this strip of linen around the wound to bind it closed and to keep it clean."

Without argument, he raised his arms, and allowed her to wrap the fabric around his chest. But when her hands brushed his skin, he drew in a sharp, ragged breath. A low groan caught at the back of his throat, his body alive with desire.

"I hope that holds. I only wish I could have done more."

"You've done enough."

She took a step back. "If you wish to keep up your strength, you really should try to eat something."

"I have no appetite." *At least not for food.* He wanted her more than his next breath. It would be easy to lay her down upon the bed of moss and bury himself to the hilt in the softness and warmth of her silken sheath, to slake the desire threatening to consume him body and soul.

Without conscious thought, he narrowed the gap between them—their bodies so close he could feel her heat. He tucked an errant strand of hair behind her ear, his fingers lightly brushing the creamy softness of her cheek. Wrapping his hand around her waist, he pulled her against his chest and dropped his head to capture her slightly parted lips. His groin stirred and his rock hard shaft pressed against the softness of her belly. Did she have any idea what she did to him?

Instead of pulling away, she swayed against him, and her lips parted more. Without hesitation, he ravaged and plundered her mouth. She tasted of mint and desire—even better than he'd remembered.

"Connor! Are you ready to ride? There's no telling how close the English garrison might be, and we best be on our way. With a price on the lass's head, I—" Alasdair stopped in his tracks, his mouth ajar.

Connor's hands immediately fell to his sides, and he stepped away. His brother's untimely arrival not only interrupted the moment, but it catapulted him back to reality. He pressed his fingers to the bridge of his nose and closed his eyes.

What just happened? How could one wee lass cause such havoc in my life? If not for Alasdair, I might have done something I'd regret...something we'd both regret. I must remain in control and keep my wits about me.

He'd always faced challenges head on. Stood firm in his convictions and fought for what he believed in—ready to battle to the death if necessary. Yet one sultry look from those large jade eyes, one sigh from those luscious lips, and he'd dissolved into a puddle of desire. One touch, one kiss, and he was ready to risk all for a few moments of ecstasy that held no future. He looked at Cailin, her lips red from his attention, her pupils dark with desire. Giving his head a shake, he silently vowed not to touch her again, to fight temptation and stay his course. A task that would be easier said than done.

To let his heart rule his head would be a mistake, but his gut twisted in knots, his mind filled with thoughts of her writhing beneath him as they coupled in a mating ritual as old as time. Since the moment he'd laid eyes on her, she haunted him day and night. He'd been guarding his heart for so long that these emotions were foreign, and certainly unwelcome. Determined to regain control of his emotions, he stiffened his spine and straightened his trews.

"Give me a minute, and we'll be on our way." After pulling his shirt over his head, Connor slid his sword into his baldric and slung it over his shoulder. "We still have a long ride ahead of us, and we best not tarry any longer." He spun around and headed to where Bryce waited with the horses.

Chapter 7

Thunder rumbled in the distance and lightening streaked across the sky. After six hours of nonstop rain, there appeared to be no end in sight. Connor glanced down at the woman tucked in his arms. Her small hand curled against his chest. The slow rise and fall of her breasts and her slightly parted lips left him longing for a kiss. *If only this were another time and place.*

Bryce rode up beside him. "She trusts you."

"She's exhausted and doesn't know me well enough to trust me."

"You're wrong, Connor. She would not sleep like a babe in your arms if she dinna feel secure. Claim what you will, but bringing her along with us is more than just a good deed. I'd wager you were moonstruck."

"When I pledged fealty to Robert the Bruce, I vowed to protect all of Scotland's sons, and daughters. Lady Cailin needs my help, and nothing more." Connor shifted his weight in the saddle. His shoulder throbbed and his legs were numb, but neither of these discomforts rivaled the painful bulge beneath his trews. If they had to ride much farther, he'd likely go insane with lust and need.

Pelted by icy rain, the woolen cloak he'd wrapped around Cailin's shoulders did little to keep her dry. She shivered in his arms and snuggled against his chest. "The storm is getting worse. We'll have to stop soon and find shelter for the night. Her clothes are drenched and she'll catch her death of cold."

"You're not thinking about going to Glasgow? Someone is sure to spot us."

"Nay. A wee bit further to the north is the village of Kirkintillock. There is an inn where we can get a hot meal and a dry place to sleep."

Alasdair joined his brothers. "Do you think it wise to stop in a public place? A little rain never hurt anyone. In fact, it has done wonders for the lass. With her face washed clean, she is quite comely."

"You and Bryce could not wait to stop and eat this morning."

"Aye, but we stopped in a secluded spot. Not in a village where mayhap we'll be recognized or captured," Alasdair replied.

Bryce agreed. "By now, the English will be combing the countryside. I vote we keep moving. We've traveled in far worse weather than this before. Do you remember the battle in Lanarkshire? It rained nonstop for three days and nights."

Connor nodded. "Aye, like it was yesterday. But we are hardened warriors, trained to do battle in any type of weather. Cailin is not. She needs to get out of these wet clothes."

Alasdair shook his head. "We're all soaked through, but each mile we travel brings us closer to Kildrummy Castle and safety. The Bruce is waiting on news from Perth."

"Robert will understand, and my decision stands. We'll stop at the inn and take our chances. If either of you wish to go on without us, I'll not stand in your way."

The discussion ended there, but when they reached the outskirts of the village, Alasdair spurred his horse, and rode on ahead. Bryce answered Connor's question before he asked it. "He goes to check out what lays ahead. We tossed a coin, and he lost. If there is any sign of danger, he'll ride back to warn us. If all is clear, he'll meet us at the inn."

Connor nodded and kicked Thor into a trot.

The inclement weather appeared to work in their favor. The streets were deserted. "Wake up, we're here," he murmured in Cailin's ear.

"Where are we?" Her hand came up to stifle a yawn.

"We are in the village of Kirkintillock. The rain has shown no sign of letting up, so we're stopping here for the night."

Cailin shivered. "I—is it safe to stop?" Her teeth chattered. "P—please dinna do so on my account."

"We dinna have a choice. The storm worsens, and if we're careful, no one will take notice." As if on cue, a bolt of lightning illuminated the sky, followed by a loud clap of thunder.

Connor dismounted and pulled Cailin from the saddle, her legs giving out as soon as her feet touched the ground. His arms enveloped her and he pulled her close. "Easy, lass. You've been on horseback for a very long time, and you're bound to be stiff. Even a veteran warrior has wobbly legs after spending so many hours in the saddle."

She placed her hands on his chest and tried to push him away. "You must let me go. If anyone sees us like this, they'll wonder why you are holding a lad."

"No one, aside from beggars and fools, is out in this weather." Connor closed his eyes, losing himself in her scent—an even bigger mistake than pulling her into his arms. The tantalizing scent of rain and crisp mountain air, laced with a hint of pine, clung to her skin like dew on a delicate spring blossom. His heart quickened to an unsteady rhythm, and his breath caught in his chest. A firestorm of primordial need swept through his body, igniting every nerve and fiber in its path. As his ability to stay his desire waned and it appeared he might succumb to temptation, reality once again reared its ugly head. They could never be together and if they tarried any longer, the English would find them and see them executed. Drawing on his last ounce of self-control, he released his grip and took a step back. "We best go inside. Can you walk?"

"Aye. The feeling has returned to my legs." Cailin followed, but came to an abrupt halt and touched her cheek. "The rain has washed away the soot."

Connor traced her jaw with his finger. Her delicate features would give one reason to question, but the faint bruising around her left eye gave the illusion of a lad who had been in a brawl. "Follow me. Keep your head down and speak to no one. The inn will be dark and smoky, the patrons more interested in their ale than those who come and go. If we are careful, no one will notice."

They entered the inn and Connor quickly scanned the room. His brothers sat at a table near the hearth. Alasdair had a tankard of ale in his hand and was asking an attractive, buxom barmaid for another when they approached the table.

"Sit down brother, l—laddie." He gestured to two empty chairs. "I've asked the innkeeper's daughter to bring us some venison stew, a loaf of bread, and four more tankards of ale. That will stick to your ribs and warm your insides, little brother." He slapped Cailin on the back.

The blow almost knocked her off her feet. Connor glared at his brother, then checked on Cailin. With downcast eyes, she huddled in the chair beside him and said nothing.

The barmaid returned, carrying a tray with four tankards of ale, trenchers, eating knives, and a steaming loaf of bread. "Your stew will be ready in a few minutes. If there be anything else you need, just ask. My name's Emma." She leaned forward, batted her blue eyes at Connor, and dragged her fingertips along his forearm in a blatantly suggestive manner.

The waitress's low-cut bodice afforded him an enticing glimpse of ample breasts. Connor quickly turned away. He was riled enough already. "That will be all for now. *Tapadh leibh.*" He thanked her and picked up his tankard of ale.

"You're very welcome. If you're sure there is nothing else I can do for you, I'll see to the stew." With a shrug, she turned on her heels and headed toward the kitchen.

"She's taken quite a fancy to you, brother." Alasdair grinned. "It must be a terrible curse to be blessed with such a pretty face."

"She was just being friendly." Connor kicked his brother under the table.

"Ouch! What did you do that for?" Alasdair rubbed his shin and scowled at Connor. "I only speak the truth."

"You speak too much, and most of it is nonsense."

Bryce ignored the banter between his brothers and wasted no time helping himself to the bread. He broke off a piece and handed it to Cailin. "Have some while it is still warm, and before Alasdair digs into it."

Emma returned with the stew and placed it on the table. She dipped the wooden ladle into the bowl, filled a trencher, gave it to Cailin, and winked. "Can I get anything else for you, lad?"

Cailin tugged the wet cap down around her ears and shook her head.

"Mayhap you'd like to hang your wet cloak by the fire to dry. There's quite a puddle of water under your chair."

Cailin almost choked on the small piece of bread she'd popped into her mouth. Coughing and sputtering, she tried to find her voice.

Connor patted Cailin on the back and grinned at Emma. "He tends to be shy around women." He handed her a tankard of ale and watched as she gulped it down.

"He'll soon get over it." Emma circled around the table and stood behind Cailin's chair. "You may be a tad small now, but if you grow up to look anything like your brother, you'll be chasing away the lassies."

"Emma! Stop bothering the gents. Your mother needs you in the kitchen." The innkeeper stood by the bar, his arms crossed over his chest and tapping his foot.

Connor waited for Emma to get out of hearing range, and then leaned close to Cailin's ear. "She has a point. You're never going to warm up if you keep that wrapped around you. Let me hang it by the fire." He reached for the cloak.

Cailin pulled away, holding the garment in place. "N-nay, I-I'm fine. W-what if someone sees through my disguise and betrays us to the English?"

"Dinna *fash* yourself, there are no soldiers here. Then again, the English have never been fond of our bonny Scottish weather." Alasdair tore off a large chunk of bread and tossed it in his mouth, then spoke while he chewed. "The decision to stop here might not have been such a bad idea after all." He swallowed his food, raised the tankard to his lips, and drained the contents in one gulp. After a loud belch, he dragged the back of his hand across his mouth.

Bryce shook his head. "A wild boar has better manners."

Ignoring the insult, Alasdair smiled at Emma when she placed a trencher of stew and a knife in front of him. "Could you bring us more ale and another loaf of bread?" He tossed some coins on her tray before digging into his meal with gusto.

Connor watched Cailin push the food around on her trencher. "Is there something wrong with your stew?"

"I'm not hungry." She shoved the trencher away.

"You dinna eat enough to keep a bird alive." Bryce scooped up some stew. Popping the hardy mixture of flavors into his mouth, he chewed with gusto.

With his mouth full and gravy running down his chin, Alasdair surveyed her platter. "I'll eat her portion if she dinna want it."

Connor moved Cailin's trencher out of his brother's reach. "Best you eat while you can. There is no telling when we'll be able to stop for another hot meal. I'll not have you fainting from hunger." Connor handed her a knife. "Eat."

As they finished their meal in silence, Connor kept a close eye on everyone who entered or left the inn. By the time they'd finished, most of the patrons had gone home or had retired to their rooms for the night. Only a few stragglers remained.

"Would you like another round of ale?" Emma asked with a broad smile.

Alasdair nodded. "That would be great."

"We've had sufficient, thank you." Connor held his hand in the air. "Could you ask the innkeeper to stop by our table? I'd like to speak to him."

"If you change your mind, just call for me." Emma accepted payment for the meal, tucked the coin in her apron, and then headed for the kitchen. "They dinna want anything else, Mum!" When a stocky woman came to the door and held out her hand, she promptly dumped the money into her palm, then turned and spoke to the innkeeper.

Ambling past the scarred tables and drunk patrons, the heavyset man approached them. "My daughter said you wished to speak to me." The innkeeper glanced down at Cailin's untouched trencher of food. "Did you not like the stew, lad?"

Connor spoke before she could answer. "The meal was excellent, but he's had a bit too much ale. We are in need of lodging for the night. Do you have any vacant rooms?"

"The storm has brought in more travelers than usual." The innkeeper stroked his chin while he pondered the question. "I'm afraid that we've only one room left with a very small bed."

"The lad can take the room. We saw a barn behind the inn. If you've some fresh straw and a couple of horse blankets, it will do fine for Bryce and me." Alasdair slapped his younger brother on the back.

The innkeeper's wife marched over to the table, her stare fixed on Connor. "Where might you be sleeping? We run a reputable establishment."

Connor frowned at the question. He hadn't thought that far ahead. While it was true Cailin needed a warm place to sleep, he wasn't about to let her out of his sight. If he left her in the inn alone and anything happened during the night, there would be no time to fetch her and make their escape. However, if forced to spend the night in a room alone with her, there was no telling what might happen.

"Speak up, man. Where will you be sleeping?" When he failed to answer, she narrowed her eyes, planted her chubby hands on her ample hips and tapped her foot. "Do you think me a fool, and blind as well? Anyone with eyes can see the lad is a lass. I run a respectable inn, and she'll not be plying her favors under my roof."

"Now Cora, give them a chance to explain." The innkeeper placed his hand on his wife's shoulder.

"They are married." Alasdair answered her before Connor had a chance to speak.

Cora gasped. "Married? Why she's little more than a bairn."

"Of course they're married. I've never known a husband and wife to be more in love?" Bryce bit down hard on his lower lip, in an obvious attempt to stifle a grin.

Cora spun around to face Connor. "Speak up, man, are you married to the lass, or not? If the glower on your face is any indicator, something is amiss, and while you are at it, you can explain why she is dressed like a lad?"

Connor helped Cailin to her feet. "I'm her husband." He kissed the back of her hand, and then held it in the air for all to see.

"What say you, lass, is it true? Is this man your husband? You look as timid as a wee kirk mouse." Cora took Cailin's free hand and patted the back of it. "Dinna be afraid to tell the truth."

A hush fell over the room. Connor tightened his grip on

her hand. "Tell her."

"A—aye." Cailin coughed and cleared her throat. "He is my husband." After speaking the lie, she glanced down at her feet.

A broad smile tugged at Cora's lips. "Well, if you were not married before, you are now. James, get the key and show them to their room."

"Right away, Cora, my love." James hurried off to do his wife's bidding.

"What did she mean?" Cailin whispered.

"Dinna question me now. I'll explain later." Connor turned, and faced Cora. "We appreciate your kindness."

"You still have not explained why she's dressed this way."

"Her father is a tyrant and dinna approve of our marriage. This was the only way we could be together, and not be discovered." Connor quickly changed the subject. "If you're agreeable, my brothers would appreciate the use of your barn."

"Aye, for a fee." Cora held out her hand. "There's fresh hay in the loft and on the morrow, they may join you and your wee wife to break their fast. I'll have my husband fetch some blankets."

"This should cover the room, and the use of the barn." Connor placed a small bag of coin across the woman's palm and watched as she counted it. "Now, if you could give us a minute alone, I need to speak with my brothers."

Connor waited until she was out of hearing range, then spoke to Cailin. "Stay here. I'll be right back." He held out a chair, waited for her to sit down, then stomped across the room to where his brothers were waiting. "Step outside. Now!" He shoved open the heavy oak door, and the three men left the inn.

"Thunder and damnation, what were you thinking?" Connor threw his hands in the air, then spun around to face his brothers. "Why in the name of Saint Stephen did you have to tell them we were married?"

Alasdair's grin broadened as he leaned in close. "Relax, little brother, I only did what was necessary. You should be thanking me, not shouting at me."

"Thanking you? Because of your big mouth, I had to declare that Cailin was my wife. Have you any idea what this means?"

"Aye, and it got you the room, and a wife to warm your bed," Alasdair replied smugly.

"Aye, it got me a wife I dinna want."

"I thought about claiming her for myself, but dinna think it would sit too well with you or the lass."

"You're a sniveling, slimy bastard. I'm a warrior, and you know that I never planned to marry. Especially to a woman who has proved to be trouble since the day we met. I've half a mind to kick your arse from here to kingdom come."

The smile left Alasdair's face, and he closed the gap between them. "Go ahead and try."

Connor raised his balled fists, but Bryce stepped between them. "Stop this before you get us all thrown out, or you shame the lass and ruin her reputation. Correct me if I'm wrong, but did you not say we needed to be discreet and not attract attention?" Bryce kept his voice low and nodded in the direction of three men who had wandered outside and were doing their best to eavesdrop.

Connor waited until the men wandered out of earshot, then continued to rant. "That was before my brothers betrayed me and declared me married to a bairn."

"I can think of a lot worse fates than sleeping in a warm, soft bed, nestled between that bonny lassie's thighs," Alasdair goaded.

"*Haud you're wheest!*" His patience pushed to the limit, and despite the threat of an audience, Connor raised his fist, ready to attack his brother. "Cailin is a lady. She is not a whore."

"Calm yourself, Connor, and dinna make a scene. Alasdair only seeks to pull your leg. He's had a bit too much ale, and meant no disrespect."

"I dinna know why you *fash* yourself. We've both seen the way you stare at her. You look at her like you could gobble her up and would kill any man who dared to look at her." Alasdair elbowed their younger brother in the side. "Tell him, Bryce."

"He has a point. You do stare at her like a lovesick hound. Face it, Connor, the lass has caught your fancy. Besides, that old woman was not about to give you a room unless she thought you were properly wed. You said it yourself, the lass is exhausted and needs a warm place to sleep. Now she can dry her clothes and you can warm her bed." Bryce smiled and patted Connor on the back.

"There'll be no bed warming do you hear me? No bedding. Period." Connor's jaw clenched, and he fought the urge to knock both their heads together. "I'll not be trapped into a marriage I dinna want. I have no use for a wife, and the sooner you get that through your thick skulls, the better. Once we reach the Bruce's camp, I'll do what is necessary to have this amended. In the meantime, I will see her safe, and nothing more."

"Suit yourself, but for now, you best go tend to your wife before anyone gets suspicious." Bryce turned and headed for the inn. "While you do that, I plan to finish my ale, then find myself a warm, dry spot to sleep in the barn."

Just as Connor was about to follow his brothers, he caught sight of two English officers sauntering up the street. He brushed past Bryce. "There's no time to escape. I must get Cailin safely tucked away in our room before the soldiers find her."

Alasdair slid his hand over the hilt of his sword. "Bryce

and I will see to our English friends. Take the lass to your room and stay there."

Connor nodded. "Be careful." He entered the inn and rushed to Cailin's side. "We need to leave now." There could be no mistaking the concern in his voice.

"What is it, what's wrong?"

"English soldiers are in the village proper, and we need to get out of here before they reach the inn." Without further explanation, he took Cailin's hand and dragged her toward the stairs.

"If you need anything, lad, just ask," James called out as they reached the above floor.

"Thank you, we will." Connor didn't take the time to look back, but he could still hear James talking to Cora as he escorted Cailin down the hall.

"Och, young love is grand. I remember a time when I was as anxious to get you into my bed. I carried you in my arms, taking those stairs two at a time."

"You're an old fool, James." She paused and Connor imagined her staring after them. "I still say there's something amiss."

He guided Cailin to their room and unlocked the door. "Go inside and put the bar in place. Dinna answer unless you are certain it's me."

"Where are you going?" Cailin grasped his arm, her nails digging into his flesh.

"I need to see what the English are about. Bryce and Alasdair may need my help. Wait here until I return."

"I refuse to remain hidden away while you—"

"This is not the time to argue. Either you promise to stay in the room, or I'll tie you to the bed and you'll have no choice in the matter." He grasped her by the shoulders and pushed her into the room with a little more force than intended.

"You wouldn't dare." She planted her hands on her

hips, standing her ground.

"Aye, I would. But if you dinna keep your voice down, there will be no need to hide. The English will surely find us."

"It's too dangerous."

"I'll only go as far as the top of the stairs. If I hide in the shadows, no one will see me." He grasped the doorknob, pulled the door closed, and waited until he heard the bar slide into place.

Connor made his way down the narrow hallway and crouched at the top of the stairs. From this vantage point, he could see the main floor of the inn. Holding his breath, he waited, and watched.

"We'll have two tankards of Ale and make it quick, wench." An English lieutenant threw open the oaken door and bellowed at Emma. Another soldier followed, close on his heels. After scanning the room, the two men sat down at a table near the hearth.

Bryce and Alasdair slipped into the inn behind them, but lingered near the door.

Rather than send Emma to wait on the soldiers, Cora delivered the drinks herself. "Will you be having anything to eat?"

"No. But keep the ale coming. This abominable Scottish weather has chilled me clear to the bones." The lieutenant threw some coins on the table and picked up his tankard.

"As you wish, m'lord." Cora scooped up the payment and curtsied politely. "You lads are a far piece from your garrison on this *dreich* night."

"It's always damp and dreary in this godforsaken country. My feet have not been dry since we left London. I—"

The soldier continued to rant until his commander abruptly cut him off. "We are searching for a young woman who escaped custody, and we have reason to believe she may be headed this way."

Cora shrugged. "A young lady, you say? What did the lass do to warrant being held and hunted by the king's soldiers?"

"She murdered an English officer." When the lieutenant stood, he towered over Cora. "The wench tempted the poor sot, and when he tried to claim his due, she murdered him."

"Denied the man his God given right to breed her, did she?" Cora clucked her tongue and shook her head. "Where did this happen?"

"In the village of Dunkeld. The woman's name is Cailin Macmillan. We mean to find her and see her punished."

"She dinna come through here. Mayhap, they are traveling south, and not north." Cora turned, and walked away with a smug grin on her face.

The lieutenant stepped into the middle of the room and banged a knife against his pewter tankard. "I am Lieutenant Winthrop, and this is my assistant, William Jones. You all heard what I told the old woman. There is a reward of twenty pounds in sterling for the woman. Have any of you seen her?"

Connor watched as his brothers shifted in the shadows, Alasdair sliding his hand over the hilt of his sword.

Dinna do anything to gain their attention. They're only asking questions and flaunting their authority.

Connor held his breath and prayed his brothers would stand fast. The bounty the soldiers offered would mean a fortune to those present, but he hoped their loyalty to Scotland would prompt them to hold their tongues.

The soldiers moved about the room, questioning the patrons. "Have you seen this woman?" Jones paused, and waited for a man sitting at a table by the bar to answer.

"I've not seen anyone like that around these parts. With an entire English garrison of at least one hundred men camped less than an hour ride to the east, and an even larger one stationed in Glasgow, a person would have to be daft to come through here if they were trying to avoid capture." His response appeared to satisfy Jones, and divulged the location of the English encampment.

"What about you, old man?" The lieutenant kicked the chair of the first man's companion, toppling it over, and sending him crashing to the floor.

Connor fought the urge to go the elderly man's defense.

"Nay. She's not in Kirkintillock." The man rubbed his elbow and climbed to his feet.

After getting nowhere with their questions, the soldiers returned to their table and picked up their tankards of ale. Before taking a drink, the lieutenant issued a warning. "The sooner you Scottish vermin learn your place, the better. When a man is murdered, especially one of the king's men, it is punishable by death. To conceal the murderer's whereabouts makes you an accessory to the crime, not to mention it is an act of treason."

Despite the threats, and promise of a hefty reward, not a soul spoke up. While it appeared to escape the officers attention, Connor saw Bryce nudge Alasdair's shoulder and whisper something in his ear, before the two men slipped out the door.

Chapter 8

Connor had barely made it through the door when Cailin rushed to his side. "Are they gone?"

"Aye, for now. I dinna think they will return tonight, so best you get undressed and into bed. We'll get a good night's rest and leave before first light."

Her face flushed and she took a step back. "For a maiden to share a room with a man who is not her husband is scandalous, and I'll not do it."

Cailin didn't need to remind him of her innocence. To stay the course, and not go insane with primal need, would be a miracle, and a true test of his resolve. His self-control already pushed to the limits, Connor steeled himself for a night alone with an alluring, desirable woman he craved with every fiber of his being, and had vowed not to touch.

"Like it or not, we are married." He pushed past her, stomped across the room, and tossed his saddlebag into the corner. The leather satchel hit the floor with a loud thud.

"How dare you tell those people we're married? I insist you set things to right and find another place to sleep." She followed on his heels, and grabbed his arm.

He spun around to face her. "I dinna have a choice."

"No choice! You could have told them I was your sister, your cousin, or—"

"That old woman is no fool. She saw through your disguise and wasn't about to let us share a room unless we were married."

"She believed your lie. That we were married in secret because my father dinna approve."

"Would your father approve if we married?"

Instead of a clever response, Cailin hesitated for a minute, and lowered her head. "Nay. He has his own plans for me."

"Then I dinna tell a lie. As long as those English bastards are in the village, we need to stay hidden, and together." Connor stepped away, picked up a log, and tossed it among those already smoldering on the hearth. When he turned around to face her again, he mumbled a curse under his breath.

With downcast eyes, she stood at the foot of the bed. Her body shivered and her teeth chattered.

I'll not allow myself to feel sorry for her. If I must keep her at arm's length, I will. If I must be gruff and cruel to save my sanity, so be it. "Best you stop your haivering and get out of those wet things before you catch your death of cold."

Cailin glared up at him. "I will not get undressed in front of you." The look of determination in her eyes and the proud jut of her chin showed the strength of her conviction. "If you were a gentleman, you'd sleep in the barn with your brothers." She defiantly wrapped the sodden cloak around her shoulders, turned her back to him, and lowered her voice to a barely audible tone. "You'll not touch me, Connor Fraser. Not if you value your manly parts."

He placed a firm hand on her shoulder and spun her around. "Those are bold words, and no way for a wife to speak to her husband. Mayhap I should take you over my knee and paddle your arse, teach you to *haud yer wheest.*"

"I'll not hold my tongue, and if you think I would stand by while you paddled my arse, you're sorely mistaken. I'm not your wife, or your property. When I marry in earnest, it will be before a priest, and to the man I love. He'll ask for my hand, and court me properly. You had no right to trick me into marriage."

"I had no plans to marry you or anyone else. Desperate

times called for desperate measures, and I'll say, and do, what's necessary to protect you. When asked if I was your husband, you dinna deny it."

"I thought it was merely a ruse to procure a room, and to hide our identity. I had no idea we'd truly be married."

"Marriage by declaration is legal and binding according to Scottish law. If there were any other another option at the time, I'd have taken it. Once Alasdair told them we were married, I had no choice but to go along with his claim. The last thing I need or want is to be saddled with a wife."

"Saddled with a wife? Why, I'll have you know that many a handsome lad asked permission to court me. I refuse to be married to a man who does not love me."

"I'm a warrior, and have no use for a wife. Once we reach the Bruce's camp, I'll see the matter rectified. Moreover, your silly notion of love is a myth that only fools believe, and I refuse to fall into your trap. If truth be known, you've been trouble and a pain in my backside since the moment we met. It was a cruel trick of fate's that I happened upon you on the riverbank, and the sooner I'm rid of you, the better."

Her bottom lip quivered, and her eyes glistened with unshed tears, but she made no attempt to reply. He hated to treat her in such a cruel, heartless manner, but to admit his true feelings would benefit no one. It served no purpose to let her know that he thought her the most amazing, beguiling woman he had ever met, and that he wanted her more than his next breath. Once they'd rejoin the Scottish forces at Kildrummy Castle and he'd seen her safely sequestered, he would continue to fight for the cause, mayhap never see her again. No, he'd not tell her how he felt, and leave her pining for something that could never be. He vowed to remain strong, to squelch the desire to take her in his arms and comfort her. To stay the unbridled passion that heated his blood and ripped through his body like a wildfire out of control. To crush the urgent need to sheath his aching shaft deep within her velvet warmth and claim his bride.

"If I am so much trouble, mayhap you should leave me here. Continue to Kildrummy on your own and forget we ever met. Better yet, send me back to Dunkeld. Let my father deal with this matter as he deems fit. I'll not beg for your help." She sat on the edge of the bed, lowered her head, and clutched the sodden cloak around her shoulders.

Guilt tugged at his heartstrings. She sat before him, frightened, exhausted, chilled to the bone, and his insensitive attitude made things worse. For the first time since they'd met, the fire was gone from her eyes. He wanted to hold her, and tell her everything would be all right, but he knew if he did, it would not stop there.

"You cannot go home. The minute you set foot on Macmillan land, the English will arrest you." Against his better judgment, he sat on the bed beside her, slid his hand over hers, and gave it a comforting squeeze. It made him shudder to think what might happen if they held her prisoner. "What's done is done, and we will have to live with it for now." His voice softened. "Best you get out of these wet things and hasten yourself into bed. I'll stoke the fire, and then join you."

Cailin sprang to her feet. "I will not share a bed with you!" She began to pace the room like a cornered animal. "I'm a maiden, and when I bed a man, it must be the husband of my heart. Not a man who takes me to wife out of necessity."

His jaw clenched, a ball of anger rising from the pit of his stomach. "Enough. I feel like I'm banging my head against a stone wall." With his fists balled, he stood and proceeded to an old oak shelf in the corner of the room, pulled down a tattered fur pelt, and laid it on the floor before the hearth. "I'll sleep here. Now, get undressed, climb into bed, and try to get some sleep."

"How can you think about sleep when English soldiers

could return at any time? Mayhap we should leave now and travel under the cover of darkness."

"Bryce and Alasdair will keep an eye on the English and handle things if need be. I'd trust no one else to guard my back."

"Handle it how? Enough blood has been shed on my account. If anything happened to one of your brothers because of me, I would never forgive myself."

"My brothers will do what is necessary to keep you safe. Best you get undressed and into bed. On the morrow, we have a long journey ahead of us."

"I must tend to my needs. Please, I bid you give me a moment of privacy."

The flush of embarrassment stained her cheeks, and the pleading look in her eyes melted his heart. *How can a woman be so damned irritating, and yet adorable and desirable at the same time?* He pressed his finger to the bridge of his nose and shook his head. His patience and resolve spent, he counted to ten beneath his breath before he answered. "There'll be a chamber pot under the bed. I'll turn my back while you undress and tend to your needs."

"Mayhap you could you wait in the hall? It will only take a few minutes."

"Nay. I cannot take the risk of being seen, and I dinna intend to leave you alone. Turning my back is the best I can do." He faced the opposite side of the room and blew out a sigh of frustration. "See to your needs, and then put your wet clothes in a pile at the foot of the bed. Once you're under the pelts, I'll hang your things by the fire to dry."

Albeit lumpy, a warm bed certainly beat a pallet on the cold hard ground. Yet sleep evaded Cailin. With Connor but a few feet away, how could she close her eyes? Her stomach tumbled, her breath caught, and her heart beat wildly at the thought of him. True, he was arrogant, and stubborn. At times, his words, and actions were cruel and insensitive, but she could not forget the tenderness of their first kiss, his bravery when he rescued her on the riverbank, and his dedication to the people and causes he held dear. She could easily fall in love with this man.

On the other hand, Connor didn't believe in love and had no use for a wife. He'd made it perfectly clear that he'd declared them wed out of necessity, not love. Their marriage a charade, one he planned to have annulled when they reached the Bruce's camp. To consummate such a union would be a sin. To accept him as her husband, a mistake that could only lead to heartbreak. So why did she want him so badly? Why did she ache to be held in his strong arms while he kissed her senseless? Why was she ready to toss aside all that was proper for a night of passion with a man she'd just met?

She knew why. Her mind wandered back to the first, fateful day they met. The feel of his lips upon hers—sensual, full, kissable lips that teased, caressed, and offered so much promise. She imagined what it would be like to lay beneath him, his deft hands roaming her body and taking intimate liberties. When an unfamiliar throbbing and a rush of wetness between her thighs suddenly became too much to bear, she brought her fingers to her mouth and stifled the urge to moan aloud.

Tortured by wanton, sinful desires, she lay naked beneath the covers. Her pulse quickened, and her heart pounded wildly against her ribs. Her breasts grew heavy, and the friction of the pelts caused her nipples to tighten and tingle each time she moved. She'd never ached like this before. Nor had she longed for a man to touch her in forbidden places the way she did now.

Her hands fisted in the covers, and she fought the overpowering urge to go to him. *Nay...I'll not surrender to this madness. When I choose to lay with a man, he will be a man I love, and one who loves me as much or more.* With that oath, she punched the pillow and rolled to her side—determined to get some sleep.

An hour later, she still tossed and turned. If anything, her desire to lay with Connor grew stronger by the minute. When he moaned in his sleep, his injured shoulder came to mind. She sat up in bed, the covers pooling around her waist. While he'd done his best to stoke the fire, it gave off very little warmth. Cold air enveloped her body, and a shiver ran down her spine.

He moaned again, and guilt replaced desire. How could she be so selfish? The man had risked his life to rescue her from the English, and how did she repay his valor? *By stabbing him, and then by forcing him to sleep on the floor, without so much a horse blanket for warmth.*

The least she could do was to share some of the covers. When her bare feet touched the cold plank floor, she quickly wrapped a woolen plaid around her trembling body. She grabbed a pelt from the pile on her bed and crept over to where Connor slept. The tallow candle on the table by the hearth had gone out, but the fire provided enough light for her to see his magnificent form.

Truly one of God's finest masterpieces, Connor's rugged, handsome features brought a smile to her lips. With a wisp of dark hair falling over his eyes and his peaceful expression, he resembled a lad lost in his dream—the only boyish quality he possessed. The tantalizing sight of his hard, sculpted body, and sun-bronzed skin shimmering in the firelight caused her stomach to knot with excitement. His broad chest, dusted with black curls, slowly rose and fell in shallow even breaths. Without conscious thought, her fingers curled in the fur she held in her hand. *What would it be like to bury my hand in those curls? Would they feel coarse against my naked breasts when he crushed me in his strong arms?*

Her gaze drifted downward. Well-defined calf muscles and powerful thighs appeared strong enough to cradle a woman as he pleasured her for hours.

This wasn't the first time she'd seen a man with a finely honed physique. She'd seen Connor without a tunic when she'd mended his wound. She'd watched the men of her clan training in lists—their lean toned bodies glistening with sweat as they pushed themselves to their physical limits. However, this was her first glimpse of a man's most private parts.

At the sight of his manhood, her eyes widened with amazement, and her mouth went dry. She had no control over the rush of heat coursing through her veins, and her body reacted on its own accord. While she was no expert, it was plain to see the Almighty had blessed Connor with a bountiful endowment. She swallowed hard. How could a woman possibly accommodate a man so large?

The sudden urge to taste, touch, and explore every inch of his body shocked her to the core. Given her prim and proper upbringing, she should never have taken such liberties. Instead of feasting her eyes, she should have covered them or, at the least, covered him. Regardless of his marriage declaration, this man was a stranger, and she had no business staring at him in this manner—especially when he was unaware of her scrutiny. The first thing she'd do when they reached Kildrummy Castle would be to visit the chapel and beg the Almighty's forgiveness.

Her curiosity and desire in check, she carefully lowered the pelt over his sleeping form—startled when his hand clamped around her wrist. Before she could react, he dropped her to the floor and pinned her beneath his body, the blade of his dirk pressed to her throat.

"Are you daft? What are you doing prowling around the room in the dark? I could have slit your throat."

She twisted her wrist in an attempt to break free, but his

grip held firm. "You're hurting me. Please let me go."

He released her arm, slipped the dirk back into its sheath, and rolled away. "Never sneak up on a man when he's sleeping," he admonished on a ragged breath.

"I dinna mean to wake you."

"A warrior sleeps with one eye open, and is always prepared to defend himself should the need arise. You're lucky to still be alive. Only a fool would creep up on a man in the middle of the night, dressed as you are."

Rage blazed in his eyes as they bore into hers. The devil himself couldn't look more menacing. She choked back fear and struggled to catch her breath. "I woke up, and the room was so cold. I thought you might have need of a pelt." She dropped the fur, held her plaid in place and scrambled to her feet, but there was nowhere to go.

He rose quickly and covered the space between them. "You play a dangerous game."

"I meant only to cover you, and nothing more." She took a step backward, but could go no further. With her spine pressed against the wall, she lowered her gaze, and gasped. He stood before her, completely naked, his manhood jutting out proudly from between his thighs. The air sizzled. Her heart rose in her throat, and the sound of her pulse echoed in her ears. She felt faint.

Connor snaked his arm around her waist, pulling her against his chest. "You're forever flirting with danger, lass. To see you standing there in only a plaid is more than a mortal man can abide. He dropped his head and kissed her hard. "Mine," he groaned against her mouth.

His teeth nipped and tugged at her lower lip. Her pulse raced and her chest constricted. Could bones truly melt, completely dissolve when a person was kissed with such intensity? She was certain of it. When she finally gasped, desperate for a much-needed gulp of air, his tongue plunged in, tangling with hers.

She could feel his passion, could taste his desire. His strong hands roamed her body, leaving behind a molten trail of desire. He cupped her breasts, testing the weight of each in his palms. His thumbs stroked her nipples and all thought and reason spiraled out of control. Trapped in a boneless, heady world of erotic fantasy, she gave in to the glorious sensations bombarding every nerve, every fiber of her being. He swallowed her moans of pleasure. His tongue delved deeper, ravaging without mercy. A kiss so powerful it stormed her senses and melted her reserve. Pliant in his arms, she offered no resistance.

The raw taste of male caused her knees to buckle. She caught his woodsy scent, a hint of spice, leather, and the unmistakable male musk of his arousal. Finding it hard to remain standing, she swayed toward him for support, bracing her hands on his broad chest. When his hand slid down her back to cup her bottom and pull her into the hollow of his thighs, she thought she might perish in his arms. His heart hammered under her hands, and as he ground his hips against the cradle of her thighs, his rock hard shaft pressed against her aching core.

Feelings, scents, and senses collided as her entire body came alive. Enslaved by the erotic heat, longing knotted her stomach. Tendrils of desire slowly unfurled, unleashing a ravenous firestorm of emotions and sensations that threatened to consume her body and soul. She longed to feel him, flesh against flesh, never dreaming it could be like this between a woman and a man.

"You're beautiful, Cailin. Like a seductive siren who lures a sailor to his death, you have me in your spell. I've tried to resist, but it is no use." His lips trailed across her jaw and along the smooth slender column of her neck, coming to rest in the fragrant curve where her pulse beat wildly.

He tugged at her toga of plaid, and it fell away. Bathed in the soft amber glow of firelight, she stood naked, naked for him—her creamy skin and pert round breasts exposed. He paused for a moment to drink in the sight of her. "May the Almighty forgive me? I cannot fight my desire any longer. Sometimes, the only way to conquer temptation is to surrender to it."

His thumbs teased the rosy tips of her breasts until they stood erect. Ripe and ready for tasting, he lowered his head, taking one of her nipples into his mouth. Suckling gently at first, and then with purpose, he drew the sensitive flesh between his teeth, his lips pressed firmly against her heated flesh.

She moaned aloud, arched toward him, and fisted her hands in his hair. A frown creased her brow when he released the tip, but she purred with delight when he moved to pay equal homage to the other breast. Restless beneath his hands, her soft mewl of pleasure urged him on. Gasps and whimpers of delight caught in her throat as he explored every inch of her slender body.

But when he reached the soft nest of auburn curls guarding her nether region, her body tensed, and she struggled to break free from his embrace. "Nay, you must stop. To allow you to touch me in such a wanton way is a sin for which we will burn in Hell."

Connor smiled at her innocence, but continued his intimate ministrations. "You're wrong, lass. For a man to touch his wife in a way that gives her pleasure is not a sin. Relax, and let me show you."

Ignoring her protest, he trailed his fingers across the flat plane of her abdomen, and with a feather-light touch, caressed the delicate flesh of her inner thighs. His skilful fingers explored the secrets of her femininity, and his thumb found the pearl of womanly pleasure. A light brush across the swollen bud had her bucking against his hand. "You're so wet, tight, and ready for loving." He moaned, and dipped his fingers past the slick folds. "Close your eyes, and imagine me buried within your warmth. You're the most beautiful thing I have ever seen. Let yourself go. Give in to the pleasure."

The fire between Cailin's thighs burned so hot, she thought she'd expire from the pure pleasure of it. As he guided her toward the point of no return, she dropped her head back, and rolled it from side to side. When he increased his tempo and slid a second finger into her throbbing heat, her vision blurred, and shockwaves of pleasure rippled through her body. A molten hot mix of lust and desire pooled low in her belly. She arched her back, forcing even greater intimacy. He slid his fingers deeper into her hot, moist center, and his strokes quickened with erotic intent.

On the verge of something she had never before experienced, her body tensed, and her thighs quivered in anticipation. When she could take no more, a cataclysmic explosion of white light and mind-numbing euphoria pushed her over the edge.

Chapter 9

When Cailin cried out in release, Connor's body answered with a rush of sensations so sharp his breath lodged in his throat. The raspy urgency of her voice, and the way she bucked beneath his touch sent a surge of lust and desire straight to his groin.

It was a wonder he didn't explode on the spot. His lips covered hers, swallowing her cry of rapture. Hopelessly lost in the taste and wonder of her, he scooped her into his arms and carried her toward the bed. This was only the beginning. Before the night was over, he vowed to see her fully sated, and to find his own release.

He pried his lips from hers, then gently placed her on the mattress and watched as she languidly stretched out before him. His eyes drank in her beauty, her sensual curves, and her soft creamy skin bathed in the moonlight streaming through the casement window. Her sultry smile unleashed something primitive. Lust-fed desire fired his blood, challenging the need to be tender and protective.

Mesmerized by the longing in her eyes, a mirror of his own, his gaze fell to her mouth as swollen lips parted when the tip of her soft pink tongue peeked out to moisten them. How a simple act could be so sensual boggled his mind. Drawn by a force too difficult to ignore, he dropped his head and indulged his fantasy.

Her lips responded lovingly, mimicking his intimate caress. He moaned aloud, savoring the taste of her desire, her surrender. It was obvious she wanted him as much as he wanted her. The thought made him want to roar with pride.

Overcome with primal need, his body covered hers, pressing her sleek form into the mattress. He buried his face in the fragrant curve of her neck and took a deep breath. Her intoxicating scent was enough to drive a man wild.

"You fire my blood and addle my senses, woman," he moaned against her ear. He raised his head, resting the bulk of his weight on his elbows and forearms, and stared into her eyes. The soft jade orbs darkened to an emerald green and filled with passion. "Will you have me, wife?"

She nodded. "Aye, I will have you, m'lord."

"Connor. Say my name."

"Aye, Connor, I'll have you."

A possessive feral growl rumbled in his chest as he captured her mouth with his own. But this time, he showed no tenderness, no restraint. He kissed her hard, took possession, and meant to see his needs fulfilled. He was about to do the most foolish, reckless thing he'd ever done, and damn the consequences.

There'd be plenty of time to savor and explore every inch of her luscious body once he'd found his release. He slid his hand between their bodies, seeking her most intimate place. When he found his mark and dipped his fingers inside her waiting heat, her hips softened, and her body wept for him. He released a feral groan of approval. The urge to dip his head and taste the sweet nectar coating his fingers was overpowering, but the need to bury his aching shaft in her hot velvet sheath proved greater.

He nudged her legs apart with his knee and nestled his body between her thighs. She wanted him. He could feel it in his soul. The throbbing tip of his thick hard shaft pressed against the slick swollen flesh of her intimate center, but instead of accepting his offering, her body tensed, and her nails dug into his shoulders.

With her wide eyes brimming with tears and a look of fear on her face, she asked, "Will it hurt? I'm told the first time comes with a terrible pain."

He withdrew slightly and tightened his embrace. "I will never hurt you *liuadhe,* my beloved. Try to relax. There will be a brief feeling of pressure when I break through your maidenhead, but it will be quickly replaced with pleasure. I promise to be gentle." He bit his lower lip and drew on his last shreds of self-control, fighting the overpowering urge to ram his aching rod to the hilt.

Despite his reassurance, her grip tightened on his shoulder, and her body trembled. "I'm frightened. I have never done this before, and dinna know what to do."

"That makes it all the sweeter. Let me teach you the way of it, *leannan.*" He nudged her thighs further apart and entered her slowly.

Once inside her, he lay very still, giving her a moment to adjust to the newness of their joining. "When a man and woman couple, the glorious feeling is like no other. Relax, sweet, and let this moment of ecstasy take you to the stars."

Instinctively, she raised her hips to accommodate him, and he eased in a little farther, but paused when he met the resistance of her maidenhead. Her velvet sheath was so tight and slick, his shaft thick, hard, ready to erupt. He tried to hold back, but the unbridled passion firing his blood and the crushing desire to claim her as his own, challenged his last ounce of reserve.

Her arms wrapped around his neck, and she nibbled on his ear lobe. The warmth of her breath on his skin and her soft moans of pleasure when he shifted inside her, tipped him over the edge. When her hips rose from the bed and she arched toward him, he thrust hard and deep, spilling her maiden blood.

As the barrier of her innocence gave way, she gasped, and he saw a flicker of pain flash in her eyes before she could conceal it. He closed his mouth over hers and swallowed her painful sob. Tears rolled down her cheeks, but she didn't utter another sound. He began to move in a slow, steady rhythm, and he felt her relax in his arms.

Bonded by pleasure, their bodies fit together as if made for each other. They moved as one—every thought and sensation centered on their joining. As the tempo increased, her feminine muscles pulsed, milking his arousal, and drawing him deeper. What started as ripples of pleasure quickly built to a tidal wave of uncontrolled desire. When she gripped his body and pulled him toward her, he quickened the pace, stoking the inferno that raged between them. Short, sharp pants mixed with squeals of delight as her body bucked and writhed beneath him. When she held her breath and her thighs began to quiver, he knew she was close. Her head dropped back, her muscles tightened around his arousal, and she called out his name. He thrust one more time, shouted out an ear-piercing war cry, and joined her in an explosive release of his own.

Afraid he might crush her with his weight, he rolled to his side, taking her with him, and cradled her against his sweat-soaked frame. She curled her fingers on his chest, gazed up at him, and smiled. In one swift move, he pulled her beneath him, and made love to her again. But this time, he took it slower, gently guiding her through the erotic experience, savoring the wonder of discovery in her eyes.

Afterward, though sated and exhausted, sleep evaded him. They'd made love until the wee hours of the morning. Exhausted, she lay, peaceful, in his arms. With his lips lightly pressed against Cailin's brow, he muttered softly, "Heaven is missing an angel this night. You have given me a glimpse of paradise, and I swear that I saw the Almighty himself." He shifted in bed, being careful not to wake her.

The tangle of plaid swaddling her sleek body barely covered her modesty and one lovely breast. To his delight, the other delectable rose-tipped globe remained exposed for his viewing pleasure. He'd suckled those perfect mounds for hours, and it took every ounce of self-control not to dip his head, drag the pert bud between his teeth, and sample her again.

Were he a gentleman, he'd cover her nakedness, but to cloak such beauty would be a sin. His eyes widened as he took in every line, every delicate curve of her luscious body. Her shapely legs went on forever, and when wrapped around his waist, enveloped him in the purest form of ecstasy. He brushed a stray curl from her cheek—still flushed with the afterglow of their passion. The musky scent of their lovemaking hung heavy in the air, and the ache in his groin intensified.

Cailin's beauty, and the sultry seductive way she responded to his touch left him awestruck, but he found her streak of feistiness, tenacity, and intelligence equally desirable. She was everything a man could want, and she'd awakened something primitive from deep within his soul. Emotions and needs he'd believed were dead, buried forever. With passion and desire reborn, his manhood sprang to life. He refused to think about the future. For this night, this moment, she was his, and his alone.

When she moved, a wince of pain clouded her delicate features, and guilt tugged at his heart. She had come to him a maiden—offering him the most precious gift he'd ever received. Knowing this, he should have taken things slower. Instead, the idea of her innocence had aroused and excited him beyond his wildest dreams.

She accepted him with such eagerness, and trusted him with her heart. In turn, he'd behaved like a drunken warrior that hadn't lifted a woman's skirt in a year.

A soft sigh escaped her lips, and she snuggled against his side. He could watch her sleep forever, bathed in the afterglow of the most earth-shattering coupling he had ever known. His chest swelled with emotion, yet his stomach twisted with regret.

Stop it, now! This night will end, and she is not yours to keep. Yet, after tasting her passion and claiming her as his own, how could he ever let her go? What if he'd planted a babe in her belly? Could he turn his back on mother and child? The thought troubled him greatly. But he knew the English would not give up their search. As long as they hunted her, Cailin would never have a minute of peace. He had sworn his oath to the Bruce and could not turn his back on his king and country. Like it or not, the time would come, and for her safety, they would have to part ways. When that day came, it would devastate him.

Startled by a rap on the door, Connor sprang from bed, drew his sword, and headed across the room. The knock came again, only this time louder.

"M'lord, please open the door. I must speak with you."

He recognized the innkeeper's voice and glanced toward the window. The sun had yet to rise. "What is it, James? Why do you come to us at this early hour?"

"Please, m'lord. I must speak with you on a matter of great importance. I dinna think it wise to discuss what I have to tell you in the hall."

He heard the concern in the man's voice and opened the door a crack. He watched James shift his weight from one foot to the other as he rang his chubby hands in front of him. Connor quickly glanced back over his shoulder in the direction of the bed. Satisfied that Cailin was adequately covered, he opened the door wider. "Why do you disturb us? Is there trouble afoot?"

James entered the room, and Connor closed the door behind him. "I apologize for waking you so early, m'lord, but you must get up and be on your way. As we speak, your brothers ready the horses."

"Why must we leave before daybreak?"

"English soldiers came into the inn right after you retired. They accused the lass of killing an officer and offered a reward for her capture. My patrons were questioned, but no one betrayed you."

"I was watching from atop the stairs and am grateful no one gave us away?"

"Mayhap they feared the wrath of my wife more than that of the English." James chuckled. "They know Cora would flay any man who dared to speak up and cut them off without a drop. Most men would rather risk death than lose their whisky. However, my guess is that they are just tired of the English tyranny."

"When they didn't search the rooms, I assumed they had left without incident, and dinna return."

"Well in their cups they were when the lieutenant and his aide decided to return to their billet. Your brother followed them and returned a short time later. I dinna asked them what happened, but I had my suspicions. When Malcolm MacTovoch came barreling into the inn before dawn and said he'd found two dead English soldiers behind his barn, I knew what had transpired."

"You think my brothers killed these men?"

"According to Malcolm, someone ran them through. No one except Cora and I know what really happened to them. If asked, the villagers can say without a lie that the two men left the inn hail and hardy." He glanced toward the bed and lowered his voice. "Best you wake the lass and make ready to leave. It is not safe for you to tarry. Cora prepared some food for you to take along."

"Thank you. Tell my brothers we come anon." Connor offered his arm. James grasped his wrist, and the two men exchanged a hardy shake.

"I've two daughters of my own. If any man tried to have his way with one of them, they'd not live to brag about it. Best you rouse the lass and be on your way before the English arrive looking for their friends."

"Connor?"

"See to your wife." James winked, then slipped into the hall and closed the door behind him.

"What is it, Connor?" Her sultry voice was still husky from sleep. "Why does the innkeeper come to us so early?" She sat up in bed, her eyes full of questions.

"Shhhh, *dinna fash yourself, leannan.*" He slid beneath the pelts and pulled her into his arms. "Bryce and Alasdair are readying the horses. They thought it best we leave before sunrise and bid the innkeeper wake us." He didn't see any reason to tell her about the dead English officers.

"You said the soldiers were gone. Do you think they'll return so soon?"

"I'm not willing to take that chance. Best we put some distance between Kirkintillock and us before daybreak. Come, *liuadhe*. If we linger any longer, I won't be able to tear myself away. The overwhelming urge to love you again challenges my ability to think like a rational man."

With a feather-light touch, Cailin drew a seductive line down the center of his chest, her hand coming to rest in his lap. She wrapped her fingers around his burgeoning manhood and smiled seductively. "I like it when you don't act rationally."

Connor sucked in a gulp of air. "If you keep that up, I will not be able to stop." He captured her lips and groaned. "Och, if only this could be another place and time. You are bewitching, *liuadhe*. Holding you in my arms and thrusting inside you is all I can think about."

"Then make love to me again, husband."

"We dinna have the luxury of time and must be away, before the English garrison resumes their search." He kissed her brow, then climbed out of bed.

"Aye, more's the pity." She heaved a lamenting sigh, pulled the covers up around her neck, and sank back against the pillows.

Connor snatched the shirt he'd left drying by the hearth

and slipped it over his head. After pulling on his trews, he tugged on his boots. "Get dressed and meet me downstairs." He quickly returned to the bed and handed Cailin her clothes. "For the moment, the English threat has passed, but there is no telling when more soldiers will arrive and resume the search. Make haste, and I'll see to my brothers."

Cailin descended the wooden staircase to find Connor, Cora, and Bryce waiting for her. James trotted down the stair a few minutes later, carrying a basket of bed linens, and sporting a mischievous grin. Cora took the basket from her husband and, after the pair exchanged a few words, she returned to the group.

"Good morning, sister. How fare you this fine day?" A broad grin crossed Alasdair's face as he entered the inn. "I trust you slept well."

"Day? It is the middle of the night." Bryce brought his hand up and stifled a yawn.

Unable to face her new brothers by marriage, she lowered her gaze and muttered softly. "I slept very well." Certain they knew exactly what had transpired, heat rose in her cheeks.

"At least your man let you get some sleep." Cora slid her arm around Cailin's shoulder and ushered her to a chair by the door. She glanced in Connor's direction and gave him a knowing look. "Mind you ride with care, m'lord. The wee lassie is bound to be sore."

"I'll be sure she is not overtaxed. We'll see to the horses, and then be on our way." Connor left the inn with his brothers in tow.

Cailin sat on the chair, twisting the corner of her plaid in her hands. "How did you know?" She raised her head, her eyes locking with Cora's.

The older woman's lips curled in a wry grin, and she lightly touched Cailin's cheek. "Do you mean aside from the fact that you have the glow of a woman well loved? I was once your age. My James was a handsome brawny man in his youth. I well remember our wedding night." Her smile broadened as she patted Cailin's shoulder and lowered her voice to a whisper. "James also brought down the sheets to be washed."

Cailin nodded, and lowered her eyes in shame. The sheets bore the undeniable proof of their lovemaking and the loss of her innocence. Had she made a mistake? Was she too willing to surrender her maidenhood to a man she hardly knew? She chewed on her bottom lip—worried she'd made a foolish decision. When Connor had made sweet love to her, she had no reservations or doubt. Now, she wondered how things would all pan out. She was married to a man that didn't love her. He'd made no secret of the fact that he planned to have their marriage annulled when they reached the Bruce's camp. Would she be able to say goodbye and watch him walk out of her life forever? Where would she go, and what if she carried his child?

She could never return to Dunkeld. Her father would be furious and married or not, he would call her a whore. She'd been promised in marriage to Laird Murray, and Duncan would never condone her actions. Spoiled by the loss of her virginity, no man of status would want her.

"Are you all right, dear? You're looking very pale all of a sudden."

"I'm fine, Cora. I'm sorry about the sheets."

"Dinna *fash* yourself, my dear." She patted Cailin's hand, and then moved behind the bar. "Since there is no time for you to break your fast, I've fixed you something for the journey. I'm sure your husband has an appetite this morn, and that big fellow looks like he doesn't miss many meals." She laughed, and then handed her a large haversack. "There are some apples, a wedge of cheese, dried venison, bannock, and a few meat pasties to tide you over until you can stop and replenish your supplies. James has seen that the wineskins are filled with ale and water."

"Thank you. I'll never forget your kindness."

"It is no trouble at all. James and I are happy to help."

"What happened last night?" Connor asked as the three brothers entered the barn. "James said the English soldiers who came to the inn were found slain behind a farmer's barn."

"We followed them and made sure they posed no threat, but we dinna kill them. When they left the inn, they were well in their cups and in no shape to make it back to their camp." Bryce moved to Lucifer's side and tightened the cinch on his saddle. "They dinna appear to pose any threat. We figured if we left before dawn, we'd be long away before they made it back to the garrison."

Connor's brow furrowed. "You took a great risk and could have been killed. What if someone saw you following the soldiers?"

"There were no witnesses. What happened to them after we left them is a mystery. They were flaunting a hefty reward. Mayhap someone overheard and decided to relieve them of it."

"In any case, we must leave Kirkintillock," Connor said as he circled Thor and checked the saddle. "I wish we had another horse. Cailin weighs no more than a child, but it is still a burden for Thor to carry us both."

Alasdair climbed onto his horse's back and glanced down at his brothers. "There'll be many farms along the way.

Surely we can find a suitable mount for your lady wife."

"Aye. Best we be away," Connor replied, and led Thor out of the barn.

Chapter 10

After putting a comfortable distance between them and the inn, they slowed their pace. Alasdair rode up beside his brothers. "We appear to have made away clean. If the English were going to catch us, they'd have been upon us by now."

"Aye, but I won't rest easy until we reach Kildrummy Castle and I know the lass is safe." Connor glanced over his shoulder at Cailin. Astride the spirited bay palfrey, purchased from a farmer on the outskirts of Kirkintillock, she proved to be a competent horsewoman. To her credit, she managed to keep up the grueling pace, riding through miles of rugged terrain without a word of complaint, and never once did she slow them down.

Connor frowned, and guilt twisted his gut. "She doesn't belong here. She should be dressed in an elegant silk gown, reading poetry, listening to music, or entertaining guests. With her intelligence, beauty, and poise, she'd make an excellent chatelaine, and be the envy of every man in Scotland. Instead she is forced to keep up an inhuman pace on horseback, is dirty, exhausted, and wearing a lad's clothes." Torn between regret and desire, he shook his head and released a heavy sigh.

He'd taken her innocence, a precious gift he could never return, yet he'd carry the memories of those few hours of bliss in his heart forever. The relief he'd felt when they found the horse for Cailin to ride was insurmountable. To travel the last leg of their journey with her nestled on his lap, her sweet womanly fragrance filling his senses, her warm supple body molded against his aching groin, would have been pure torture. Now if he could just maintain a safe distance between them and stay the nagging urge to take her in his arms and kiss her senseless, he might just make it to the Bruce's camp a sane man.

While he found it difficult to hide the longing in his eyes, he could not forget that once they reached their destination, they'd have no choice but to go their separate ways. Cailin deserved far more than he could offer. He'd have the Bruce repudiate their marriage declaration. It was the best thing for everyone involved, or so he tried to convince himself.

He cursed his weakness, for allowing lust and desire to get the better of him. When he'd bedded a woman in the past, he always remained in control. Once his partner reached her womanly pleasure, he'd release his seed into the sheets. Yet with Cailin, it was different. They moved together as if they were one, and the need to find his sublime release while joined in ecstasy overrode all sense and reason. Could Cailin be with child? Nay! He slammed his fist on the pummel of his saddle. Fate would not be so cruel.

"You look preoccupied, brother." Bryce rode up beside Connor.

"I'm fine."

"Mayhap we could stop and rest. I'd wager the lass could use a bit of a break. Surely after six hours in the saddle, every muscle in her body must ache in protest. I know mine do."

"Dinna stop on my account." Despite her stoic declaration, she shifted in the saddle, stretching her back and rolling her neck.

"The horses need tending, and we can all use a chance to stretch our legs." Connor reined in Thor and surveyed the area.

"I could use something to eat." Alasdair rubbed his belly and longingly eyed the haversack of food hanging from Bryce's saddle.

Bryce rolled his eyes skyward. "His arse could be

numb and his legs about to fall off, but it is his stomach that concerns him the most."

"If you'll stop your blasted bickering, we'll break here, and Alasdair can fill his stomach." Connor quickly slid from the saddle, and braced his hands against the small of his back. Twisting from side to side, he worked out the kinks. He rolled his shoulders several times and moaned as the tension eased. After the rigors of the day, and a night spent making love to Cailin, he was exhausted. Not that he was about to admit that to his brothers.

Bryce seized the palfrey's bridle and held his hand out in Cailin's direction. "Do you need a hand dismounting?" He glanced over his shoulder at Connor, his smile full of mischief.

Connor cursed, and without giving thought to his actions, he shoved Bryce out of the way. "I'll help her." He gave his brother a menacing look, wrapped his hands around Cailin's slender waist, lifted her from the saddle, and carried her toward a nearby shade tree.

Her hands splayed across his broad shoulders as she pressed her slender body against his chest. Connor felt the catch in her breath as his hand trailed down her back and settled over her bottom. *I can feel every beat of her heart as if it were my own. With her luscious lips slightly parted and her head tilted up, she is ready for the taking. All I have to do is...*It took his last ounce of self-control not to dip his head and claim her waiting lips.

He placed her on the ground and took a step back. "Best you tend to your needs. We'll not be stopping long. Once we've given the horses a chance to rest and have had a bite to eat, we'll be on our way." Despite her crestfallen look, he steeled himself against the overwhelming urge to envelope her in his arms and apologize for his boorish behavior.

"Have I done something to displease you?" Her eyes searched his for answers.

Even though she had the heart and spirit of a tigress, she looked so young and helpless. She stood before him in a lad's clothes, her cheeks smudged with dirt. Strands of auburn hair framed her heart-shaped face. With her slender fingers intertwined, she held her dainty hands in front of her belly—hands that hours before had worked their magic on his body, stroking his manhood to life and sending shivers of desire to his very core.

Without conscious thought, he tucked a stray strand of hair behind her ear, then brushed the dirt from her cheek with the pad of his thumb. "You've done nothing wrong. If we wish to reach Kildrummy Castle on the morrow, there are still many miles to cover before this day is spent. Go tend to your needs, and mind you dinna wander beyond that group of bushes." He pointed to a thicket near the river.

He watched the gentle sway of her hips as she walked away. A lump formed in his throat at the thought of never making love to her again. He shook his head in an attempt to bring his randy body under control. He had to be strong, not only for his sake, but for hers as well. Why the Almighty sent this angel to him, knowing they could never be together, was beyond his comprehension. Was this a test of his honor and fortitude, or a form of penance for his sins? If a test, he'd failed miserably. If penance, he could think of no crueler form of punishment.

Bryce approached his brother from behind and slid his hand over his shoulder. "What are you going to do?"

"Do?" Connor asked, his eyes never leaving the spot where Cailin had disappeared behind the bushes.

"About the lass? We covered a lot of ground today and if we keep up this pace, we'll be at Kildrummy Castle by noon tomorrow. You'll have to make a decision soon."

"I have made my decision. Once she is safely sequestered, I will rejoin my fellow patriots in our bid to free Scotland of English tyranny."

"It's not that simple, and you know it. Your marriage by declaration is as binding as any vows taken before a priest. Like it or not, you now have a wife to consider."

"I wed out of necessity, not by choice. There isn't a court in Scotland that would expect me to honor a declaration made under such duress. Robert has the power to disavow a marriage if he so chooses."

"Mayhap you had no choice about the marriage declaration, but you did when it came to bedding the lass. What if she carries your babe? Can you just walk away, never to see your bairn or wife again?" Bryce shook his head. "You're not that kind of man. You may deny your feelings, but I know you, brother. You are in love, and I dinna believe you could desert her."

"Cailin will be better off without me. I have nothing to offer a wife." However, the possibility that she might carry his child did weigh heavy on his mind.

"You have yourself to offer. If only you would stop being so stubborn and unlock your heart."

"I'm a warrior sworn to fight and, if necessary, give my life for the cause. Should I die in battle, I dinna want to leave behind a wife and children to mourn my passing. Not like our—"

"Da?" Bryce finished his sentence. "But you do have a wife, and mayhap a bairn on the way. Are you prepared to walk away and not look back? The decision is difficult, but I have faith you'll make the right choice."

"I told you the decision is already made. Now leave me be." Connor stormed off in search of Cailin.

"You at least owe the lass an explanation," Bryce called after his brother's retreating form.

Cailin sat on a large bolder overlooking a stream that meandered through the valley. She'd picked a daisy and plucked the pearl-white petals one by one.

Connor strode up beside her. "We need to talk." His

voice held a serious note.

"About what?" She looked up at him, her eyes wide with questions.

In a feeble attempt to appear nonchalant, Connor reached up and picked a leaf from a low hanging branch. After examining the frond and nervously shifting his weight from one foot to the other, he finally spoke. "We need to talk about last night. It should never have happened, and I'm very sorry," he blurted out before she had a chance to respond. "If I could turn back the time, I would give you back your innocence and not behave like a randy lad in heat."

"I offered myself to you freely. You took nothing that I dinna wish to give." She proudly looked him in the eye. "You made it very clear that you dinna want a wife. You declared us married to protect me, and I will not hold you responsible for what happened between us. I dinna blame you if you wish to have the marriage dissolved."

Taken aback by her candor, Connor stood transfixed, searching for his voice. "I should have been stronger and fought temptation. You're a breathtaking young woman and have so much to offer. You have barely seen eight and ten summers and are unfamiliar with the ways of passion between a man and a woman. I took advantage of your inexperience, and I'm sorry."

She held her hand up in protest. "Please, m'lord, I bid you leave me some shred of dignity." With downcast eyes, she nibbled on her bottom lip.

She does that to keep it from quivering, as she tries to hide the fact that I have broken her heart. He had not known her for long, but he had memorized every little quirk and adorable gesture. He'd committed to memory her delicate features, winsome smile, and the sultry sound of her voice. Not to mention her soft mewls of pleasure when they made love.

His heart clawed at his chest, begging for release. He

wanted to take her in his arms. He longed to hold her close, to tell her that everything would be all right, and that they would be together. He wanted to promise her a future, but it would be a lie.

The war with England was coming to a head. Given what he'd learned on his mission to Perth, the Scottish forces were about to face a most formidable enemy in Aymer de Valence.

He'd vowed on his father's grave to avenge the death of his family members and had pledged his fealty to Robert the Bruce. His sword, and life, belonged to Scotland, and he could not let Cailin burrow any deeper beneath his skin than she already had. Robert would be granting her a boon if he disavowed the marriage. She deserved a husband who could be there to protect her. Moreover, if God saw fit to bless her with a child, that child would need a father who could be there to show him right from wrong, could teach him to hunt, to fight, and to be a fine, and decent man—or a respectable woman if the babe was a lass.

He closed his eyes for a moment and pictured Cailin growing round with a babe in her belly. The adorable way she'd waddle across a room as her time grew near. He could hear the soft lilt of her voice as she sang a sweet lullaby to the babe tucked safely in her womb and imagined the fierce look of tenacity and determination on her face as she battled the pains of labor to bring the bairn into the world. His mind's eye conjured up the image of a babe suckling at her perfect, round breasts. He couldn't picture anything lovelier.

He envisioned a bonnie wee lassie with her mother's dark auburn curls, soft green eyes, and beautiful smile. A smile that would melt not only her da's heart, but that of any man who dared to look upon it. She'd be petite and delicate, yet filled with spice and sass. Like her mother, no man would ever tell her what to do.

His mind shifted to a dark-haired lad, his brow furrowed,

the muscles straining to pull back on the bowstring—prepared to let loose an arrow for the first time. He'd missed the target by a mile, but it wouldn't matter. Filled with pride and determination, he'd pluck another arrow from the quiver, and under the watchful eye of his da, he'd practice until he got it right.

But it was a life he'd never know. Another man would sire Cailin's children. The thought hit him like a kick in the gut. After tomorrow, he'd never know the bliss of holding her in his arms again. While he'd been the one to take her innocence, another man would warm her bed. The ideal man she'd so adamantly described on the night they wed would love her with all his heart and marry her by choice, not out of necessity.

Unfortunately, wishing he could be that man didn't make it so. His fate had been sealed the day he watched his father and brother be slaughtered by the English. That was the day a fourteen-year-old boy became a man on a mission.

But Cailin had breached the curtain wall around his heart of stone. He'd let down his guard and allowed Cupid's arrow to pierce the vulnerable organ, causing it to beat with a wild fury he'd never known. Now he had to heal that wound and bury those emotions even deeper than ever before.

"I wish I could be the man you've dreamed about. If I had the power to change things, I would." He held out his hand in her direction. "Come, we can cover a few more miles before making camp for the night." When she didn't respond, he squatted down beside her, and ran his hand along her cheek. He felt the dampness of tears on his fingertips. "You must be hungry. Let us rejoin my brothers before Alasdair eats everything Cora packed for the journey." His attempt to lighten the mood and change the subject failed. She continued to stare at the ground, her eyes brimming with tears.

Cailin shook her head. "If you please, I'd like a few

minutes alone with my thoughts."

He nodded. "Take as long as you need. I'll have Bryce put something aside for you to eat." With a heavy heart, he headed back toward the horses.

Her shoulders slumped as she leaned against a moss-covered tree trunk. She blinked away the tears and raised her chin—determined to be brave and to face the future with her head held high. She'd managed to survive her first eighteen years without Connor Fraser, she could survive the rest of her life without him. Or could she?

Despite the dire circumstances under which they met, he caused her heart to soar. However, the same heart that swelled with joy as they made love sank like a stone beneath the icy waters of a loch at the thought of him walking out of her life forever. She knew it was inevitable, but didn't think it would be so soon. She'd actually begun to hope that by the time they reached Kildrummy Castle, he'd change his mind, might even fight to keep her by his side.

She loved him and knew beyond any doubt that she could never feel this strongly for another man. He awakened the woman in her, unleashing emotions she'd never known existed. He made her feel beautiful, desirable, and for the first time in her life, like someone who truly mattered.

Until now, she'd merely existed. Locked away in her father's keep, she'd spent her entire life alone, dreaming of the day that someone would love her enough to accept her for who she was. She meant nothing to her father, but Connor risked his life, and that of his brothers, to protect her from Borden. Despite his aversion to marriage, he declared them husband and wife to save her reputation and to protect her identity. He'd made love to her with wild abandon and even though it was only for one night, he showed her what it was like to lie in the arms of man who thought her the most precious thing in the world.

Her heart ached so badly, she was certain it would shatter beyond repair. So much had happened in the space of a few days that it felt as if she'd aged ten summers. Would she ever find some semblance of order in her life? Or was she destined to spend the rest of her days alone, trying to stay one step ahead of the English executioner?

What she longed for was simple. She wanted a home, a man who loved her, and babes. Bairns she could shower with affection and attention. Babes that would grow up knowing their parents loved and cherished them. She wanted all of these things, but more than anything, she wanted Connor. But she refused to beg for his affection.

"Are you ready to leave?"

Lost in thought, she didn't hear Bryce approach. She dragged the heel of her hand across her tear-stained cheeks in an attempt to hide the fact that she'd been crying and coughed to clear her throat. "Aye, I'm ready."

Bryce grasped her hand, helping her to her feet. "My brother is a hard-headed fool. He would not know a good thing if it jumped up and bit him in the arse. Be patient, lass. I'm certain that by the time we reach Kildrummy castle, he'll be begging you to stay."

"Connor is a good man and will do what he thinks is best." Feeling another bout of tears coming on, she turned and headed toward the horses.

As she approached, Connor moved to her side. "Are you all right?" he asked, his voice laced with concern.

"Aye, I'm fine." In truth, she was devastated.

"You haven't eaten," Bryce pointed out as he reached into the haversack and pulled out a meat-filled pastry.

"He's right," Connor whispered in her ear. "You need to eat something and keep up your strength." He placed his hand against the small of her back and steered her toward

Bryce. His touch sent a shockwave of desire up her spine, but she refused to believe it meant anything more than a gesture of kindness.

"Cora is an excellent cook." Bryce held out the pastry in her direction.

"I'll say. They're delicious." Alasdair picked up the haversack, reached inside, and grabbed another.

"You should know. You've already eaten three." Bryce snatched the sack from his brother's hand. "Not to mention the fact that you've also eaten several oatcakes, half a loaf of bannock, some venison, and cheese. You had best eat something, lass, before it is all gone."

"A piece of fruit would be fine. I'm really not very hungry." Bryce handed her an apple. She could feel Connor's eyes upon her as she took the first succulent bite. When she glanced in his direction, he licked his lower lip—his dark eyes fixed on a trickle of juice running down her chin. Using a small square of linen, she wiped it away.

Connor cursed and turned on his heels. "Once you've finished, we'll leave. We've already tarried long enough."

Chapter 11

Connor cupped his hand over his eyes and peered up at a cloudless azure sky. Judging by the position of the sun, it was near noon, and if they continued at their current pace, they'd reach Kildrummy Castle in time for the evening meal.

Bone weary from travel and lack of sleep, he shifted in the saddle and brought his hand up to stifle a groan. Telling Cailin that their lovemaking had been a mistake was the right thing to do, but banishing her from his thoughts and dreams was not an easy task. He'd tossed and turned all night—tormented by the look of disappointment on her face and haunted by the knowledge that once they reached their destination, he'd have to let her go. In time she would get over it and move on with her life, but could he?

He muttered a curse under his breath. He'd begun to question his priorities again and had to stop yearning for things he could never possess. Despite the memories of their night of unbridled passion, stolen moments, and what might have been, he'd made his decision, and meant to stick by it. He vowed to be strong and to resist temptation.

A tree branch snapped on the trail ahead of them. Connor held his hand in the air, signaling to the others to stop. As he quickly surveyed the area, he reached over his shoulder and slid the claymore from the baldric on his back—the scrape of steel against leather the only sound breaking the eerie silence. "Hold fast, and make ready."

"What is it?" Bryce rode up beside his brother.

Connor narrowed his eyes and scanned the surrounding area again. "I heard something up ahead. Wait here while I check it out. Keep your head on a swivel, and dinna leave

Cailin unattended. Guard her with your life if necessary."

"You know I will. Be careful." Bryce moved to her side and grabbed the reins of the palfrey.

"Why are we stopping?"

Bryce brought his finger to his lips to silence her.

Before Connor could spur Thor into action, a man bellowed from behind a large oak tree only a few feet away. "Halt, and state your business."

Connor slid from the saddle, tossed Thor's reins to Bryce, and then took up a fighting stance in the middle of the trail. "Come out and face me like a man, you cowardly buffoon." He stood his ground when two huge men dressed in Highland plaid and sporting two-handed claymores, stepped into the clearing.

"Who do you think you're calling a buffoon?" The older of the two men swung his claymore in a circle above his head.

"There are only two of you guarding the trail? I expected more of a challenge." He glanced at Bryce, shrugged, and smiled.

"Connor, behind you!" Cailin shrieked when the older man lunged forward. As the attacker's blade arced through the air, he turned and lifted his claymore in time to deflect the blow.

"You're getting old, Cameron." Connor laughed, and lowered his weapon. "There was a time when I would have never heard you coming. Nor would I have bested you in a fight."

Cameron scowled. "I'm as spry as ever and will challenge any man who tries to prove differently. Especially a cocky young pup, who is still wet behind the ears." He lowered his blade and took a step in Connor's direction with his arm outstretched.

Cailin leaned toward Bryce. "You know these men?"

"They are two of Robert's most trusted guardsmen.

We've known Cameron since we were lads." Bryce dismounted and joined his brother in greeting their comrades.

"Best we make haste." Alasdair joined them. "We can catch up on old times once we're inside the castle walls and have spoken with Robert."

"He's right. The Bruce has been anxiously awaiting your return, and it's not wise to tarry here any longer." Cameron's eyes shifted from Cailin to Connor. "Where did you pick up the lad?"

"It is a long story, my friend." Connor swung his leg over Thor's back and pulled himself into the saddle with ease. "A story best told over a tankard of ale, mayhap two or three." He kicked his horse, urging him forward.

Elaborate earthen works, a high stone curtain wall, a twin-towered gatehouse, and dry moat protected Kildrummy Castle from attack on three sides. Of French design, the back of the D-shaped structure bordered on a deep ravine, making it virtually impossible to breach the walls from behind. Four separate towers of equal height rose like giants above the parapets, but it was a single stone tower—at least seven stories tall—that she found most impressive. If an enemy managed to get into the bailey, the laird and his family could take refuge at the top, while his men rallied at the base to protect them.

"It is magnificent," Cailin said as they approached a massive drawbridge.

Iron groaned, and chains rattled as the portcullis rose, granting them entrance to the castle bailey. Atop the parapets a crowd waved and cheered as they passed beneath the gate. However all grew quiet and heads turned when the daunting figure of a man stepped out of the center tower and descended the stone staircase.

The man strode across the bailey with an air of authority, and purpose. With his tall burly stature, broad shoulders, red hair, and piercing blue eyes, he could have been an older version of Alasdair. The family resemblance was unmistakable.

"Welcome home lads. We are glad you made it back safely."

While introductions were forthcoming, Cailin already concluded that this strapping man in his mid forties must be Connor's cousin, the famous Scottish patriot, Sir Simon Fraser. She watched the older man approach. Nibbling nervously on her lower lip, she couldn't help but wonder what the future held. Now that they had reached Kildrummy Castle, would she be safe? Would Connor acknowledge her as his bride, or go ahead with his plan to have their union dissolved? He'd made his feelings about marriage clear, but she hoped he would change his mind. She had fallen in love with the man, but refused to be a millstone around his neck. Should he decide to go through with the annulment, she would not protest.

Cailin glanced down at her soiled clothing. Suddenly self-conscious of her disheveled appearance, she released a soft sigh. She was about to meet Connor's revered cousin and eventually the newly crowned king and queen of Scotland. What would they think of her?

Connor climbed from his horse and handed Thor's reins to a young squire. "See that he has a good rubdown and plenty of oats, Blair."

"Aye, m'lord, I'll take good care of him. I'll fetch Taren, and have him come for the other horses." The boy led Thor toward the stable.

"We were expecting you two days ago. Robert was starting to worry that something was amiss." Simon frowned. His eyes narrowed and he pointed at the blood on Connor's shirt. "From the look of things, he was right."

"It is a scratch, and already forgotten."

"I am sure Marion will have something to say about that. Once you've spoken to Robert, she'll want to see that your wound is properly cleaned and dressed."

Bryce and Alasdair dismounted and together they approached Simon. "It is good to see you, cousin, and I've certainly missed Marion's cooking," Alasdair remarked, and rubbed his belly. "Bryce could use a few lessons."

Bryce scowled at his brother. "Marion has you spoiled, and you dinna complain about my cooking until now."

"Can I help if she knows how much I appreciate the fact that despite her title of chatelaine, she likes to venture into the kitchen from time to time and cook my favorite meals? Besides, a man can only eat so many oatcakes and so much dried venison."

Simon laughed. "Things never change." After greeting his cousins, he moved toward the palfrey. "And who might this laddie be?"

Cailin's heart rate kicked up a notch as she awaited her husband's reply.

Connor moved to the left side of the horse and lifted her from the saddle. He placed his hand in the small of her back, and urged her toward his cousin. "This is Lady Cailin, of Clan Macmillan."

"Lady?" Simon's mouth gaped open.

Connor nodded. "She was forced to don a disguise to hide from the English."

Her heart sank. She had her answer.

Simon arched a brow. "Macmillan? Are you a kin to Laird Duncan Macmillan of Dunkeld?"

She smoothed her hands down her trews and brushed the dust from her tunic. "Aye, he's my father."

"And Connor's father-by-marriage," Alasdair blurted, before his brother had a chance to explain.

Simon's head snapped in Alasdair's direction. "Did I

hear you correctly when you said the lass is Connor's wife?"

"Aye. They declared themselves married in a tavern two days ago. When he bedded the lass, he made it official." Alasdair covered his mouth and snickered.

Connor moved in his older brother's direction with his fist balled. The glower of deadly intent on his face was unmistakable. "Will you ever learn to hold your tongue?"

Bryce quickly stepped between them and placed his hands on Connor's shoulders, halting him in his tracks. "Dinna do anything to embarrass the lass. You can get even with Alasdair later. In fact, I'd be more than happy to help."

Cailin was grateful for Bryce's timely intervention, but it didn't change the fact that Connor had no intention of letting their marriage stand. Tears burned her eyes, and while she held them at bay, she could not hide the heated humiliation that rose in her cheeks. If the events of the last few days weren't enough, she now found herself in the midst of strangers, each one ready to pass judgment, despite the fact that they didn't even know her.

"Is this true?" Simon returned his full attention to Connor. "What in name of Saint Stephen would possess you to marry? You were on a mission for the Bruce, not off on a lark. Do you care to explain?"

Connor stepped forward. "English soldiers accosted Lady Cailin, and I was able to intervene before they raped her. Unfortunately, one of her assailants wasn't pleased about surrendering his quarry and left me no choice but—"

"To kill him." Simon finished the sentence for him. "The news of his death spread across Scotland like a wildfire, but according to the rumors, he died at the hand of a woman. And you saw fit to bring her here?"

Connor squared his shoulders and faced his cousin. "We could not leave her to face punishment for treason and a murder she dinna commit, so we brought her with us. I'm sure Robert can find her a place of sanctuary."

"Sir Simon!" Blair shouted as he raced down the castle steps and across the bailey to where the men stood talking.

"Slow down and tell me what all this *haivering* is about." Simon rested his hand on the lad's shoulder and waited for him to catch his breath.

"King Robert heard of your cousins' return and wishes to see them right away. He bid me tell them to make haste."

"Thank you, lad. Tell Robert we come anon." Simon patted the boy on the back and sent him on his way. He turned to address his cousins. "Come, we will meet with Robert and discuss this later." He called out to a young woman standing near the foot of the stairs. "Maggie, take Lady Cailin into the castle and have Hugh find her a chamber in which she can rest and freshen up. Also, see if you can find her something decent to wear."

"Aye, m'lord." The young woman bobbed a curtsey. "I'd be happy to see to the lady's needs."

Cailin ran a shaky hand through her tangle of curls, but it did little to tame the windblown mess. Her eyes flashed in Connor's direction. "M'lord?"

"Maggie will see to your needs, and I'll join you once I have spoken to Robert."

"If you'd come with me, m'lady, I'll see you settled." Maggie moved toward Cailin and curtsied.

Given no choice in the matter, Cailin nodded and watched as the men headed up the stone steps. As they were about to enter the castle, an elegantly dressed woman appeared at the door. With her titian hair piled high upon her head and her lovely violet gown, she appeared quite regal. *Is she the queen?*

The woman crossed herself and hugged each brother before taking a step back. "Thank the Lord you have returned. Other than being a little bedraggled from the trip, I must say you all appear to be hale and hardy."

"Alasdair was just telling everyone how much he has

missed your cooking." Bryce glanced at his brother and flashed him a cynical grin.

"Was he now? Well, I'll just have to make him some of my meat pasties and ask cook to dress a fine fat hen for the evening meal." She narrowed her eyes. "He does look as if he's dropped a stone, and we cannot have the lad wasting away."

Marion's attention shifted to Cailin. "Who is this lad?" Her voice trailed off, and she narrowed her eyes. "Saints alive, the lad is a lass." She gasped and quickly covered her mouth with her hand.

"She's Connor's wife," Alasdair said, his bold announcement gaining him an elbow in the side from Bryce.

Simon trotted down the stairs, took Cailin by the arm, and escorted her to where Marion waited. "Lady Cailin, may I present my wife, Lady Fraser." He slid his arm around the woman's waist, and pulled her against his side.

"She doesn't look like a lady. She looks more like a homeless beggar. Wait until Lady Jenna hears about this." The rancorous whispers came from somewhere in the crowd, but Cailin had no idea who had uttered the cruel remarks. The urge to search for the culprits was overwhelming, but she refused to let it rattle her. Staring straight ahead, she raised her chin and bobbed a curtsy. "It is an honor to meet you, Lady Fraser."

Marion stepped forward. She tucked two fingers under Cailin's chin and lifted until their eyes met. "Come, my dear, you must be exhausted from your journey. Once you've had a chance to rest and freshen up, we'll sit down and try to sort through this—" She hesitated.

Mess…mistake…disaster. Cailin mentally finished her thoughts. Tears sprang to her eyes, but she managed to blink them away. "Thank you, Lady Fraser. I'd very much like a chance to freshen up."

"Please call me Marion, my dear. We are family now.

The men must attend to matters of great importance. In the meantime, we shall see about getting you settled."

Chapter 12

With her head high, Cailin accompanied Marion into the great hall. Maggie followed close behind. Despite the stares, snickers, and whispers from the servants milling about the room, she refused to give them the satisfaction of knowing their unkind words had cut through her like a knife.

"Dinna pay them any mind. They're not happy unless they have something to gossip about." Marion stopped abruptly and called for the castle steward. "Hugh! Mayhap you could find more chores that need tending. It appears the only things working in this room are these people's tongues."

On the far side of the hall, an elfin looking man dropped what he was doing and waddled toward them. As round as he was tall, his tufts of grey hair stuck out wildly from his head in every direction. Cailin stifled the urge to chuckle.

Marion continued to address the servants. "In case you have not heard, my husband's cousin, Connor, has taken a bride. Lady Cailin is to be treated with the same respect you show to me. Anyone who doesn't see fit to do so, will answer to my husband or myself."

A grin tugged at Cailin's lips. The speed with which the people scattered and returned to their chores was most impressive. Torn between embarrassment and gratitude, she had no doubt that under different circumstances she and Marion would have become good friends.

 Marion turned and spoke to Hugh. "Lady Cailin needs a chamber in which to rest and bathe. No offense dear."

Hugh stopped a few feet away. "A lady you say?" He cocked his head and scanned Cailin from head to toe.

"Please stop gawking at the lass, Hugh, and see her

settled. Maggie, fetch a tray of food from the kitchen and take it up to her chamber. Lady Cailin must be famished after her long journey." Marion crossed her arms over her chest and impatiently tapped her toe on the stone floor.

"I'll see to it right away." Maggie curtsied, then went to do her mistress's bidding.

"I meant no disrespect, Lady Fraser. There is an empty chamber on the third floor of the Snow Tower. Does she have a chest with her belongings?" Hugh asked.

Cailin shook her head. "I dinna have time to pack my things. I have only the clothes on my back, but a chance to freshen up sounds divine."

"Follow me, and I'll show you to your chamber." Hugh moved toward a large stone staircase at the far end of the hall, but paused partway and glanced over his shoulder. "Will the lady's husband be joining her? Mayhap it would be better to take her to his chamber instead."

"I'm not sure if—" At a loss for words, she glanced at Marion.

Marion placed her hand on Cailin's shoulder and gently squeezed. "After he has spoken to the king, I'm sure Connor will join her. The chambers on the third floor are larger, and more suitable to the needs of a newly married couple."

After he has spoken to the king, we may no longer be married. The thought caused Cailin's heart to clench. She closed her eyes and drew in a slow deep breath. When she opened them again, Marion was staring at her.

Marion silently studied her for a moment, and then spoke to Hugh. "Could you give us a moment alone?"

"Of course, m'lady, I'll see to the servants while I wait." He bowed, and stepped out of hearing range.

"Come, sit with me for a few minutes." Marion pointed to a pair of overstuffed chairs beside the hearth. Once seated, she patted the chair beside her and waited for her to sit down. "You seem uncertain if Connor will wish to join you."

"I'm afraid our marriage was not planned. In fact, he may already have seen it dissolved. From the day we met, he made it very clear he was dedicated to the cause and has no use for a wife."

"Nonsense. I have known him since he was a wee lad. Connor may be a master at hiding his feelings, but there is no mistaking a man in love."

"He is not in love with me. The only reason he declared us married was to protect my reputation, and to keep me safe."

"Are you in love with him?"

Cailin lowered her eyes and twisted her hands in her lap. "I do love him, but I will not force him to stay in a marriage he doesn't want."

"Has he told you he does not love you?"

"Nay, but he hasn't told me that he does."

Marion raised her elegantly sculpted brow. "The words dinna come easily to a man. Since you are not certain what is in his heart, I think it only fair to give him a chance. I assume he saw the marriage consummated."

"Aye, we are husband and wife by word, and deed." The heat of a blush rose in her cheeks.

"My husband's cousin is not the sort of man to take advantage of a woman, and then turn his back on her."

"I gave myself to him freely, and I will not hold him to a marriage he did not want."

"You might carry his babe. Have you thought about that? Will you give up so easily?" Marion badgered.

"It is what I must do. Even if it breaks my heart." Her voice trailed off to a whisper. She glanced away, fighting the swell of emotion rising from the pit of her stomach. She slid her hand over the flat plane of her belly. "He wants no commitments or responsibilities to tie him down. If the Almighty sees fit to bless me with a babe, I will love the bairn with all my heart and raise it on my own."

"Connor is so much like his cousin." She reached over and patted Cailin's hand. "When we first met, Simon was serious, brooding, and so handsome he stole my breath away. He, too, had dedicated his life to Scotland's cause, and claimed no interest in marriage or family. It dinna help that my father forbid me to see him. He had grander plans for me and my sisters."

Cailin's eyes widened—surprised by the similarity in their situations. "How did you find your way around those obstacles?"

"Och, we did not have an easy go of it. Things worth having seldom are. I refused to back down from what I wanted. Eventually love took its course, and Simon decided he would rather live with me than without me. We have been happily married for twenty-one summers, and have two lovely daughters to show for it. Connor is a very good man and has a lot of love to share. He has kept his heart guarded for so long he's not sure what to do. Given time, he will come around."

"If only that were true, I would be willing to wait."

"Would you like me to show the lady to her bower?" Maggie rushed across the room, startling both women.

Hugh followed close on her heels. "I'm sorry, m'lady. I wasn't able to stop her in time."

"Forgive me, m'lady." Maggie said, her eyes trailing the floor.

Marion rose from the chair and faced them. "It's all right, Hugh, she meant no harm." She offered Cailin her hand and helped her to her feet. "While you are staying with us, Maggie will serve as your maid and tend to your needs. Hugh, please show Lady Cailin to her chamber."

"This way m'lady." He motioned with a sweep of his hand and continued his trek toward the stairs.

Marion smiled. "Go with Maggie and Hugh, my dear, and I'll see that everything you need is sent up directly. After you've rested, join us in the great hall for the evening meal."

Cailin nodded. "Thank you, I'd like that." Confiding in Marion had lifted her spirits, and gave her a reason to hope. She seldom shared her innermost thoughts with anyone, especially a stranger, but Marion's kindness and motherly demeanor made her feel welcome and at ease. Perhaps it was because she'd grown up longing for her own mother's love. Eildth did her best, but it was not the same.

A moan of pure pleasure escaped Cailin's lips as she lowered herself into the tub. Her body cried out in protest, and the fragrant hot water felt like Heaven. While she considered herself as fit and hardy as any man, the grueling three-day journey through some of the most rugged terrain in Scotland had left her exhausted, and painfully acquainted with muscles she never knew existed until now.

Cailin closed her eyes. She needed to rid her mind of Connor, of the events of the last few days, but failed at her attempt. His face was all she could see. She remembered the feel of his powerful hands as he gently explored every inch of her body and brought her to the point of ecstasy more times than she could count. The rude comments and whispers of the villages and servants when they heard that she and Connor were married also played on her mind. *Jenna won't be pleased, someone in the crowd had remarked.* She opened her eyes. "Who is Jenna?"

Maggie added another bucket of hot water to the tub. "Lady Jenna?"

"I overheard her name mentioned when I arrived in the bailey and wondered who she might be."

"Och, I suspect you will meet her soon enough. But it is not a meeting I would rush if I were you." The pleasant look on Maggie's face was replaced by a scowl of disdain.

"Who is she?" Cailin persisted.

"She's the only daughter of Nigel Bruce. He's the king's brother and was the laird of Kildrummy Castle before the Bruce and his wife and daughter moved in."

A sudden pang of uneasiness niggled at Cailin's belly. Given Maggie's reaction when she heard Jenna's name, mayhap she was someone best avoided. But curiosity got the better of her. "I heard someone say she would not be pleased to hear Connor was married. Should I be concerned?"

"Lady Jenna is not fond of surprises. Most would call her vain and overindulged by her father. Nay, she will not be pleased to hear that Laird Connor has taken a wife. She's made no secret of the fact she planned to wed him herself." As if something had bit her tongue, Maggie covered her mouth and turned away.

"Was there a betrothal or understanding between them?" It was obvious that Maggie had already said more than she had intended, but she had to ask.

"A betrothal was never publicly announced, but to hear her speak, you would think so. She decided the day he arrived that she would be his wife, and warned the other lassies to stay away. What Lady Jenna wants, she usually gets."

"Does Connor feel the same way about her?" The thought that he may have taken her innocence while another woman waited for him was a bitter pill to swallow.

"Everyone knows he has sworn his sword and his life to the cause. Lady Jenna, on the other hand, has her own agenda. She is accustomed to having her way and is not above trickery and lies to get what she wants. She even asked her uncle to speak to him on her behalf. I would not want to be in the room when she learns of your marriage"

There are few secrets in a keep. Always abreast of the castle gossip, the servants were privy to a lot more than they cared to admit. If there was a dalliance going on under the laird's nose, they knew. "Are you certain that Connor has no feelings for Lady Jenna?"

"It would take a man with a fist of steel to keep that one in line. Lady Jenna is not only selfish, but she has an evil streak that makes me shudder." Maggie's face blanched and she shook her head. "Your husband may be a brave and noble warrior, but he is no match for the likes of her. She would chew him up and spit him out the first time she dinna get her way. Mind you watch your back, m'lady. I would not put it past her to try to come between you. She is not to be trusted."

"I'll keep that in mind." Cailin closed her eyes and lay back in the tub. At this moment, Jenna Bruce was the least of her worries. Getting Connor to realize his true feelings and to salvage their marriage was her only concern.

Maggie tossed a log on the fire, and then stirred the embers with a poker. "Best you get out of the tub before the water cools."

"I suppose you're right. If I stay here any longer, I am sure to nod off." Cailin sighed and sank lower in the tub, the water covering her shoulders. "It just feels wonderful to be clean and warm."

Maggie placed a length of toweling on a chair beside the tub. "Are you hungry? Cook prepared a tray with some cheese, fruit slices, bread, and honey." She moved toward the four-poster bed in the middle of the room and pointed to a small table beside it.

Cailin wrapped herself in the toweling and stepped out of the tub. "I am very tired. I think a rest might prove more beneficial than food. In fact, if you have other things to tend to, I'm sure I'll be fine on my own."

"Lady Marion sent these garments for you to wear." Maggie laid a kirtle, a night rail, a pair of slippers, and an exquisite emerald gown, the neck and sleeves trimmed in gold thread and pearls, on the bed before her.

"These are lovely." Cailin picked up the gown and ran her hand over the fine fabric. She had never seen anything so beautiful. Her father had always provided her with clothing fit for the daughter of a laird, but never had she worn anything this extravagant.

Maggie handed her a night rail in exchange for the gown. "Put this on, and I'll set the other clothes on the chair by the door. After you've had a chance to rest, I'll return and help you dress. I have also taken the liberty of washing your clothes, hanging them by the fire to dry."

"Thank you for your help and kindness, Maggie." Cailin brought her hand up to stifle a yawn.

"You are welcome, m'lady. Now, try to get a wee bit of rest, and I'll be back in an hour to check in on you." She bobbed a curtsy and left the room.

Cailin let the toweling drop to the floor, pulled the night rail over her head, and climbed into bed. Exhausted and emotionally spent, her eyes drifted closed as soon as her head hit the down-filled pillow.

Chapter 13

Unable to get Cailin off his mind, Connor paused at the casement window and stared into the bailey below. He envisioned her standing there in her tattered tunic and trews, her dirt-smudged cheeks, and her auburn hair, a windblown mess. When he'd left her in the bailey, her eyes had widened with uncertainty and questions. It took every ounce of self-control not to turn back and pull her into his arms. To tell her that everything would be all right, that he loved her, and would see her safe. Instead, he'd let duty take precedence and had left her in the care of strangers. Was she resting? Or was she roaming her chamber as confused, lost, and filled with uncertainty about the future as he was?

Connor never dreamed a woman could lay claim to his soul. Despite his efforts to deny the lust and desire firing his blood, she had somehow managed to breach the walls that protected his heart. Walls that until now, he believed were impenetrable. She had burrowed so far beneath his skin, he wasn't certain he'd ever get her out. She made him question his chosen path, and her kisses left him dizzy with need. He wished that he could turn his back on duty, hang up his sword, and walk away from everything he stood for. Like a gem of great value and rare beauty, Cailin was a prize to be coveted—a treasure for which he felt unworthy. He'd been a warrior for so long that he'd forgotten what it was like to feel, and she deserved to be loved without reservation.

"Sit down, lad." Simon motioned to the empty chair beside him. He leaned toward Robert and lowered his voice. "I've never seen him like this."

"You should have been traveling with him these last

few days. I think the lass addled his brain." While Alasdair's comment didn't get a rise out of Connor, it did gain him an elbow in the side from Bryce.

Robert stroked his bearded chin and looked at Connor. "If the situation with the lass has you rattled, dinna *fash* yourself. Simon explained what happened. We've all made mistakes, or let the desire to tup a beautiful woman cloud our judgment. I'll see the marriage repudiated and find a safe place for her to hide from Edward's henchmen."

Connor clenched his fists, slammed them on the table, and glared at Robert. "Cailin is not a whore. She's a lady, and she needed my help." The words came out before he could stop them.

Simon sprang to his feet, his glower fixed on Connor. "Counsel your tongue. You are speaking to the King of Scotland, and I'll not have you—"

Robert rested his hand on Simon's forearm. "It's all right, my friend. I'll excuse his insolence, but only once." His voice hardened to one of authority as he continued. "I meant the lady no disrespect, and will grant you quarter, but if it ever happens again, I will not be so lenient."

Connor reined in his emotions before he spoke again. "I was out of line, Robert, and for that I apologize."

"Rescuing the lass from those bastards was a very noble deed, but you dinna have to pay for it with your freedom. Fortunately, I'm in a position to see you liberated from a marriage you dinna want. That being said, tell me what you learned in Perth." Robert tapped his finger against the side of his tankard as he awaited an answer.

"When Longshanks made the Earl of Pembroke his ambassador to Scotland, he gave him leave to raise the dragon banner in retaliation for the death of Red Comyn. This, of course, means he intends to take no prisoners, and show no mercy."

In addition to his cousin and two brothers, the Bruce

had summoned his four advisors and three of his most trusted warriors. A rumble of comments erupted after hearing what Connor had to say. Robert raised his hand to silence them. "How many men does he have?"

"At last count, his forces numbered three thousand. Following the news of Comyn's death, Longshanks named his son the Prince of Wales, and knighted over two hundred warriors. During the feast that followed, two elaborately decorated swans were paraded through their midst. At that time, Edward made known his plan to avenge the death of Comyn, and to squash the Scottish resistance. They are calling it the Oath of Swans."

"Like Comyn, Aymer de Valence is a man driven by his lust for power. His desire to avenge his brother-in-law's death only adds more fuel to an already raging fire. The situation needs careful scrutiny before we make a move." Simon raised his tankard and took a drink before he continued. "I met de Valence on several occasions and dinna trust the man."

"He bears watching, but this battle is imperative if we wish to unite the clans and drive the English out of Scotland." Robert picked up a piece of parchment, and handed it to Simon. "This missive arrived from de Valence earlier today. He has thrown down the gauntlet, and I intend to meet the challenge. If I ever hope to gain the support and respect of the Scottish people, I cannot back down from this."

"I understand, but we must proceed with caution," Simon reiterated.

"We will not advance until the troops are ready. At last count, we numbered close to forty-five hundred men, and I'll leave it to you and your cousins to get them into shape." Robert emptied his tankard of ale, stood, and moved toward the door. "If you gentlemen will join me, we'll retire to the great hall for the evening meal. We have planned a feast in honor of your return. As for the matter of your annulment, Connor, consider it done."

The king's words hit him like a fist in the gut. Suddenly uncertain if he wanted his marriage to end, Connor took a step in Robert's direction, but a hand planted firmly on his shoulder halted his advance.

Simon stood beside him, and shook his head. "There's no telling what the outcome of this battle will be and you've not known the lass long enough to make a commitment of marriage. Best you let her go."

The sound of a door closing disturbed her slumber. Cailin woke with a start and sat up in bed. "Maggie? Is that you?" Cailin called out, but no one answered. Still half asleep, she slid to the edge of the bed and dropped her legs over the side.

She stretched and rubbed her eyes. The fire in the hearth had burned to ashes and all but one candle had gone out. Her stomach growled and she remembered the tray Maggie had left on the table beside the bed. She picked up a slice of apple and popped it into her mouth, followed by a wedge of cheese. The combination of flavors exploded on her tongue, and her stomach rumbled again. She was hungrier than she thought. As she reached for a bit of bread, she noticed a piece of parchment, propped against the pitcher of ale. Cailin picked up the note, broke the seal, and began to read.

You are not welcome here. Connor is not for you. The sooner you realize that and leave, the better. If you choose to stay, you will be sorry.

There was no signature, but it didn't take a scholar to deduce that the note was left by Jenna, or another lass who fancied Connor for herself. Little did they know that if he had spoken to the king, he might already be free to marry the woman of his choice.

Anger twisted her gut, but Cailin calmly folded the note

and placed it on the tray. She would not allow herself to be intimidated or forced to leave until she was ready. If Connor chose to have their marriage annulled, so be it. However, if he decided to give their marriage a chance, she'd not give up her husband without a fight.

She went to the chair, picked up the kirtle, and gasped. Holding it at arm's length, she examined the garment. The front of the muslin undergarment was shredded to ribbons. When she lifted the gown, she sucked in another sharp breath. Ugly red stains marred the emerald fabric. Wine or blood? She wasn't certain, but she had no doubt it was meant as an additional warning.

Thanks to Maggie, her own clothes were laundered and drying by the fire. She dressed quickly, brushed her hair, and prepared to join the other in the great hall. How she'd explain her appearance and Marion's gown, she had yet to decide.

Cailin scurried down the hall and as she rounded the corner, she bumped into Maggie. She stumbled, but managed to steady herself by using the wall for support.

"Forgive me, m'lady." Maggie stepped back and bowed her head. "I was on my way to offer you some assistance with dressing and should have been watching where I was going. Lady Marion is right. I'm an accident waiting to happen and must learn to be more careful."

"I'm the one at fault. I was lost in thought and not paying attention." Cailin ran her hands down the front of her tunic when she noticed Maggie staring at her. "Is something amiss?"

"Why are you not wearing the gown Lady Marion sent up for you?"

Cailin dragged her lower lip between her teeth and glanced away. While Maggie had been very kind and accommodating, the note and desecration of the gown had left her feeling unsettled. Uncertain as to whom she could trust, she decided it best not to mention the incident or her suspicions about Jenna until she had more proof.

"I'm afraid it dinna fit. Lady Marion is—um—more generously endowed than I." Judging by the grin on Maggie's face, her lady's maid agreed with her observations.

"Aye, Laird Fraser has nothing to complain about there." Maggie giggled and covered her mouth with her hand.

Cailin gestured toward the stairs. "It must be late, and I dare not keep my hosts waiting any longer."

"It was near sundown when Lady Marion asked me to check on you. She said if you were too tired to come down for the meal, a tray could be sent up to your chamber."

"I'm fine, and welcome the chance to meet the king and queen." In reality, butterflies worried her stomach, and an uncomfortable feeling of foreboding she could not explain washed over her. Dismissing her fear as nerves and excitement over meeting royalty, she smiled at Maggie. "Shall we proceed?"

"When you first arrived, Sir Simon bid me find you as suitable gown. If he sees you dressed in these clothes, he will not be pleased. I have a gown you could wear. It is not as fine as the one Lady Fraser sent for you, but if you would like, I can fetch it."

Cailin nodded. "If you dinna mind, I would welcome the offer of another gown."

"I'll get it right away, and meet you in your chamber."

People of all ages and social classes filled the great hall, eager to partake in the evening meal and the festivities that would follow. Three musicians tuned their instruments in one corner of the hall and a group of jugglers practiced their skills in another. Servants carried wooden trays laden with roasted meat, pheasant, smoked salmon, potatoes, turnips, and leeks, and the succulent aromas filled the room. Others carried pitchers overflowing with ale and wine.

The sights, sounds, and smells brought back memories of the elaborate feasts her father hosted during special events and holidays. For the first time in days, Cailin actually felt a little homesick. She missed Myrna, Eildth, her cousins, and Aunt Bess. However, those feelings quickly passed when she reminded herself that Borden's men would arrest her the moment she set foot on Macmillan land, and her father would do nothing to stop them. She would never return home, and had to accept it.

As Cailin and Maggie approached the dais, heads turned in their direction and a hush fell over the room. She nervously smoothed her hands down the front of her blue wool gown and willed her legs to move.

"Dinna pay them any mind, Lady Cailin, they are just curious is all."

Maggie's reassuring words did little to calm her insecurity, or to ease the knot that twisted her stomach when she glanced up the dais a few feet in front of them. A regal looking couple sat at the laird's table. She assumed they must be the newly crowned King and Queen of Scotland. Lady Marion flanked the queen and Simon sat beside the Bruce—the two men immersed in conversation. Connor, Alasdair, and Bryce sat to Simon's right, while a young girl of ten summers and a man who appeared to be in his early forties sat beside Marion.

"I am pleased that you could join us, Lady Cailin. Come, and have a seat." Lady Marion smiled, then gestured to an empty chair beside Connor. "Thank you, Maggie, that will be all for now."

Maggie curtsied. "Enjoy your meal, m'lady. I'll assist you in your chambers when you are ready to retire." That said, she turned and moved toward an empty seat at the end of one of the trestle tables.

On shaky legs, Cailin climbed the two dais steps, aware that all eyes were upon her. She approached the proffered seat, but stopped abruptly, stumbled, and struck her hip on the edge of the table when a raven-haired beauty shoved her out of the way.

The young woman bowed to the king and queen. Without hesitation, or an apology to Cailin, she sat in the chair beside Connor. She grabbed his forearm and leaned in close. "I'm so glad you have returned to me unharmed. I've missed you so much."

Bryce stood, wrapped his arm around Cailin's waist, and whispered in her ear. "I'm afraid Lady Jenna likes to make a grand entrance. I'd be very honored if you would share a meal with me." He held out the chair beside him.

Cailin didn't sit down. Instead, she placed her hand on the table to steady herself and stared at her husband. *Say something. You may not wish to be married, but how could you humiliate me like this?*

Connor flashed an apologetic look in her direction and shrugged. "I'm sorry," he mouthed, but said nothing aloud to discourage Jenna.

Jenna's smug expression and coy smiled triggered a sudden stab of jealousy. Cailin was more certain than ever who had destroyed Marion's gown and left the threatening note.

"May I present Queen Elizabeth de Burgh and her husband, King Robert I," Marion said, breaking the uncomfortable silence.

Cailin turned to face Robert and Elizabeth and curtsied. "It is my honor to meet you. I thank you for your kindness and hospitality."

"Dinna mention it," Elizabeth replied. "Please have a seat, and enjoy the meal."

"Aye, sit before the food grows cold," Robert added as he filled his trencher with roasted meat and vegetables.

As Cailin slowly sank into the chair beside Bryce, he leaned in and spoke in a low voice. "Trust me when I say that there is nothing between them. At least not as far as Connor is concerned."

"It certainly does not look that way. She is climbing all over him, and he has done nothing to dissuade her."

"He cannot slight Jenna in public and risk insulting the Bruce or her father. Jenna may be a little—um—" He stumbled for the right words. "She's very overbearing, and forward, but her father does not see it. To push her away in front of the clan would be an embarrassment for Jenna and her family. Out of respect for Nigel and Robert, Connor tolerates her bold advances."

The swell of emotion that rose in her throat threatened to cut off her ability to breathe. Had Connor taken her to his bed, knowing Jenna was awaiting his return? How could she compete with Jenna's unearthly beauty and lineage? She could not really blame Connor for choosing the niece of the king. But, that didn't make it hurt any less. Watching Jenna fawn all over him was like having a dagger run through her heart over and over again.

Bryce moved the trencher they shared closer and handed her a knife. "You need to eat, lass."

"I've lost my appetite." Cailin's eyes were fixed on her husband. *Any closer, and she'll be sitting on his lap.*

As if on cue, Jenna moved her chair closer to Connor. "I was concerned when I heard about your encounter with those nasty English soldiers. Some people go looking for trouble with no regard for the consequences." She glanced over her shoulder at Cailin, then quickly returned her attention to Connor. With one hand resting on his forearm, the other on his thigh, she leaned in, her lips nearly brushing his ear. "Thank God, Uncle Robert saw fit to rectify the horrible mistake you made. I cannot imagine being forced to endure a marriage to a little chit that you dinna love. Now you're free to marry the woman of your heart."

Connor grunted, but said nothing.

If possible, Jenna leaned even closer, offering Connor a glimpse of ample breasts spilling over the top of a too tight bodice. "You deserve a wife of status and breeding. Uncle Robert and my father are both in agreement. If you wish to court me, they'd be most pleased. Is that not right, Father?"

"I have no objection if you wish to court her," Nigel said with his mouth full.

Connor shifted in his chair, but made no offer of marriage. Was he shocked by Jenna's brazenness and manipulation, or just embarrassed about being caught in a deception? Regardless, Cailin could not sit there and listen to any more. She slowly rose from her chair and faced the king and queen. "I am suddenly not feeling well. The journey must have taken a greater toll on me than I thought. My sincere apologies your majesties, but I must leave." Fleeing the dais, she rushed toward the door.

Connor cursed, peeled Jenna's hand from his arm, and sprang to his feet. "Cailin, wait!" he shouted, but she did not stop, nor did she turn around. He cursed again. What was wrong with him? Mayhap Alasdair was right and she had addled his brains. There was a time when the attention and ministrations of a beautiful lass like Jenna would have been welcome. Now all he wanted to do was to find Cailin, and explain.

"Things happen for a reason," Simon said. "Let the lass be, Connor."

"What do you know about such things?" Marion snapped at her husband, then turned to Connor. "Dinna just stand there, lad, go after her."

"If you'll please excuse me." Connor bowed toward

Elizabeth and Robert, then left the dais, unaware Jenna followed on his heels. When they reached the hallway, she grabbed Connor's right arm, halting his advancement.

"Connor, wait. Dinna make a fool of yourself. She is not for you."

He spun around to face her. "If you dinna let go of me, I'll not be held responsible for my actions." He twisted his arm to break free of her grasp, but she tightened her grip.

"I'm counting on it, m'lord. Do with me what you will. I know you want me." She pressed her supple body against his chest and ground her hips against his thigh. "You know we're meant to be together. Make love with me, Connor." Her hand slid down his chest and across his belly, her fingers brushing his groin. "I've forgiven your dalliance with that little whore, and now that you're rid of her, we are free to wed."

Connor cursed and took a step backward. "I have no interest in courting you now or in the future and have never done anything to make you think otherwise. I have no intention of marrying you. The sooner you understand that, the better."

Anger flashed in her blue eyes, and she dug her nails into the flesh on his arm. "A few moments ago, you asked for my hand. Father even gave his blessing. How could you deny me now? Why would you lead me on?"

"I have never led you on, and I dinna ask for your hand. You're the one who spoke of courting and marriage, not I. Your father is a good man, and I have the utmost respect for him. Because of that, I dinna want to slight him by showing you any disrespect. You're a bonny lass, and you deserve much better than a man like me." He went for the gentle, subtle approach. Let her down easy, and hope she would get the hint.

Jenna's scowl softened, and she closed the gap between them. "You jest with me, Connor. You're exactly the kind of man I want." Before he could offer a rebuttal, Jenna stood on her tiptoes, pressed her mouth to his, and slid her tongue along the pursed seam of his lips. "Come now, I know you can do better than that," she scolded when he did not respond to her bold advances.

Connor grabbed Jenna's wrists, and held her at arm's length. "Enough! You have pushed me past my limit, woman." He glanced up to see Cailin watching them, and immediately wondered how much of the conversation she had heard. What was she thinking? He had his answer when she turned and ran from the castle.

His patience spent, Connor shoved Jenna out of the way. "Go back to the great hall, lass. You've done enough damage for one night. I just hope that she'll listen to reason."

Jenna clung to his arm in an attempt to stop him from leaving. "You cannot possibly choose her over me. I have so much more to offer. She is a fugitive, and when the English find her, she will hang by the neck until she is dead."

"Hold your *weist*." Connor raised his balled fist in the air. He had never struck a woman, but it took every ounce of willpower not to hit Jenna. She had pushed him past his limit and perhaps ruined his chances with Cailin. "I have no interest in you or your wanton offer, and never will. Be gone with you, or I will not restrain my anger in future." No longer concerned about offending her, he broke free of Jenna's grasp and raced after the woman he loved. Setting things straight was all that mattered, and damn the consequences.

He found Cailin atop the castle parapet. A heavy rain was falling, and her clothes were drenched. Shivering, she stood with her arms wrapped around herself, staring into the darkness.

"Cailin," he softly spoke her name to alert her of his presence, while being careful not to startle her.

"Don't come near me!" Cailin held her hand up in his direction. "Go back to Jenna, and leave me alone."

"Please come inside, Cailin. We need to talk."

"I have nothing to say to you. Please go."

Connor sucked in a sharp breath and froze in his tracks when her foot slipped on the slick stones.

She grasped the wall for support. "Dinna come any closer," she cautioned.

"All right. I'll keep my distance, but you need to hear me out. There has been a grave mistake."

"I have made mistakes, too. Trusting you was the biggest one of all. You took me to your bed knowing Jenna awaited your return. I was a fool to believe you might actually have feelings for me."

"You're wrong. I do have feelings for you, and need you to believe me when I say that I've never been interested in Jenna. In the past, I've tolerated her behavior out of respect for Robert and her father, but I've told her it must stop."

"That is not how it appeared when I saw you together in the hallway, and it is certainly not what Jenna thinks. A person would have to be blind not to notice the way she looks at you and touches you. Dinna lie to me, Connor. I saw you kiss her."

"You must listen to me. I dinna kiss her, she kissed me. As far as the way she touches me—" Before she knew what he was about, Connor closed the gap between them, grasped her wrist, and pulled her into his arms. "There is only one woman I want to touch me in that way."

Cailin struggled to break free and pounded her fists on his chest, but he tightened his embrace. "If what you say is true, why do you allow her to touch you in that manner? Why did you ask the king to annul our marriage?"

"Out of respect for her father. Jenna, well, Jenna likes to get what she wants, and I dare not cause a scene in front of her father. Robert annulled the marriage because he thought it was what we both wanted...I thought it was what I wanted. But we were both wrong."

"I do not believe you. The day we met, you told me you never planned to marry, and you made it very clear you planned to have the marriage repudiated."

"I have very strong feelings for you, *liuadhe*, but I have sworn an oath to Robert, to fight for Scotland's freedom. Each time I enter a battle, there's no guarantee that I'll return. I dinna want to leave behind a wife to mourn my passing."

"No one asked you to shirk your duty. I understand how important your honor is, and that you have dedicated your life to the cause. If I knew you cared for me, even a little, I would wait for you as long as it took."

Her words touched his heart and melted the last of his resolve. Connor lowered his head, and his mouth crashed down on hers in a hungry kiss. Her lips parted, and his tongue slid past her teeth, sampling the sweet mysteries of her mouth. She tasted of salty tears, mint, and surrender. He closed his eyes, allowing the scent of lavender soap, mixed with her sweet fragrance, to fill his senses. He tightened his embrace and plundered her mouth.

"Why in the name of Saint Stephen are you standing the rain? Come in before you both catch your death of cold." Simon stepped out from the shadows with Robert at his side.

Startled by the intrusion, Connor released his hold on Cailin and took a step back.

"I have made arrangements for the lass, but I refuse to discuss them in the pouring rain." Robert turned and entered the castle. Simon, Connor, and Cailin followed.

Robert shook the water from his tunic, and addressed Cailin. "At first light, Cameron will escort you to St. Agnes Priory. There you will remain sequestered until the English are banished from Scottish soil and your name cleared of all charges."

"The same priory in which my cousin Mary resides?" Connor asked.

Simon nodded. "It is far enough away from the English

border, and I know Father Paul will grant her sanctuary. Your cousin will be there to lend her support."

Connor slid his arm around Cailin's waist and pulled her against his side. While he hated the thought of being separated, he knew the English would not give up their search until they'd recaptured her and made her stand trial. If she stayed at Kildrummy Castle, it would not take long for the word to get out, and Borden would come for her. Despite his feelings for Cailin, he had to honor his word to Robert and join his fellow patriots in Perth. Once he was gone, there would be no one to protect her. Mary was more like a sister than a cousin. Knowing Cailin would have someone he loved and trusted to lean on provided some consolation.

Connor tightened his embrace and tucked her head beneath his chin. "It is only temporary. Once I return from Perth, I will come for you."

Cailin nodded her agreement, but she said nothing.

"It is settled. Now that we've dealt with this matter, I have other things that require my attention." Robert turned to leave.

"Wait!" Connor called out. "I have one more request." A request he never thought he'd make.

"And what might that be?" Robert crossed his arms over his chest and tapped his toe impatiently.

"If Lady Cailin agrees, I would see us handfasted."

"What are you saying?" Cailin gasped. Her eyes widened, searching his eyes for answers.

"I wish to give us time to test the strength of our relationship, and if I should die in battle, it cannot be said that what has gone on between us was indecent or immoral. If a child should result from our joining, he will have my name, and no one will call him a bastard. After a year, if you wish your freedom, I will not contest the decision." He sucked in a sharp breath and waited for her reply. "Do you agree, lass?"

Robert raked his fingers through his hair and shook his head. "Correct me if I am wrong, Connor, but did you not request an annulment and then ask my niece for her hand?"

"Those were Jenna's words, not mine. Your niece is a beguiling woman and will make a fine wife for the right man. But, I am not that man." Connor tightened his hold on Cailin. "The annulment was a mistake, but a handfast will serve us better. I dinna want to embarrass you, Jenna, or Nigel in front of the clan, so I had planned to speak to you after the meal."

Robert scraped his hand across his chin and shook his head. "I must admit, I am disappointed. Jenna is a spirited lass and needs a husband who can keep her on a tight rein. Nigel will not be pleased, but while he hates to admit it, he is also aware that Jenna is impetuous and headstrong. I will do what I can to smooth things over." He looked at Cailin. "What do you say, lass? Do you agree to a handfast?"

Cailin hesitated for a moment, then smiled up at Connor. "Aye. I would be honored, m'lord."

Before she had a chance to change her mind, he scooped her up in his arms and carried her past Simon and Robert. "I trust you'll see to the papers concerning our agreement. I'll sign them in the morning."

Chapter 14

Cailin marveled at the way Connor climbed the steep stone steps two at a time. She huddled against the hard broad plane of his chest, desperately clinging to the hope that a handfast was not a mistake. Soaked through to the skin and chilled to the bone, she shivered in his arms, her teeth chattering. She snuggled closer, searching for the heat and security only his embrace could provide.

He strode with purpose down the narrow hallway. "We need to get you out of these wet clothes and do something to warm you." He paused outside her chamber, shifted her weight in his arms, and kicked the door open. The massive oaken slab yielded to the powerful blow and slammed against the wall with a thunderous crash. He stepped into the chamber, using his elbow to close the door, and carried her like a precious cargo across the room.

It wasn't until they reached the hearth that he let her slide down the front of his body—one torturous inch at a time. Her heart beat wildly. She burned with erotic heat, ached with urgent need, and wished they could stay wrapped in each other's arms forever. When he released her, an unbearable sense of loss washed over her.

Connor added more wood and peat to the fire. He stirred the smoldering embers until they burst into flames. "That should warm things in a hurry."

Things are already heating up nicely, she thought when he grabbed the hem of his sodden shirt and tugged it over his head. Sun-bronzed skin glistened in the firelight, every sculpted ridge of muscle highlighted. Water dripped from his hair in rivulets that ran down his chest, collecting in the coarse dark curls. He wiped his tunic over his head and across his upper torso before tossing it on a chair by the hearth.

Her gaze traveled south. Wet trews clung to his slender hips, outlining the bulge of his arousal and powerful thighs. He was magnificent, and the sight of him standing before her like a virile Norse God took her breath away. Was this real, or a dream? If it was a dream, she wanted to sleep for an eternity.

Her breath caught and her pulse kicked up a notch, the way it always did when she looked at him. When he closed the gap between them and began to unlace the bodice of her gown, all uncertainty faded into oblivion.

"You need to shed these wet things." His husky voice was thick with passion.

Her hands covered his, halting his action. "I'll do it." But her cold fingers trembled nervously, and she could not manage the task.

"You're a *thrawn* lass, and much too independent. Something we'll need to address." He grasped the ribbons on the bodice of her gown and continued where he had left off.

"You can try, m'lord, but those who know me say I'm as stubborn and tenacious as they come. Mayhap, you should have considered that before you asked for the handfast," she replied in a playful tone.

"Och, aye, I have given your temerity a lot of thought, and it only made me more determined to tame you, lass." His dark eyes remained locked with hers as he finished with the laces, and then slowly peeled the wet gown from her shoulders.

Stripped naked to the waist, she shivered as the cool air touched her damp skin. Her nipples tightened into taut peaks, and she longed to feel his hot moist breath on her skin as he suckled and teased the aching buds. He smelled of wind and rain, of spice, and the potent masculine musk of his arousal—the combination of scents, intoxicating.

Jenna's face flashed before her eyes and brought her crashing back to reality. *How could he want me when Jenna is so beautiful, has a voluptuous figure, and so much to offer him?* Lowering her gaze, she wrapped her arms around herself and took a step back.

"What is it, *liuadhe*? Why do you pull away and cover yourself?" He slid two fingers beneath her chin and lifted until their eyes met.

Cailin peeked out from beneath her lashes. "I—I'm sorry." It made no sense for her to feel self conscious. He'd already seen her naked, and they had made love more than once, but she hadn't known about Jenna.

"You're sorry about what?"

"I'm not as pretty or as buxom as Jenna. Nor am I the niece of a king."

He grasped her wrists, gently unfolded her arms, and held them out to the side. "Never hide from me, *liuadhe*. You are the most beautiful woman I have ever laid eyes on. No one fires my blood or stirs my desire the way you do." He pulled her into his embrace, lowered his head, and captured her lips.

The taste of wine and spices made her swoon. Her lips softened and parted, welcoming his sweet invasion. His teeth tugged at her lower lip, while his tongue stroked with an intimate rhythm that drove her beyond thought and reason. Her head spun with uncertainty, yet her body quickened with desire, every nerve alive and on fire.

Skillful hands closed over her breasts, caressing, and kneading. He rolled the aching tips between his fingers, while his mouth devoured hers, swallowing her tiny whimpers and sobs of pleasure. When his lips traveled along her jaw to the sensitive spot beneath her earlobe, she dropped her head back and moaned aloud.

"Never doubt your beauty, or feel you are unworthy,"

he whispered in her ear. "You're perfect, and you're mine." A possessive growl rolled in the back of his throat as he dipped his head and drew one of her aching nipples into his mouth.

His breath was warm and moist against her skin, his tongue branding everywhere it touched. When he dragged a nipple between his teeth and his fingers deftly fondled the other, she arched her back to give him better access. The sensation bordered on pain, but was so exquisite that she wanted more. He licked, suckled, and nibbled without mercy. The throbbing between her thighs intensified until she thought she might perish from need.

He raised his head and smiled. "I think this one needs attention, too." His mouth closed over the neglected nipple, and she swooned. He feasted on her breasts while his hands tugged at the sodden gown still draped around her hips. It slid away easily, and he helped her to step out of it without breaking the intimate contact.

While one hand continued to fondle and tease her breasts, the other trailed down her ribcage and across her stomach, coming to rest in the nest of curls at the apex of her thighs. She gasped from both shock and pleasure. When he sought out the burning bud of her arousal, she opened to him and offered herself for the taking.

He slid his finger along the slick swollen folds, and then dipped it inside. "Och, lass, you are so hot and wet, ready for loving. Your nectar flows like honey."

Connor lifted her, and she wrapped her legs around his waist. As he ground his hips against hers, she could feel the rock hard proof of his desire straining against the confines of his wet trews. She dropped her head, burying her face in the strong curve of his neck, and let out a soft sigh. Her body was on fire and wept with desire. It cried out to be touched, relieved of its tension. May the Almighty forgive her brazenness, but she wanted this man inside her, and she wanted him now.

"I want you, too," he moaned in her ear, as if he knew her thoughts. "I could take you here and now, but I want to savor this night." He carried her toward the bed and gently laid her upon the down-filled mattress. After stripping off his trews in record time, he tossed them on the floor and joined her.

He curled his tongue across his upper lip, while his burning gaze took in every inch and curve of her body. "You're too exquisite for words."

She sucked in a sharp breath when he slid his hand between her thighs and eased them apart. "Please, take me, and end this torture." She writhed and sobbed with pleasure when his fingers brushed across her throbbing heat.

"Soon, *liuadhe*. I want this to be a night we will both remember."

Her body tensed with excitement and anticipation. Something wild and primitive bubbled up from deep within her core. Something she could not explain, and had no desire to stop. Bombarded by intense sensations, heat flared and desire awakened. She reached for him without reservation. "I want to join with you," she muttered on a strangled sigh.

He released a feral growl and pulled her into his arms. "Your wish is my command."

In one swift move, Cailin found herself buried beneath him, pressed into the mattress as he captured her mouth in a ravenous kiss. His hands roamed her body, fondling bare nipples, caressing fevered flesh, and taking intimate liberties, but it wasn't enough. She wanted more. Her arms wrapped around his neck, and she moaned in his ear. "Take me, now."

"In good time, *leannan*."

Her hands slid across his broad shoulder, over his chest, and the flatness of his belly. The sensual trail continued until she finally reached his rock hard shaft. She explored his arousal with a feather light touch, and his body jerked.

A feral growl escaped his lips. He grasped her wrist

and pulled her hand away. Rising up on one elbow, he gazed into her eyes. "My body craves release, and if you touch me again, this may be over before either of us wishes. I promise you will be well rewarded." He nuzzled her neck. "First, I want to taste you fully."

He nipped at her bare shoulder, sending a shockwave of desire rippling through her entire body. His lips left a searing trail of kisses across her shoulder and the swell of her breast. When his mouth closed over her nipple, she moaned with pleasure. He gently kneaded and fondled the other breast as he suckled and teased. Again, she reached for his shaft, but he grasped her wrist.

"Be patient, *liuadhe*. I have so much more to show you." He kissed his way down her rib cage, across her belly.

That's easy for you to say. I want you now! Her mind screamed out like a wanton harlot. Her body hummed with desire and cried out for release. There couldn't possibly be more.

She was wrong.

"Let me look at you." He nudged her thighs farther apart, and then gently separated the folds of her heat. "So beautiful. Like a delicate pink flower waiting to be picked." His finger slowly circled the bud of her arousal in a way that made her squirm beneath his touch. Caught up in the intensity of the moment, Cailin couldn't find her voice. Before she could protest, his head dipped between her thighs, and he drew the folds between his teeth, carrying her away on a title wave of unbridled passion.

The languorous circling of his tongue made her writhe with delight. As his ministrations increased, so did the pulsing between her thighs. She moved restlessly beneath his lips. When he lifted her legs and placed them on his shoulders, her hips softened, and sexual energy reached a fevered peak. Wild with urgent need, she grasped his head and let her legs fall to the sides, giving him full access.

He slid one finger into her aching heat, followed by another, creating fullness and pressure so intense that her toes curled from the divine pleasure of it. As he pumped his fingers in and out, he kept the same rhythm with his tongue, lapping hungrily, moving faster, and stroking until she neared the precipice of release.

Delirious with passion, she began to pant. Her body tensed and her legs quivered. He must have known she was close to edge because he quickened the pace with his fingers, stoking the fire that raged inside. He suckled at the pearl of ecstasy, his tongue still working its magic. She had never been possessed in such a physical way, the endless barrage of pleasure and excitement almost too much to bear. It was as though he had completely forgotten his own need and focused solely on hers. Her body ablaze, she mindlessly thrashed beneath his touch in her quest for the apogee of pleasure, and sweet release.

Tendrils of desire unfurled, and her body began to quake. She shouted out his name, but he did not stop his sensual assault. The erotic heat burned low in her belly, and beyond, working its way to the surface with each slide of his fingers, each lap of his tongue. Consumed by a firestorm of emotion and sensation so sharp she couldn't breathe, he brought her to completion.

But it didn't end there. The sweet agony seemed to go on forever. Wave after wave of pure pleasure racked her body, and Connor refused to release her from the exquisite torture. Not until the last ripples of ecstasy ceased and her body relaxed, did he raise his head.

"I cannot hold back any longer." He pressed a kiss to the skin on her inner thigh, and then raised himself over her like a mighty beast.

When the tip of his shaft pressed against the wetness of her heat, she trembled with excitement. She shifted her bottom, then with one quick thrust, he entered her on the most intimate level.

They moaned in unison as he settled between her thighs and began to rock his hips. Unlike their first joining, there was no pain, only pleasure, and a sublime sensation of completion. She could feel every inch of his swollen member and savored the stretch and fullness. The musky scent of her climax mingled with the unmistakable scent of his arousal. Every thought and sensation centered on the joining of their bodies and the sublime pleasure that lay ahead.

He could never get enough of her. Heaven only knew he had tried to resist her charms, had done his utmost to deny the lust that fired his blood and made him ache with primordial need. He'd lost the battle before it began.

He buried his face in her hair. Like potent mead, her intoxicating scent boggled his mind and addled his senses. He raised his sweat-soaked frame, withdrew his shaft, then plunged in to the hilt. She moaned in delight. Her arms wrapped around his neck and she pulled him close, while the muscles of her heat contracted around him and drew him deeper.

Cailin was not trained in the ways that brought pleasure to men, but instinctively knew what drove him wild. She moved beneath him, matching his rhythm stroke for stroke. A ravenous heat ripped through his body, consuming everything in its path. His rapid breathing grew heavy, and his heart hammered against his chest. His vision blurred, gut clenched, and the fire in his groin intensified with each stroke. Her hands slid down his back, her touch pure sizzle. When she slid her hands over his bottom and pulled him into the cradle of her thighs, Connor knew the end was near. He buried himself, and they moved in unison.

He ached for release, and longed to spill his seed, but

first, he wanted to see her fulfilled once more. Connor slid his hand between their bodies, found her pearl of pleasure, and began to stroke it lightly. Her body arched, and she bucked beneath his touch. Her muscles tensed, and her thighs began to quiver. His mouth came down on hers, their breaths and moans mingling. Without breaking his rhythm, he continued to thrust into her with unbridled passion.

The tempo between them reached a fevered pitch. Cailin's body convulsed. She dropped her head back and rolled it from side to side. The feminine muscles tightened around his cock to the point of pain—a pain so exquisite and mind-blowing that he rode the wave of her release, thrust one more time, and plummeted over the precipice in an earth-shattering climax of his own. A mighty battle cry sprang from his lips as he spilled his seed and collapsed on top of her.

Concerned that his weight was too much for her to bear, he rolled to his back without breaking their connection. She raised her head and smiled at him. A smile that not only melted his heart, but one that made his manhood spring to life once again.

She straddled him and wiggled her bottom. When she tried to move, his hands grasped her hips and held her in place. "Are you never sated?"

"I can never get enough of you. Do with me as you will, lass, but keep in mind we have the whole night ahead of us."

"I pray you will keep your word, and make this a night I will not soon forget." Cailin lowered her head and captured his lips with a brief, but passionate, kiss.

Connor brushed away the tangled curls that hung around her face. "I give you my word." He wrapped his arms around her shoulders, pulled her toward him, and kissed her soundly.

He honored his promise and gave her a night of memories that may have to satisfy them both for a very long time—mayhap forever. They made love three more times before collapsing in exhaustion. When sleep finally threatened to claim them both, he cursed beneath his breath. In a few hours, the sun would rise, and she would leave Kildrummy Castle. She would go into hiding, and he would rejoin the cause. While he knew it was for best, the thought of never seeing her again did nothing to ease the ache in his heart.

Chapter 15

Connor languorously stretched, then rubbed the heel of his hand across his eyes. For the first time in years, he'd let down his guard and allowed himself to dream. But the moments of bliss were too brief. Soon, Cameron would come for Cailin and, albeit for her own safety, the knowledge that he may never see her again was like a dagger through his heart.

Peacefully cradled at his side, she rested on his shoulder, her cheeks still flushed from the heat of their passion. She affected him on so many levels, and his body craved hers in a way he'd never known. Maybe Alasdair was right. She'd bewitched him. Cailin addled his brains and scrambled his senses. After the intimacy they shared, how could he let her go?

Daylight filtered through cracks in the closed shutters, and prisms of color danced across the stone floor. He cursed the sun for having the audacity to herald the new day. He cursed the night for ending when he had all but offered his soul to the devil if it could go on forever. He cursed fate for bringing her into his life, only to snatch her away.

Cailin stirred, released a soft sigh, and opened her eyes. "Why do you frown?" Her voice was husky and thick from sleep.

"It is morning, and you will soon be on your way." He almost choked on the words. "If I could turn back the clock, I would. Alas, I'm a mortal man, and have no power to do so."

"Is the priory far?"

"A full day's ride. If you and Cameron make good time,

you'll arrive before sundown. Simon sent a missive to Father Paul and told him you are coming. You will like Mary. The two of you are of a similar heart and mind."

"Has she taken her vows?"

"Not yet. Mary has been at the priory since she was four and ten. She has chosen to stay for one more summer, and then she must make her choice. At that time, she will either take her vows or leave the priory to marry one of the many lairds who have asked for her hand."

"Does she love any of these men?" Cailin brushed the hair from his brow.

"Love has nothing to do with who she'll marry. If she decides to leave the priory, Simon will choose the man he feels most fitting."

"I see." She laid her head on his shoulder. "When will Cameron come for me?"

"Too soon." He sucked in a strangled breath when her long slender fingers curled in the dark curls covering his chest.

"I wish I could stay here with you." She snuggled closer and pressed her lips to the side of his neck.

"You cannot stay here, *liuadhe*. When Robert's army departs for Perth, I am honor-bound to go with them. Should the English find you, I won't be here to protect you." He kissed the top of her head, closed his eyes, and moaned aloud.

"How long will you be away?"

"I dinna know." He bit his lower lip and refrained from telling her that he might never return. He would not underestimate Aymer de Valance. Many men would die before the battle was over.

Cailin clutched his hand to her breast. "Never forget that I hold your heart in mine, and know that I await your return?"

Tears welled in her eyes, but to her credit, she held

them at bay. His heart clenched. "It would be easier for me to forget how to breathe. The first time I kissed you, the earth moved. I have committed to memory every luscious curve and sensual dip of your body." He skimmed his hand across the swell of her perfect breasts, and then gently lifted her chin. "Every time I close my eyes, I'll see your face, your sweet smile, and the look of surrender in your eyes when we make love. These are the memories I will carry into battle."

She nestled against his side. "I wish we could stay like this forever. Swear you will come back to me unharmed."

"You must be brave, and accept what destiny has planned. As long as I know you're safe." The sight of tears trickling down her cheeks rendered him speechless. All she wanted was a glimmer of hope. To know that he'd return to her, that they would spend the rest of their lives together, but he couldn't make any promises. He had no idea what fate had in store, and his heart that had found new life weighed heavy with despair.

A knock on the door served as a stark reminder that their time together grew short. "Aye, who is it?" Connor asked, even though he knew the reason for the intrusion.

"Cameron. I've come for the lass. If we want to reach the priory before sundown, we must be away." He waited a few minutes, and when Connor didn't reply, he continued. "Maggie has prepared a tray of food, and once the lady breaks her fast, we'll depart. The king also wishes to see you in his chamber before you join Simon and the others in the lists."

"Leave the tray by the door, and I'll see her ready to leave within the hour. Tell Robert I come anon." When the sound of Cameron's footfall faded, he glanced down at Cailin. "It's time."

Her arms encircled his neck, and she nuzzled against his ear. "Nay. Please, stay with me just a wee bit longer. Join with me again."

When her hand fell to his lap, her fingers wrapped around his burgeoning flesh and danced across the tip. His body ignited, bursting into flames. He groaned aloud and grasped her wrist. His inner voice warned that making love to her would be a mistake and prolong the agony of their separation. But, he was only human. A possessive growl rolled in the back of his throat. "Be careful what you wish for, lass." Yielding to temptation, he rolled her body beneath him and captured her lips in a voracious kiss.

Aye, he would take her again, and leave them both with a memory that would live in their hearts forever.

Cailin nibbled on an oatcake, and rinsed it down with a swallow of ale. After a night of rigorous lovemaking, her appetite should have been enormous, but she found it difficult to choke down a mouthful of food. Connor had gone to see the Bruce, and soon he would join her in the bailey to say goodbye. Heartbroken, she had no idea how to ease the pain. Even though her husband hadn't said it outright, she knew the battle in Perth would be fierce and might be his last. Something in her gut told her that they may never see each other again. She slid her hand over the flat plane of her belly and closed her eyes. She prayed the seed Connor planted would prosper. If he didn't return, she'd have a part of him to hold, love, and cherish.

"Are you ready to leave, m'lady, or do you need help gathering your things?" Maggie crossed the room, paused by the table, and picked up the tray. "You've hardly eaten a thing. Are you feeling poorly this morn?"

"I'm fine, and I dinna have much to pack." She gathered her meager belongings, the clothes she'd wore on her journey, a change of undergarments, and a simple wool gown. She'd declined Marion's generous offer of silks and finery, and had opted for more serviceable attire. There would be no need for such things in a priory.

"Best you make haste. Cameron waits for you in the bailey. Cook packed some supplies for you to take along, so be sure to tell Cameron when you are feeling hungry. You know how men can be. They'll ride forever and not stop until they reach their destination."

"I'll keep that in mind." Cailin stuffed the clothing into a canvas sack.

"Forgive me for being forward, m'lady." Maggie bowed her head and shuffled her feet. "I know this is none of my affair, but are you sure you're all right? If you're worried about Lady Jenna, don't be. It is obvious your betrothed loves you. I'm sure he will not stray, no matter what she does to get his attention. When he returns from battle, he will come for you and carry you away to his castle in Beauly."

Cailin knew that Jenna would do her utmost to win Connor's affection in her absence, but she believed he would remain true. Being separated from the man she'd come to love, and the fact that after everything they'd shared, he had not yet told her that he loved her weighed heavy on her mind. What if he died in battle and she never saw him again? The idea of going to the priory frightened her, but she'd spent the better part of her life with her emotions in check, and her dreams unspoken, so why should this be any different? For her safety, and to throw the English off her trail, an announcement had been made that she'd be returning to her father's castle in Dunkeld while Connor was away.

"I trust Connor, and have faith he will not stray." Cailin rose slowly, gathered up her skirt, and made her way to the door. "Come, we dinna want to keep Cameron waiting." She left the room and headed down the hall toward the stairs. Maggie followed.

"There you are. I was about to come looking for you." Cameron approached the two women as they entered the bailey, then held out his hand in Cailin's direction. "Give me your haversack and I'll secure it to the horse."

Maggie stepped forward, handed him another canvas sack and two horns of ale. "Cook packed some provisions for you to take along. Mind you stop along the way to eat and give Lady Cailin a chance to rest and tend to her needs."

He nodded, took the items from Maggie, the sack of clothing from Cailin, and then moved to where the horses stood saddled and waiting. "Connor speaks with the king and said he'd be here before we leave."

"You dinna think I'd let you leave without saying goodbye." Connor strode across the inner courtyard toward them. Bryce and Alasdair accompanied him.

Her heart leapt at the sight of him. She ran in his direction and threw herself into his arms, clutching his shirt. Despite her effort to hold them back, tears rolled down her cheeks.

"Hush, lass, dinna weep. Cameron will see you safely to the priory and the Lord willing, when I return from Perth, I'll come for you." He wiped away the tears with a gentle sweep of his thumb, before pulling her into an all-encompassing embrace.

He released her, took a step back, and handed her a parchment bearing the royal seal of Scotland. "My pledge of handfast. Should anything happen to me, this is your claim to my name, land, wealth, and property."

She clutched the scroll to her breast and shook her head. Without him by her side, it all meant nothing. She tried to hand it back to him. "I dinna want this. It is you I love and desire, not your money or your land."

No woman had every truly loved him unconditionally, and her words touched him deeply. To know of her affection and devotion should make him happy, but instead, it caused him great pain. Should he die in battle, she may someday fall in love and choose to marry. The thought of her in another man's arms and round with child—a babe that was not of his loins—evoked a rage that threatened to consume him body and soul.

He wanted to hold her forever and to declare his undying love. Instead, he released her. Taking her hand, he led her toward Cameron. "I'm entrusting you with her life. Have a safe journey, my friend."

Cameron nodded. "You know I'll do what's necessary to see her safely to her destination."

The forlorn expression on her face was enough to break his heart, but Connor steeled himself against the swell of emotion burning in his chest.

He watched while Cameron lifted her into the saddle. When she glanced in his direction, Connor quickly lowered his gaze. He knew if their eyes met, he'd race to her side, pull her from the horse, and carry her back up to his chamber.

He couldn't bear to watch them leave, so he turned away and walked toward the castle. Only when the sound of horse's hooves faded into the distance did he dare to glance over his shoulder.

She was gone.

Bryce joined him and slid his hand over his shoulder, giving it a comforting squeeze. "That can't have been easy."

"It was Hell." Connor blew out a ragged breath.

"Best you put the lass out of your mind," Alasdair said curtly. "We have a battle to fight, and you need a clear head. You should not have gotten involved with her in the first place."

"Shut up," Bryce snapped. "Can't you see the man is in pain?"

"Alasdair is right. I should never have allowed myself to get involved with Cailin. She deserves far better than I can ever give her. She'll be safe at the priory, and we dinna know what the outcome of the battle will be. It is best for all that she leave."

Bryce shook his head. "If only it were that easy. I hate to bring up another sore subject, but what do you plan to do about Jenna? You know she won't rest until she gets her way."

"I'll not be swayed by that she-devil. She can try, but I will not bend."

"Lady Jenna has other ideas. I ran into her last night. She was prowling the hall like a cat in heat. When she dinna find you in your chamber, she made her intentions clear to me. The lass is determined to win your heart at all cost. I would not let my guard down if I were you."

"I'm a grown man and can look after myself. I dinna need my little brother to tell me what to do."

"You're vulnerable right now, and she'll try to take advantage of that. She knows a lot more than she should, and I dinna trust her to hold her tongue. If you anger her, she may use that information to get back at you, or worse at Cailin."

"She may be a selfish, spoiled brat, but I dinna believe she would do anything to dishonor her family," Connor countered. "In any event, Cailin is safely away, and I have no interest in Jenna."

Bryce shook his head and clucked his tongue. "A woman scorned can be a dangerous enemy. Keep your head on a swivel."

"I'll take your warning into consideration," Connor said as he began to climb the stairs. Alasdair accompanied him.

"Wait for me," Bryce shouted as he took the stairs two at a time and joined his brothers as they neared the top. "The men have been fighting in the lists since daybreak. If we hurry, we can join them."

"Aye, I could use a good training session right about

now. I have a lot of energy to burn off," Connor said and entered the castle.

Cailin chewed on her lower lip as she glanced around the priory cell. A dismal place at best. Aside from a small bed with a lumpy straw-filled mattress, a wooden chair, and a dilapidated table, the musty smelling room was empty. Walls of stone held no tapestries or adornments, and the cobbled floor was devoid of rugs and rushes. The single tallow candle, her only source of light, had almost burned down to a snub. An iron brassier in the corner of the room housed the smoldering remnants of a fire long burned to ashes. A Bible, its cover tattered and worn, sat on the table. At least she'd have something to read.

She moved to the window. The rusty hinges groaned when she pushed open the wooden shutters in time to see a spectacular sunset. Truly God's Pallet, the twilight sky still held a brilliant pink and orange hue, streaked with dark grey and purple. She caught the scent of the flowers planted in a small garden beneath her window and inhaled deeply, savoring the fragrance. She'd leave the shutters open to air out her room.

Cameron stood in the courtyard, speaking with Father Paul, but she was too far away to hear their conversation. Uneasiness settled in her belly, and she fought the urge to rush outside, to beg him to take her back to Kildrummy Castle and Connor. They'd only been apart for a few hours, but she already missed him more than she ever anticipated.

"Good evening. Is there anything I can get for you?"

Cailin spun around, staring at the petite, titian-haired young woman standing in the doorway. She was the image of Marion. While she was dressed in the drab woolen robes of a nun, her blue eyes danced and sparkled with life as she spoke. Her broad smile was most inviting.

"I dinna mean to startle you. I'm Mary Fraser, and you must be my new cousin." She stepped into the room and closed the door behind her. "Father sent word that you were coming, and he explained the reason you needed to seek sanctuary in the priory." She joined Cailin beside the window. "You're very comely. I can see why Connor is so taken with you."

The heat of a blush rose in Cailin's cheeks. "I am pleased to meet you, Mary. Connor spoke fondly of you as well."

"I remember a time when he called me a pest. He said I could prattle on more than any lass he had ever met." She laughed and touched Cailin's arm. "Och, you're as cold as ice. Come away from the window, and I will stoke the fire."

"I'm fine." Cailin glanced out the window and watched Cameron mount his horse. After a curt nod to the priest, he rode out the gate. He was leaving, and she had no choice but to stay behind in the hopes that Connor would come for her soon.

Mary peered out the window and smiled. "It was wonderful to see Cameron again."

"Connor told me he'd trust no one else to see me safely to the priory." Cailin stepped away from the window and sat on the edge of the bed. When Mary reached for the shutters, she held up her hand. "Please leave them open. I like the fresh air, and the flowers smell lovely."

Mary sat on the bed beside her. "Once you're settled, I'd be happy to show you around. The priory is not a grand dwelling, but you'll be safe here." She stopped talking long enough to take a breath, then continued. "I'm anxious to hear about my family and to know how everyone is faring. I miss my mother and sister. Having you here will be wonderful. You must be famished. I'll ask the cook to prepare you a tray."

"I appreciate your kindness, Mary, but we ate along the way, and I am not very hungry. If you could show me where I can go to tend to my needs and where I can get a basin of water, I'd like to wash up and go to bed. Mayhap you could show me around the priory in the morning and we could talk then."

"Forgive me for prattling on. You must be exhausted from your long journey. There is a chamber pot under the bed and an outdoor privy." Mary pointed out the window at a small stone building. "I'd be happy to bring you a basin of water to wash up and a pitcher of ale to quench your thirst. We will have plenty of time to talk and get acquainted once you've rested."

A mix of jealousy and sadness washed over Cailin, and Mary's disappointed expression didn't make things any easier. She couldn't help but envy Mary and the relationship she had with her family. She craved a mother's love and a father's adoration. When Simon spoke of his daughters or of Connor and his brothers, warmth and affection lit up his eyes. Marion's love and devotion for her brood was unquestionable. If anything, she felt more alone than ever.

Cailin fought back the tears and the ball of emotion that rose in her throat. Her father didn't care if she lived or died. He'd offered her to Borden to win his favor, and she was certain that after her escape, he'd not attempt to find her. After surrendering her innocence to Connor, she was useless to her father as a bargaining chip. At best, he might be able to marry her off in exchange for a few head of cattle or a small parcel of land. If she was ever cleared of the murder charge and Connor chose not to honor the handfast, she refused to return to Dunkeld.

Cailin slid her hand over her belly. Did she carry Connor's babe? If so blessed, she vowed the child would never know the pain of longing. She would love their little one with all her heart and cherish it always. On the other hand, there might be no bairn, and she'd forever feel empty and alone. The melancholia that gripped her was difficult to mask.

"Are you certain that you're all right?" Mary asked.

"Aye. I'm just tired."

"Then we must see you settled and into bed. I'll go and fetch you some water." Mary pulled a basin from under the bed and headed for the door.

"Wait," Cailin called after her. "I'm being selfish. Your family has been so kind to me, and you must be anxious to hear how they fare."

"I am, but I understand if you're too tired. It can wait until morning if you wish to rest," Mary said with a hint of renewed anticipation in her voice.

"After the kindness you've shown me, it would be cruel for me to make you wait. Sit down." Cailin patted the bed beside her. "I would be happy to share the news of your family."

"Our family." Mary sat down, took Cailin's hand, and gave it a comforting squeeze. "Dinna worry, you'll be safe here, and Connor will come for you as soon as he can. I know he will."

Cailin forced a smile. "I hope you're right."

Chapter 16

Bone-weary and ready to drop from fatigue, Connor slid from the saddle. He'd prowled the battlements until the wee hours of the morning, woke up before dawn, and then worked in the lists. After soundly defeating every warrior who dared to challenge, he mounted Thor and pushed the powerful warhorse until he neared collapse.

For weeks, he'd repeated this grueling routine, rain or shine. Nearly two months had passed since Cailin left for the priory, yet memories of their time together plagued his waking hours and haunted his dreams.

Connor cursed beneath his breath. He'd never known such weakness, and it had to stop before he went insane or dropped from exhaustion. They'd be leaving for Perth any day, and he needed his wits about him. There wasn't time for woolgathering about mesmerizing eyes the color of emeralds, soft feminine curves, silken hair that rivaled an autumn sunset and smelled of heather. He had to stop longing for what could never be. He had done what was necessary to protect her reputation, but she was safely sequestered, out of his life, and all the better for it. In time, she'd forget about him.

"Can I take your horse, m'lord?" A young lad stumbled out of the stable, rubbed his eyes, and covered his mouth to stifle a yawn.

"Aye, Gavin. After you've given him some oats, water, and a good rubdown, you may return to your pallet." He handed over the reins, then moved toward the castle. "A tankard of ale, mayhap two, and then I will seek my own bed," he mumbled as he climbed the stone steps.

Alasdair elbowed Bryce in the ribs, and pointed toward the door leading into the great hall. "It appears the prodigal brother has returned. About time he found his way home." He gulped down a tankard of ale, and then belched loudly.

Connor raked his fingers through his hair and heaved a weary sigh. The last thing he needed was Alasdair's cynicism. When he entered the hall at this late hour, he'd expected to find it empty. Dreading an interrogation from his brothers, he debated about turning around and going straight to his chamber. Instead, he plunked himself down in a chair beside Bryce. Without saying a word, he reached for a pitcher of ale.

"The sun set hours ago, and you missed the evening meal, again. We were beginning to worry." Bryce pushed a wooden platter in front of Connor. "There is still some pheasant and turnip, if Alasdair doesn't snatch it up."

"If he's not home in time for meals, he has only himself to blame." Alasdair dragged a piece of bread across his trencher, sopped up the last bit of meat drippings, and tossed it in his mouth.

Connor grunted and reached for an empty tankard. "I'm not hungry." After filling the pewter mug to the brim, he downed the contents.

Bryce moved the food closer. "You really should eat something. This morning you dinna come down to break your fast, and after working in the lists, you failed to join us for the noonday meal. Instead, you saddled Thor, rode out at full speed, and dinna return until after dark. Again. You're going to drive that poor horse into the ground."

"Thor is of sturdy stock, and when I want a nurse-maid, I'll hire one. Until then, mind your own affairs." Connor refilled the tankard and brought it to his lips.

"You need to stop pining for Cailin and do something about it." Bryce grabbed Connor's wrist when he reached for the pitcher again. "Drinking yourself into oblivion won't solve anything. Nor will it help to starve yourself. I've never seen you brood like this. Not even after Mam and Da died."

Connor clenched his jaw and glared at his brother. "I dinna brood. And if you value your life, brother, you'll let go of my hand."

Bryce didn't budge, nor did he back down. "For weeks you've skulked around the castle like a volcano ready to erupt. You speak to no one, except to growl, and you barely eat enough to keep a bird alive."

"If you dinna start taking it easy on the men in the lists, there won't be anyone willing to face you," Alasdair added.

Connor wrenched his arm free of Bryce's grasp. "Mayhap you missed your calling, little brother. A bard seems like a good choice given your gift of gab and woman's heart." He refilled his tankard, and drained it for the third time. "As for the way I treat the men, Alasdair, you're exaggerating, as always."

"Tell that to Donald and Brian. They're still recovering from the wounds you inflicted two weeks ago, or have you forgotten?" Alasdair's retort was sharp, and to the point.

"They should not be training in the lists if they're not prepared to fight. Had they been paying attention, they'd not have been injured." Well on his way to being in his cups, Connor slumped in his chair. Maybe Alasdair was right. He did expect a lot of his men, but he'd not ease up and see them go into battle unprepared. As for Bryce's accusations about Cailin, he refused to admit that his heart and body ached for her. A warrior would not allow infatuation with a woman to keep him from doing his duty. She was better off without him, and he didn't need her to complicate his life. Or so he tried to convince himself.

Call it a gut feeling, but he was certain he'd die in battle—if not in Perth, soon after. The thought of giving his life for the cause had never bothered him before, but now that he'd tasted the passion, desire, and divine euphoria of bedding a woman like Cailin, he had so much more to lose.

"The men are afraid to challenge you. Many of them are sure you have lost your mind," Bryce said dourly.

"I ask no more than I demand of myself. The men must learn to fight with every fiber of their being. To enter each battle like it is the last day of their lives."

"They're aware of that, but there is no excuse for the way you are driving them," Bryce argued.

"There is no time to coddle the men. We should have left for Perth weeks ago, but Robert knew they were not ready." Connor narrowed his eyes and slammed his balled fist on the table. "If they want to whine like old women, mayhap they best don kirtles. They can take to scrubbing the floors, serving the meals, and leave the fighting to real men." He picked up his empty tankard, and then scanned the table for more ale. "I won't trust my back to a man who isn't prepared for battle."

"Your foul mood has nothing to do with the battle in Perth." Bryce moved the pitcher of ale out of Connor's reach. "When are you going to admit that you love the lass and miss her in your bed?"

"He's got two hands doesn't he?" Alasdair threw back his head and laughed boisterously.

Normally such bawdy comments would spur Connor to fight, but he stared into his empty tankard and said nothing.

"He needs to do something to take his mind off the lass," Alasdair pressed. Not ready to give up the jest, he leaned across the table and patted Connor on the shoulder. "I'm sure Lady Jenna would be happy to warm your bed."

His patience worn thin, Connor stood and faced his brother. "I told you, I have no interest in Jenna." He picked up the empty tankard and threw it against the wall.

Alasdair nodded toward the door of the great hall. "Speak of the devil."

Bryce let out a low whistle as Jenna glided across the

room.

"There you are, Connor. I've been looking for you."

Too late to escape, Connor lowered himself into the chair. He dropped his head forward and groaned.

What must I do to get through to the woman?

Smugly looking like a cat about to swallow a bird, Bryce stood and bowed. "Good evening, Lady Jenna. You're looking lovely as usual.

Ignoring Bryce and Alasdair, Jenna raised her nose in the air and focused on Connor. "We missed you at the evening meal. A big strong man like you must eat to keep up your strength. One never knows when you'll need it." She rounded the table and stood behind his chair. "Would you like me to have Cook prepare a tray? I'd be very happy to bring it to your chamber."

"No!" Connor snapped.

Jenna placed her hands on his shoulder and began to massage them. Her breath tickled his ear when she spoke. "You're tense and need to relax, m'lord. I can help you unwind. Mayhap, you would like to take a nice hot bath. I'll have a tub sent up to your chamber, and would be happy to scrub your back, or—"

"Enough!" Connor shoved the chair back, almost knocking Jenna off her feet.

Alasdair covered his mouth to hide a snicker, then raised his tankard and winked at Jenna. "I've a few body parts that need a good scrubbing, m'lady, if you have a mind to be of assistance."

"How dare you proposition me? I'm a lady, and refuse be spoken to in such a bawdy manner. I would not touch you if you were the last man in Scotland. I'd just as soon be sent to a priory like—"

Connor grabbed Jenna's arm and spun her around to face him. Was her reference to the priory an innocent remark, or was she trying to make a point? "You best counsel your tongue. One of these days, you will approach the wrong man, and he will take you up on your offer, or worse, he'll take his pleasure against your will."

Her cheeks flushed red, but the determined look in her sapphire eyes let him know she had no intention of backing off. "We were meant to be together, and the sooner you realize that, the better. Someday, you will regret the way you have treated me and beg my forgiveness." Jenna splayed her hands over Connor's chest and ground her hips against the hollow of his thighs. "That little chit will never make you happy. Not the way I can. Asking her to marry you was a noble act. Especially after you soiled her reputation, but you need a real woman in your bed. You need a woman who knows how to please a man."

Connor grasped Jenna's wrists and held her at arm's length. "Have you no shame? Only a wanton woman would flaunt herself in such a manner. Best you return to your solar and forget this foolish notion." He firmly shoved her out of his way. "If you'll excuse me, I need some air." His patience pushed to the limits, he stormed out of the great hall and climbed the steps to the parapets.

When he reached the top, he stepped onto the stone walkway and paused to draw in a breath of crisp clean air. He'd asked for Cailin's hand in this very same spot, but unlike that night, there wasn't a cloud in the star-spattered sky. A full moon illuminated the rocky cliffs and he could see for miles. Oh how he wished he could hold Cailin in his arms just one more time and kiss those pouty lips. When he closed his eyes, he could see her face. When he inhaled, he could smell her sweet fragrance. With a heavy heart, he placed his hands on the wall, leaned forward, and rested his forehead on the cold stones. "I wish I could purge you from my mind," he muttered aloud.

"You cannot go on like this." Bryce stepped onto the walkway. "I know being separated from Cailin is tormenting you. Even if you refuse to admit it."

Connor spun around to face his brother. "Are you daft, man? I said I needed some air, not your company." He leaned his back against the wall and rubbed his temples to ease the ache building behind his eyes. "Why won't you leave me be?"

Bryce shrugged. "Mayhap you should pay the lass a visit before we leave for Perth. I've no doubt that she'd be very happy to see you."

"She is safely sequestered, and I dinna want to draw any attention to the priory. Besides, she is better off without me. In time, she will realize that, and move on. She deserves a husband that will love her and be by her side." He almost choked on the unbearable words.

"If you are not in love with the lass, then you put on a good act." Bryce took a step forward and frowned. "What about the handfast? With the declaration of marriage repudiated by the king, you could have walked away. Why did you become betrothed if you had no intention of following through?"

"Despite my best effort, and against my better judgment, I fell for the lady's charms. I'm not proud of my weakness, or the fact that I allowed my heart to rule my head. To visit Cailin would only make things worse for both of us. I dinna want to give her false hope, or lead her on. This way is best."

"Who are you really trying to protect?" Bryce asked.

"You overstep your boundaries. Best you mind your tongue." Connor turned away. Bryce knew him far too well. With his hands braced on the castle wall, he peered out over the moonlit moors in the direction of the priory.

"You distance yourself to ease your own pain," Bryce said in a matter-of-fact tone. "Admit it. You love her. Despite your effort to hide it, I saw the look of anguish on your face the day she left. I've also seen the longing in your eyes when the two of you are together."

"Be that as it may, we are going into battle in a few days and may not come back," Connor said solemnly.

"Then there is all the more reason to see her before we leave. To tell her how you feel about her."

"Nay! I'll not be like our father and leave behind anyone to mourn me. I dinna want to cause her any more grief than I already have."

"I'm afraid it is too late for that. Do you ever intend to see her again?" Bryce asked bluntly.

Connor didn't answer.

"Did you ask for a handfast in a moment of weakness, or did you want to make sure no one else could have her?" Bryce badgered.

Connor spun on his heels, his fists balled at his sides. "There could be a child, and I'll not have a son of mine called a bastard."

"What about the lass?"

"I did it for her as well. I'll not have people think her a whore. With luck, there'll be no child, and once the year is up, she'll be free to move on and marry the man she deserves without shame.

"What if she carries your babe?"

"If there is a babe, Cailin will be a fine mother and do right by the bairn. Both will be better off without me."

"You're a *thrawn* man. You've run from the past and guarded your heart far too long. You need to put it behind you and start living again. Let Cailin be that new beginning." Bryce slid his hand on Connor's shoulder and gave it a squeeze.

"Things are not that simple," Connor said on a shuddering breath.

"They are only as complicated as you choose to make them. Every journey begins with a single step. Take that step, Connor. Go and see Cailin. Tell her how you feel."

"Mayhap you're right..." His resolve weakened.

"Connor, Bryce. The king wishes to see you in his chambers right away. He said it was time to ready the men." Cameron stood in the doorway, his massive size filling it. "We leave for Perth at sunrise."

Cailin leaned over the chamber pot as the acid bile rose in her throat and her stomach churned. She'd already emptied the meager contents, but the heaving refused to stop.

"Och, are you all right?" Mary asked. She crossed the room and knelt beside Cailin. "You poor lamb. You have been feeling poorly six mornings in a row."

"Fortunately, it doesn't last long. Once I've been up and about for a while, is passes." She drew in a slow, ragged breath and fought the urge to vomit again.

"Have you given any thought to what ails you?"

"The venison Cook served last week tasted off. Mayhap it was tainted," Cailin replied weakly and covered her mouth.

"We all ate the meat, and no one else appears ill. Could it be you're with child?"

The thought had crossed her mind, but she was afraid to hope. "I'm sure it was caused by something I ate. In fact, I'm certain of it. I had my courses not long after I arrived at the priory."

"When are they due again?"

Cailin counted back the days. "They were due a sennight ago, but I have never been regular, so cannot be sure."

"While I'm no expert on such things, I've heard that a woman can sometimes have her courses, even when she is with child. Are you telling me you and Connor dinna consummate the handfast?"

Cailin sat on her heels and dragged a shaky hand across her brow. The glorious nights of unbridled passion flooded her mind. "Now that I think about it, my courses were very light, and only lasted a day. I guess it is possible."

Mary's smile broadened. She threw her arms around Cailin's shoulders and gave her a hug. "This is wonderful news. Connor will crow like a proud rooster when he finds out." She leaned back, tilted her head to the side, and met Cailin's gaze. "You dinna look pleased. I'm sure my cousin will be a wonderful father."

Cailin blinked back tears, her joy overshadowed by memories of her own childhood. *What if the babe is a girl? Will Connor love and cherish our daughter, or be disappointed and shun her as my father did?* Cailin's heart clenched as she struggled to catch her breath. Familiar feelings of rejection and sadness knotted her stomach. The loneliness, longing for a mother's love and father's acceptance were things she refused to let happen to her child.

Mary brushed a stray curl from Cailin's forehead. "Are you frightened about giving birth?"

Cailin lowered her eyes. "My mother died giving birth to my twin brother, and my father never forgave me for being the one who lived. He had no use for a daughter. Men wish for sons."

"Be it a son or a daughter, a babe is a gift from God. If I marry, I hope to have at least a half a dozen bairns." Mary took Cailin's hands and squeezed them. "Giving birth must be the most wonderful thing in the world. You're a strong, healthy lass, and I have faith that all will go well.

"I fear not for myself," Cailin muttered, her hand sliding over the flat plane of her belly.

"Then what bothers you?" Mary lifted Cailin's chin. "This is a time for joy. Dinna worry about Connor. He is a skilled warrior and will come back to you. I know it."

Mary's attempt to reassure Cailin fell short. "He's not invincible. Even the bravest, most skilled warriors can fall victim to a blade. There is also the possibility that the English will find me and see me punished for a crime I dinna commit." She wrapped her arms around herself and shook her head. "What will happen to my child if they do?"

"You're safe here, Cailin. Connor will return, and he will protect you and the bairn."

"What if he doesn't return? What if the babe is born and Borden finds me? He'll show no mercy." Cailin stood and began to pace the small cell. "Mayhap, I should leave here."

Mary grasped Cailin by the shoulders, forcing her to stand still. "That would be foolish. It's not safe for you to leave the priory."

"Promise me that if Borden comes, you will protect my babe. Promise that you will care for him and see him safe."

"Nothing is going to happen to you or the bairn. What about your father? Surely you can go to him for protection, and he would welcome his grandchild."

"I will never go back to my father's keep. He showed me no affection or regard when I was a bairn and made no effort to protect me when Borden came to the castle to arrest me. If not for my own resourcefulness, I would have been taken prisoner without a protest. As sure as I am he's made no effort to find me. If I must raise my babe alone, I will. If I am arrested, and executed, I'll not have him reared by a heartless bastard. Promise me that you'll raise my bairn as your own, Mary, that you'll love him," Cailin pleaded.

"I promise," Mary said softly. She pulled Cailin into her arms and held her close. "Should the need arise, I promise to love him as my own."

Chapter 17

The acrid smell of blood and the stench of death shrouded the once peaceful Scottish encampment. Connor crept through bracken, brambles, and thistles—being careful not to raise the attention of the English. When he reached a copse of trees at the north end of what was now a battlefield, he lowered himself into a crouched position. His heart sank as he surveyed the carnage.

How could this have happened? Why did I survive when so many of my comrades perished?

The Scottish army of nearly four thousand men came to Perth prepared to fight, but when Aymer de Valence refused to meet the challenge, the Bruce ordered them to make camp outside the village of Methven. He had not anticipated a predawn raid by three thousand English soldiers.

Unable to sleep, his dreams plagued by thoughts of Cailin, Connor had gone to the stream to bathe and cool the fire in his loins. When he heard men shouting and the clash of metal, he raced back to the camp, but it was too late. Many of the men died as they slept. They never heard the blackguards coming. The Scots fought bravely, but they were caught unawares. The English took full advantage of the surprise attack, and in no time, they'd overrun the camp.

Grief-stricken, Connor hung his head. *If only I could have done something to stop the butchery. What of my brothers, and cousin? Have I failed them, too?*

With baited breath, he scanned the sea of twisted bodies, the familiar faces contorted by pain, the lifeless eyes staring up at the sky? Were Alasdair, Bryce, and Simon among them? The full impact of what happened hit him like a mighty blow to the gut. His stomach roiled and acid rose in his throat as he bent over a rock and emptied his stomach.

A tree branch snapped. He had company. His breath caught and his heart pounded like a battering ram against his ribs. He reached for his claymore and turned in the direction of the noise, prepared to fight with his last ounce of strength if necessary.

In a voice barely above a whisper, a man spoke from shadows. "Saints be praised, you're still alive."

He immediately recognized Simon's voice. Blowing out a sigh of relief, he lowered his weapon. When his two brothers and Cameron joined his cousin, he moved with stealth to where they stood. He embraced each of them in turn. "What of Robert, and the rest of the lads? How many survived?"

Simon brought his finger to his lips and ushered him into the woods before he answered. "Robert is safe. When we knew the battle was lost, we saw him away." Simon clutched his left arm. The sleeve of his tunic was red with blood. His face drained of color and he wobbled on his feet.

"You're hurt." Connor caught his cousin as he staggered forward and fell to his knees.

Simon shoved Connor away and struggled to stand unaided. "I'll live to fight another day, but I cannot say the same for the lads who fell on the field. Robert should have posted more guards around the camp. Had he done so, the blackguards would not have been able to attack under the cloak of darkness."

"The lads fought bravely and died for a cause they believed in. We will not let their deaths be in vain. We must honor their memory." Alasdair briefly bowed his head and crossed his chest. "The Almighty has seen fit to let us live, so best we not tarry. Those who survived the battle headed west to the Argyll Mountains. There we will regroup and come back stronger than ever. Aymer de Valence will rue the day he was born." He slammed his balled fist against the trunk of a tree so hard his knuckles bled.

"We cannot just leave the dead and wounded behind." Bryce drew his sword and started to move in the direction of the camp.

Connor grabbed his arm. "What do you plan to do? Too many have fallen, and we are but five men against three thousand. There's nothing more we can do for them. We must entrust the spirits of the dead to the Almighty, and as for the wounded—" Connor hesitated, his eyes downcast. "The English have shown no quarter, and there are no survivors."

Bryce took a few more steps, then planted his feet firmly in place. He took a final look at the disheveled encampment, crossed himself, and bowed his head in prayer. "*Tha ma duilich*. I'm sorry, please forgive us, dear friends. Rest assured that your deaths will be avenged."

Following his brother's lead, Connor bowed his head and prayed for the souls of those lost this day, for their families, and for Scotland.

Pangs of guilt twisted his gut. Thousands of brave men had died, yet he'd survived, and would carry the memory of this battle the rest of his days. Aye, Simon was right, they would live to see another day, to fight another battle, and owed it to the fallen to do it with pride. But when it was over, and Scotland's army had licked its wounds and rebuilt its forces, he would go to Cailin and tell her how he felt. He would beg her forgiveness and take her to wife—if she'd have him. If this day's massacre taught him anything, it was that time is precious, and not to be wasted on fear or senseless pride.

"We must be away, lads," Simon whispered. He tapped Connor on the shoulder.

"Aye, we've tarried long enough." He joined the others, and they silently made their way through a thicket of brambles and out of harm's way.

It didn't take long for news of the Scot's defeat and de Valence's treachery to spread. It was a well-known fact that Robert the Bruce had narrowly escaped and planned to retaliate. However, to divulge the extent of their loss and the near annihilation of the Scottish army would be an open invitation for the English to attack before they had a chance to regroup.

Over two months had passed since the battle near Methven and still there had been little word as to survivors, leaving many families wondering about the fate of their loved ones. Cailin was no exception.

She paced the priory cell, praying for news of Connor and his brothers, but hope of their return was beginning to wane. Without conscious thought, her hands covered the small swell of her belly. Five months along, she was starting to show. Fortunately, the morning sickness had subsided, and she no longer dreaded waking up to a chamber pot. A soft rap on the door caught her attention. Half-expecting Mary to bustle in with a food-laden tray, she slid to the edge of the bed and sat up. "Aye, who is it?"

The door opened, and Cailin's mouth dropped open in surprise when in addition to Mary, she saw Marjory Bruce standing in the doorway.

"The queen feared an attack on Kildrummy castle was immanent and sent Marjory to us for safe keeping." Mary placed her hand on emiesMarjory's shoulder and ushered her into the cell.

"Is there any word of Connor or your father?"

Mary shook her head. "Nay. I'm sorry to say there has been no word."

"I wanted to wait for my father to come home, but my step-mother would not hear of it. If Papa is wounded, he may need my help." She buried her face in her hands and sobbed, her slender shoulders heaving as she released a torrent of tears.

Cailin gathered Marjory in her arms. When the child had cried herself out, her wailing reduced to a few sniffles, she guided her to the bed and encouraged her to sit down. She sat beside her and offered a linen handkerchief. Even though her own father had no regard for her, she knew the loss and despair of being ripped from her home. To be forced to leave parents who adored and coddled you must have been devastating.

"I know you're worried about your father. The word is that he survived the battle at Methven and is hale and hardy. Your stepmother was wise to send you here." Cailin swept the tangle of blond curls from the girl's face with a gentle brush of her hand. "Did your mother and the others leave the castle as well?"

"Nay. They stayed to wait for the men to return," Mary interjected. "The castle is well-guarded, and I'm sure everyone is safe. They thought it best that the bairn join us for while."

Cailin studied Mary's face, uncertain if she was telling the truth, or simply trying to allay the child's fear.

"Mother, Aunt Mary, Aunt Christina, Uncle Nigel, and Isabella MacDuff, the Countess of Buchan, remain at the castle. Lady Fraser left a fortnight ago. She grew restless and decided to return to their home in lowlands to wait for Sir Simon's return." Marjory dragged the handkerchief across her damp cheeks.

"What of Lady Jenna?" Cailin asked with genuine concern. While the lass had shown her no kindness, she shuddered to think what the English soldiers would do to a maiden if given a chance. Her own attack on the riverbank showed her to what extent the randy scoundrels would go.

"Jenna refused to leave, despite her father's wishes. I begged her to come with me, but she would not hear of it. I am ashamed to say it, but my cousin Jenna will turn this terrible event around and use it to her advantage." Marjory sniffled, blew her nose, then crumpled the scrap of linen in her hand before she continued. "Jenna once told me that if the English ever took over Scotland, she would select a handsome lord who suited her fancy, woo him, and if necessary, marry the rogue. She claimed she would do what was necessary to remain a lady in high standing and would never cower to any man."

Tightness squeezed her chest, and Cailin fought to breathe. What if Jenna knew of her location and betrayed her to the English? "You dinna think she knows where I'm hiding and would tell?"

"Nay, I'm certain they kept your hiding place a secret. Marjory dinna know where she was going until she arrived. Even if Jenna did know, I cannot believe she would betray her family's trust or stoop so low." Mary wrapped her arm around Marjory's shoulder, and urged her to stand. "Come, sweeting, I'll show you to a chamber and help you to clean up. Cailin needs to rest."

"I appreciate your concern, Mary, but I dinna wish to rest."

Mary lightly stroked Cailin's cheek. "Your face lacks color and you have dark circles under your eyes. When I passed by your cell late last night, I noticed the light under your door. Connor would never forgive me if I dinna care for you and the bairn."

"I'm a grown woman, and know if I need to rest," Cailin replied a little more sharply than she'd intended. She didn't mean to appear ungrateful and truly appreciated Mary's concern, even if she was a little overzealous at times.

"If not for yourself, then think about the babe," Mary cautioned. "Now, climb back into bed while I see the wee lassie settled. Once I'm finished, I'll fetch you a cup of warm milk to help calm your nerves. Cook made a fresh batch of bannock. I'll bring you some with honey and a wedge of cheese."

Cailin bit back the urge to argue. Mary was probably right. She hadn't been sleeping well, her appetite was poor, and she needed to think about the babe. On the other hand, how could she rest? If wounded, Connor might need of a healer or, God forbid—she quickly crossed herself—he could be dead. The constant worry that Borden's men would find her hiding place weighed heavy on her mind. She began to pace, even more concerned about her fate and that of her loved ones. "I need to know that Connor is safe and that this place of sanctuary will remain as such."

"I dinna want to stay in this horrible place. It's dark, damp, and smells like dung," Marjory shrieked. She crossed her arms over her chest and defiantly stomped her foot. "I want to go home."

Mary threw her hands up in the air. "Och, the two of you will be the death of me." She lifted the girl's chin and sighed. "I'm afraid you dinna have a choice in the matter. I know you're worried about your father, as I worry about my own. The priory may not be a fancy place, but your mother has placed you in my care, and I mean to keep you safe. Now, be a good lass and come along."

After a moment's pause, the child nodded. "Fine, I'll go with you for now, but I'm not staying. As soon as I'm able, I plan to return home and wait for father."

Cailin bit back the urge to smile. Marjory's spirit reminded her of herself as a child. Mary was so kind-hearted and only trying to do what she felt was best for all concerned. She did not wish to cause any more grief, so she sat on the edge of the bed and waited for them to leave. However, when the door closed behind them, she sprang to her feet. Resting was out of the question. She'd go out of her mind with worry if word of Connor did not come soon. She spied the Bible on the table and picked it up. Holding it to her breast, she prayed Connor, his brothers, and all at Kildrummy Castle would be spared.

Chapter 18

With a heavy heart, Cailin peered out the casement window and drew her woolen plaid around her shoulders. Dark grey clouds loomed over the moors, threatening rain, but the fiercest storm could not rival the torrent of emotion and uncertainty raging within her breast. Several more weeks had passed, and still no word of Connor. The chill of late autumn gripped the air and soon the snow would fly. In the spring, her babe would be born, and it was beginning to look like he would never know his father.

On more than one occasion, she'd contemplated leaving the priory, rather than waiting for Borden to find her, but where would she go? As if on cue, the babe rolled, and kicked—a vivid reminder that she had a reason to live, and a reason to fight. She smiled and slid her hands over the spot, wondering if he'd used a foot or an elbow to gain her attention. "You'll be all right, little one. I'll see you safe, and protect you always." From the beginning, she'd sensed the babe would be a lad, had prayed it would not a lass. A daughter used to barter for land and alliances, or subject to the unjust English laws.

A gust of wind blew the shutters closed, locking out the world beyond the priory walls. For now she was safe, but something in her gut told her it would not last for long. She sighed, then moved toward the bed and picked up the Bible. Propped up on her lone pillow, she settled into a comfortable position and began to read aloud. After a few pages, fatigue took over and she nodded off.

When the door latch lifted, she woke with a start. "Who is it?" she called out, expecting Marjory to come bounding into the room. The child had taken to visiting every day and Mary often accompanied her. She welcomed the company, and the distraction. "Who is it?" she asked again.

There was no reply.

She slid to the edge of the bed and dropped her legs over the side. No sooner had her feet touched the floor when the door burst open and crashed against the wall.

Cailin felt the color drain from her face as her worst nightmare had come to life.

Lord Jonathan Borden stood in the doorway with a sinister grin plastered across his face. "It's about time I found you. You've led me on a merry chase and put me in bad favor with my king. We are not impressed." He stepped into the room, slammed the door shut, and moved with purpose toward the bed. "There's a gallows at Carlisle Castle with your name on it, and the executioner awaits your arrival."

Terrified, but determined not to show it, Cailin squared her shoulders and sucked in a ragged breath. With her chin held high, she slowly rose to her feet, the Bible clutched against her breast. There was no way out, but she refused to let him see her fear. "For what crime am I charged?"

"The charges are murder and witchcraft. You killed my brother, and you will pay for the crime."

"I am not a witch, and I have killed no one."

He grabbed Cailin's upper arm and the bible tumbled to the floor. His eyes traveled the length of her body, settling on the swell of her belly. An angry scowl replaced his pompous smirk. "I can see you are no longer innocent in the ways of the flesh. You denied me, yet you slept with rabble." He stroked the scar on his cheek. "Do you remember this? I've spent many a sleepless night, thinking of the ways I can make you pay...make you beg for my mercy."

"I remember you all too well, Lord Borden. I was bairn when you tried to accost me against my will. You were a guest in my father's home, and you had no right to touch me—"

"As an English Lord, I have right to bed any whore I choose, and to do with her as I wish." He twisted her arm, shoving her back against the bed. "Anywhere I choose." With his free hand, he loosened the ties on his trews.

Cailin slid a protective hand over her belly. "I am not a whore. I carry my husband's child." *My betrothed's child.*

"No marriage was sanction by King Edward."

"I answer to the rightful King of Scotland. Not the English tyrant who lays claim to my homeland."

Borden wrapped his hand around her throat and squeezed. "I could cut out your tongue for speaking such treason. But I have other uses for your lovely mouth." A lascivious grin crossed his lips. "Where is your husband now? Only a coward would run away, leaving his bride unprotected."

"My husband is the bravest man I know. He sent me here for my protection while he—" She stopped speaking before she revealed too much.

"While he what?" Borden tightened his hand around her throat. "Perhaps he was one of the fools killed at Methven, or lays dead and rotting in a field outside of Dail Righ. That is where the clan MacDougall intercepted the followers of Robert the Bruce after the battle and laid waste to what was left of his pathetic army."

"*Dail Righ*...the king's field?" After the death of Red Comyn, the clan MacDougall sided with the English, but the idea that Scots would betray their fellow compatriots was unthinkable. Her knees buckled when Borden suggested Connor was dead, but she managed to remain standing. She'd not let Borden know he rattled her. She had to be strong for Connor, and for their child. Was the blackguard fishing for information? Was he toying with her head, and her heart, hoping she would betray the man she loved, or was Connor truly gone from her life forever?

"The Scots tried to rebuild their forces in Argyll Mountains. When word reached our army, we intercepted the rebels. Those that survived the battle of Dail Righ retreated to Kirkenclif, where most were taken prisoner, or executed for treason. There, we arrested Sir Simon Fraser and sent him to England to stand trial. Found guilty of treason, Edward saw him hanged, disemboweled, and then drawn and quartered. His head sits on pike on London Bridge, along with that of William Wallace."

Her throat constricted, but she managed to hold the tears at bay. Cailin staggered at his words and struggled to catch her breath. "Sir Simon Fraser was captured and executed?" Her heart sank, and Mary immediately came to mind. She'd be devastated to learn of her father's fate. Not to mention how the death of their beloved cousin and surrogate father would affect Connor and his brothers. Scotland had suffered a great loss.

"Some of the insurgents managed to escape, but it won't be long before we round them up and see them punished," Borden continued. "Perhaps your husband is among them. If I knew his name, I could ease your mind."

The bittersweet news that Connor might still be alive caused her heart to race with joy, but it plummeted as quickly when she thought about the torture and brutal execution that awaited him if captured. That is if he was not already dead. She turned her head. "You were right when you said my husband died at the battle of Methven."

"Liar!"

"I speak the truth. Word arrived shortly after the battle. He died a warrior's death. When I learned his fate, I took refuge in the priory."

"Perhaps he did die at Methven, but it matters not. In the event he is still alive, I've sent a missive to Kirkenclif, informing the miscreants that Kildrummy Castle has fallen and the villages in the surrounding area are now under English rule. I made it very clear we'll leave no stone unturned in our search for enemies of the king or fugitives from his laws.

The news of Kildrummy's fall was another heavy blow, but she refused to betray Connor. "How did you find me?" She was doing some fishing of her own. Obviously, the person who had divulged her whereabouts had not mentioned his name.

"I got my information from a lovely and very reliable source at Kildrummy Castle."

"Jenna?" Cailin gasped. She clenched her fist and brought it to her breast. She couldn't breathe. She could only imagine what they had done to her, and the others who had refused to leave the castle.

"So you know the lovely Jenna, do you?" The evil laugh that followed his question echoed throughout the cell. "When she finished revealing her family secrets, she warmed my bed quite nicely. The little vixen wasn't even affected when we hanged her father in the bailey as a warning to anyone who may try to retaliate. Once I finished with her, I handed her over to the captain of my guard."

Vile bastard! "You violated her, and killed her father?" Despite the fact that Jenna had betrayed her and her family, Cailin wouldn't wish that fate on her worst enemy.

"You can't violate a whore." There was no remorse in his voice. "I did not have to force myself on her. She offered her favors quite willingly and asked me to take her to England as my mistress. But one can only eat so many sweets before they tire of them and move to something more delectable." His fingers skimmed her shoulder, then pawed at her breasts. "You are a very beautiful woman. It's a shame you allowed that Scottish swine to deflower you. Had you saved yourself for me, I might have been able to persuade Edward to show leniency. At the least, I'd have seen you executed without torture."

"How chivalrous. Your mercy knows no bounds."

Cailin didn't try to hide the sarcasm in her voice. His touch repulsed her, yet she stood her ground and didn't shy away.

"You're a sassy wench. I like fire in the women I bed. I look forward to taming your wild spirit."

She cringed at the thought, but her own safety wasn't her only concern. She worried about the fate of those who had treated her so kindly during her brief stay at the castle and prayed Connor was safe. She silently thanked the Almighty that Lady Fraser had gone home before the English attacked. "What of Lady Bruce and the others? How did you manage to take a castle so well fortified?" Cailin asked boldly.

"A man will do anything for a price, especially when he's offered all the gold he can carry." Borden's smug smile broadened. "It was actually a very simple plan. The blacksmith created a diversion by setting the corn stores on fire. While the guard was busy putting out the blaze, we were able to overrun the castle with little resistance. Lady Bruce is in England, under house arrest. The Bruce's sisters and the Countess of Buchan, imprisoned. The guards were executed, and any servant who refused to swear fealty to Edward sent to the dungeon to await their fate. Unfortunately, the Bruce's young daughter managed to escape before we arrived, but we will find her."

The door to Cailin's cell opened with a crash. "You killed my father!" Mary shouted as she raced across the room in Borden's direction with a dirk clutched in her hand.

Borden released his grip on Cailin and spun around to face his attacker.

He caught Mary's wrist mid-air, and twisted it sharply to the right. The dagger fell to the floor, and he kicked it out of reach. With his free hand, he delivered a backhanded blow that sent Mary to the ground with a thud.

Cailin considered going for the dagger, but knew if she did, he'd snap Mary's neck like a twig.

"I'm sorry, sir, I tried to stop her." An English soldier

staggered into the room, his hand cupping the crotch of his trews. "The bitch kneed me in the ballocks and grabbed my dagger. It took me a minute to catch my breath and to stop my stomach from roiling."

With his fist balled, Borden prepared to strike her again. "You dare to attack an English officer?"

Without regard for her own safety, Cailin went to Mary's side and squatted beside her. Drawing her friend into her arms, she shielded her against another blow. "Stop, she's a nun, and knows not what she does." She tore a small piece of fabric from her kirtle and held it to the cut on Mary's lower lip to stop the bleeding.

"She will pay for her insolence." Borden shook his fist in the air.

"You killed her father. What else would you expect?" Cailin glared up at the two men, surprised when Borden picked up the dirk, slid it into his belt, and took a step backward.

"I expect my men to be on their guard, and to keep their prisoners under control." He turned to face the young officer. "What of the girl?" Borden asked. "Have they located the Bruce's daughter?"

"We haven't found her yet, but we won't give up until we do."

"See that you don't. I plan to present her to Edward as a bargaining tool," Borden replied, before returning his attention to Cailin and Mary. "Where is she?"

"I have no idea what you're talking about." Cailin honestly didn't know where Mary had hidden Marjory, but was confident that child was tucked away and safe from Borden's grasp. She cradled Mary in her arms. "Are you all right?"

Mary nodded and sobbed. "They killed my father and must pay." She clenched her fists in Cailin's gown, burying her face against her shoulder.

"Hold your tongue, Mary. You must be brave and make your da proud."

"I'd heed the lady's advice if I were you." Borden hovered over them. "Push me any further, and I will see you both hang. I grow tired of these games. Tell me where the Bruce's daughter is hiding and I will see you are treated fairly."

"What, and deny yourself the pleasure of seeing me stand before your English judges in a mock trail, and then executed for a crime I dinna commit?" Judging by the scowl of lethal intent that crossed his face, her deliberate attempt to draw his anger away from Mary and distract him from Marjory appeared to be working. "I hate to disappoint you, but the lass is not here."

Borden grabbed Cailin by the arm, yanking her to her feet. "I've had enough of your insolence. We will leave for England within the hour. Have the men ready the horses and see they find the girl by then," Borden said to the guard. He fastened his trews and glared at Cailin. "We'll finish this later."

As he steered her toward the door, Cailin offered little resistance. She would not risk the life of her child or the safety of those in the priory.

Mary rose to her knees in a futile attempt to stand. "You cannot take her! She is innocent and soon to be a mother. What kind of monster would harm a woman and her unborn child?"

"Interfere and I will give my men leave to do with the nuns what they will, and then we will torch the priory," Borden warned as he leered over his shoulder at Mary.

Cailin raised her hand to stay Mary's attempt to stand. Enough people had lost their lives or jeopardized their freedom to help her, and she'd not let anyone else pay for her problems. "Nay, there is nothing you can do. I will go with them, and please dinna try to follow."

"A wise decision," Borden said with a cocky smile, and slammed the door behind them.

Chapter 19

When Connor burst through the door of the priory and saw Mary sitting on the floor, amidst a pile of broken earthenware and toppled furniture, panic gripped his heart. With a quick scan of the hall, he realized his worst fear. Cailin wasn't there. He rushed to his cousin's side and knelt down. "Are you hurt, magpie?" He used the name he'd called when she was a child and gently touched her shoulder to get her attention and allay her fear.

She stared up at him with dazed, tear-filled eyes, but she never made a sound.

"Lord Almighty, tell me what happened." Completely unnerved by the scene before him, he fought the urge to grab his cousin and shake her for the answers. Instead, he gathered his wits and asked again in a gentler tone. "Please, tell me what happened. Where's Cailin?" He touched her bruised cheek.

"The English attacked the priory with no regard for the sanctity of this holy place. They plundered and lay waste to anything they could get their hands on." She dragged her hand across her damp cheeks. "What if they come back?"

He gently gathered her into his arms. "Dinna cry. I'm here now, and they'll not be back. There's no reason for them to return since they already raided the place and have taken what wanted."

Mary turned her face into his chest, her hot tears soaking his tunic. "Och, Connor, they told me father was dead? Please tell me it is all a horrible lie."

He didn't want to be the one to tell her, but she had to know the truth. "Simon was captured in Kirkenclif after our stand at *Dail Righ* and taken to England to stand trial. He died a hero's death, and will be forever remembered by all." He spared her the grisly details of Simon's brutal execution, unaware that Borden's men had already told her everything.

"Why didn't you do something to stop them?"

"Your father made us promise not to follow. You know how stubborn Simon could be." When she clutched his tunic, he hesitated and glanced away, not wanting her to see the unshed tears stinging his eyes.

"Aye, Father was a wonderful man. He would never allow someone he cared about to risk their life on his behalf."

Connor hugged her tighter and tucked her head under his chin. "He was the bravest, most unselfish man I have ever known. Your father believed too many men had already perished for the cause, and for more to die before we could regroup would serve no purpose. He made us swear that we would not interfere if he were captured. We all pledged the same to each other."

"What of my mother? Is she all right?"

"Word is that she's safe, and at Oliver Castle. Alasdair and Bryce went to check on her. They plan to meet me here." His heart went out to his cousin, but his concern for Cailin mounted. Leaning back on his heels, he lifted Mary's chin. "Please tell me of Cailin. Where is she?" Something in his gut told him the answer, but he prayed he was wrong.

"She's gone, Connor. The English took her. I tried to stop them, but..." She lowered her head and twisted her apron in her hands.

With her words, the last glimmer of hope faded into oblivion. Connor's heart lurched, and he struggled to speak. "Tell me what happened." He found it impossible to hide the tremor in his voice.

"The one they called Borden arrested her. He said he was taking her to England to stand trial for witchcraft and murder. Please forgive me. I tried to stop him, but there was nothing I could do." She sobbed even louder.

"Borden." He felt as though someone had ripped the heart from his chest. The thought of Cailin, alone with the blackguard, caused his blood boil. Yet at the same time, his stomach clenched. Frightened and alone, she might be injured, or worse, dead.

He glanced down at his cousin, her face contorted with despair. With the loss of her father and the recent attack, she had enough to deal with, and he didn't want to make her feel any worse. He swept the tears from her cheek with a gentle brush of his thumb. "I'm sure you did all that you could. I must go after them. When did they leave?"

She clutched his tunic again, her expression riddled with fear. "They left a few hours ago. Borden said if anyone tried to follow, he'd kill her. You cannot go after them alone. You must wait for Alasdair and Bryce."

"There's no time to wait. Even if they have already left, Oliver Castle is several days ride from here. There is no telling what that bastard might do to Cailin, and I won't take that risk." He helped Mary to her feet and escorted her to a nearby chair. "Tell me, Mary, did she go willingly, or was she taken by force? Did Borden harm her?"

"She dinna fight him, if that's what you mean. I think she was afraid he might harm the babe if she did." Mary's blue eyes widened, and she covered her mouth as soon as the words left her lips. "I—I'm sorry. You were not supposed to find out this way."

He stared at Mary. "Cailin is with child? When? How? Why wasn't I told?" he stammered like a babbling fool.

Mary blushed at his question. "I'm not an expert in such things, but I'm certain she conceived in the usual way. Given she is several months along, my guess is that it happened the first time you tupped her. The poor lamb hasn't had an easy time of it. Only of late has she managed to keep any food down."

"Her mother died in childbirth. Do you think there is a chance she will not be able to carry and birth a bairn? That she might die?"

"Nay, she's a healthy lass." She grasped his hand and patted it. "For a woman to feel unwell in her early months is common. I'm sure she will give you many fine, healthy sons."

Mary's reassurance did little to squelch his concern. He raked his fingers through his hair and began to pace. "It might be common for a woman in her condition to suffer from sickness when she wakes, but not to be held prisoner by an animal like Borden, or dragged across Scotland on horseback. She's in grave danger, and I must go to her. I cannot stand around doing nothing while that bastard has Cailin." He gently touched Mary's bruised cheek again and examined her split lower lip. "Are you certain you're uninjured?"

"I am shaken, and my heart aches for my father, but I'm uninjured."

"What of Marjory Bruce? I'm told her mother sent her here before the castle was raided."

"She is safely hidden."

"Good, then I must go after Cailin." He placed a kiss on the top of Mary's head, then moved toward the door. "I'll see Father Paul before I leave and make arrangements for you to go home. Cameron is with me, and he'll see you and Marjory to Oliver Castle."

"You cannot go alone. Borden had at least a dozen men with him."

"A dozen English soldiers are no match for a Highlander."

"Damn your Highland pride! That is what got my father killed. It might be too late for him, but not for you." The words spilled from her lips before she could stop them. "Those men are ruthless, and will show you no mercy. You'll be of no use to Cailin if Borden kills you. I'm begging you, dinna go alone."

"I cannot rest while she's in danger. If he harms one hair on her head, I'll kill him with my bare hands and feed his ballocks to the dogs." With that oath on his lips, he stormed down the hallway toward Father Paul's cell.

Cailin shifted her weight in the saddle. The only things that hurt more than her legs and lower back were her wrists. The coarse ropes binding her to the pommel bit into her tender flesh. They'd ridden for two days, only stopping long enough to rest the horses and to relieve themselves—which she needed to do often at this stage in her pregnancy. They ate and slept on horseback. But between the babe kicking and the discomfort of sleeping upright, she got no rest. Not that she would dare relax or let her guard down around a lecherous man like Borden. At this rate of travel, they'd be in England by week's end. It was beginning to look like help was not going to reach her in time.

A young lieutenant rode up beside Borden. "There is a stream up ahead, and we've already traveled halfway to the border. I wondered if we might stop for a bite to eat. The horses need to rest, and I would wager the lady would appreciate a chance to stretch her legs. I know I would."

Borden glanced over his shoulder at Cailin. "Her comfort is of no concern to me, Williams, but perhaps you are right. The horses are tired, and this might be the perfect spot to rest." A wry grin crossed his lips. "What do you think, my lady? Shall we stop here and get better acquainted?"

She offered no response. The thought of Borden touching her made her skin crawl. But to tell him what she thought would only feed his ire.

Borden raised his hand in the air and shouted to his

men. "We will rest here."

A second officer rode up beside the two men. "I beg your pardon, Lord Borden, but do you think it is prudent to stop in such an open place?"

"I will decide what is prudent and what is not." Borden slid from his saddle and handed the reins over to his squire. "See that the horse is well fed and watered, boy."

"Aye, my lord." The lad bowed, and led the horse toward the stream.

Borden was up to something. Cailin felt it in her bones, those that hadn't crumbled or turned to mush. Lieutenant Williams lifted her from the saddle, but when her feet touched the ground, her knees buckled. While he managed to cushion her fall, she still found herself sitting in the dirt. But not for long.

"Get up." Borden wrapped his hands around her upper arms and roughly hauled her to her feet. "You best make the most of your chance to stretch your legs. We'll not be stopping for long."

"I must tend to my needs."

Without saying a word, Borden dragged her across the field to a small copse of trees and shoved her in the direction of a thicket of bracken. "Do what you need to do, and make haste."

"I cannot relieve myself in front of you and would ask for some privacy. Even your men have the decency to turn their backs."

"I'm not my men, and I have no intention of letting you out of my sight. You either go here, or not at all." The imposing tone of his voice and the menacing look on his face let her know that he had no intention of negotiating.

She lifted her bound hands in his direction. "I cannot hold my skirts and do what is necessary if my hands are tied."

Borden pulled his dirk from its sheath and cut the rope,

freeing her hands. "Don't give me a reason to regret my decision."

"Will you turn your back and give me some privacy?"

"No. Squat, and be done with it."

Regardless of her request, Borden watched her every move. She hiked up her skirts and tried to ignore the hitch in his breath, his raised brow, and the lewd stare he fixed on her exposed ankle and lower leg. *If he won't turn around, I will.* She turned her back to him, surprised when he didn't try to stop her.

After completing the task as quickly as possible, Cailin spun around and smoothed her hands down the front of her gown. "If you are finished ogling me, I'd appreciate a wee bite to eat, and mayhap some water to quench my thirst."

"Would you now?" Borden snaked his arm around her waist and pulled her against his chest. "You're a saucy wench. Perhaps I have a better way to sate your hunger, and mine, too." His hands roamed seductively up and down her spine, kneading her buttocks with each pass. He pulled her hips into the hollow of his thighs, nipped at the side of her neck, and groaned aloud.

His touch repulsed her, made her want to vomit. She braced her hands on his chest and tried to push him away. "You cannot be desperate enough to take your pleasure from a woman heavy with child," Cailin challenged.

"I'll do as I damned well please." Borden grabbed the back of her head, fisted his hand in her hair, and lowered his head. "You'll do as I tell you, and give me no sass."

His eyes darkened, but not with desire or passion. It was something sinister and evil. For a moment, she was certain she'd come face to face with the Devil. Despite her attempt to break free, he held her firmly in place. The more she kicked and clawed, the more he seemed to enjoy the challenge. He pulled on her hair, yanked her head back, and bit her neck. When she yelped, he laughed, and did it again.

She soon found her back pressed up against a nearby tree, the weight of his body making it difficult to breathe. She felt faint.

"Please dinna do this." Cailin turned her head when he lowered his, but to no avail. He held her chin and forced his tongue past her lips in a rapacious kiss. Her stomach wretched and just as she thought to clamp down with her teeth, the sound of footsteps approaching caught her attention.

Lieutenant Williams cleared his throat. "I'm sorry to interrupt you, sir, but Morrison has returned, and informed me that we may soon have a visitor."

Borden released his hold on Cailin and spun around to face his aid. He straightened his tunic and stepped away from where she stood trembling and gasping for air. "Excellent. I didn't think it would take long for him to find us."

Cailin staggered backward and brought her hand to her mouth in an attempt to wipe clean where his vile lips had been. He seemed unaffected by her actions, and the fact that someone might be following them appeared to please him. A sudden feeling of impending doom caused her gut to clench. Could it be Connor? And if so, did he have any idea he was walking into a trap?

Borden pointed to a lone oak standing at the edge of the field. "Take her to the tree and see she's bound securely. Post a guard and tell him to kill her if she gives him any trouble. When you're done, meet me by the horses." He pushed her toward Williams with a force that caused her to stumble.

The lieutenant reacted quickly, catching her before she hit the ground. Once steady on her feet, he frowned. "I'm sorry, my lady, but I must follow orders."

"Stop wasting time and do as you're told, or I'll have your bars," Borden snapped as he crossed the clearing.

Williams nodded, took Cailin by the elbow, and escorted her toward the tree. With a hardened stare, he glanced over his shoulder at Borden. "The man is a cruel, unyielding bastard. He'd hang his own mother if he thought it would gain him favor with the king. I'd be careful not to cross him if I were you."

When he looked at her, his expression softened. Was that empathy she saw in his hazel eyes? Her heart raced, as did her mind. She had to do something to warn Connor. If she attempted to run, would Williams stop her? She could try, but knew if he didn't intervene, Borden would tackle her before she got a few feet. In her condition, she'd not get far, and she wouldn't risk injury to the babe. If she called out, Connor would be more determined than ever to attempt a rescue. As she contemplated her options, the lieutenant eased her back up against the tree and gently grasped her wrists, binding them behind her. Even though he tied them loosely, the ropes aggravated her already torn flesh. Cailin bit down on her lower lip, swallowing hard against the pain shooting up her arms.

Gaining Williams's sympathy was her only hope. "Please, sir. I am innocent and wish only to go home to my family. Surely you cannot condone the torture and execution of a woman with child. If you could find it in your heart to release me, I would be most grateful."

"I do not have the authority to release you, nor do I have a death wish. Borden acts on behalf of King Edward. When you escaped the first time, our revered sovereign threatened to strip him of his title and see him hanged in your stead. There is nothing I can do nothing to help you, my lady."

"I understand, and dinna hold you responsible for my fate." She could tell by his tone of voice and the look of remorse on his face he resented having to follow Borden's orders. Despite the urge to argue her case, she decided she would say nothing more. She may need to rely on the man's sense of honor at a future time and didn't want to do anything to anger him.

Williams turned to face a soldier standing a few feet

away. "George, guard the lady, and if she gives you any trouble—" He hesitated. "Gag her." He turned and walked across the field toward Borden and his men.

If she was right in her assumption, Williams might prove to be an ally after all. He followed his commander's orders and saw her tied to the tree, but didn't tell the guard to kill her, reinforcing her suspicions. She craned her neck and tried to hear the conversation between Borden and Morrison, but they were out of earshot. She thought she heard Connor's name mentioned by two men who walked by, but nothing more. Had Borden known his identity all along?

To her surprise, eight of Borden's men mounted their horses and rode out of camp, leaving six men behind. From what she knew of Connor's Highland pride and battle skills, the reduced number from fourteen to six against one would be an open invitation for him to make his move. Did her captor know this as well?

Borden strode across the field in her direction. He stopped only a few inches away. An evil grin crossed his lips. "I'll take it from here, George. Williams will tell you what you are to do."

"Yes, sir." George snapped to attention, then trotted off to find the lieutenant. After a brief conversation with Williams, he disappeared into the woods.

"As you might have guessed, your lover has been following us for some time and has played into my hand nicely. Now that we have stopped, I have no doubt he'll make an attempt to save you."

Borden's hot breath caressed her cheek, sending a shiver of repulsion down her spine.

"Once I have dealt with him, we will continue our journey to England. If you are a good girl, I will reward you in my tent this evening." He dragged his fingers across her lips, down her cheek, and along her neck. His hand came to rest on the swell of her breast. Leaning in closer, he whispered in her ear. "I promise that once I've filled you, all thought of that pathetic Highlander will be gone from your mind forever. Well, at least until I see you executed."

His smugness fueled her anger. "Never!" Cailin raised her chin in defiance. "I would rather die than have you touch me." A quick backhanded slap silenced her.

"I will bed you. It is just a matter of when and where. Maybe I will let your lover live long enough to watch."

"How do you know that he will try to rescue me?"

Borden clucked his tongue and shook his head. "He'll come." He pulled his sword from its sheath and waved it in the air. "Do you think he'll stand by and watch while I cut the babe from your womb?" He cocked his head to one side, ran his fingers over the blade, and smiled. "I think not."

"You are a vile bastard." Cailin struggled against the ropes binding her to the tree, but to no avail. "I hope that you rot in Hell for your evil deeds."

"I'm already destined for Hell, my lady."

Cailin closed her eyes and prayed for strength. If Connor tried to rescue her, he'd be cut down before he got a few yards. If he didn't make a move, Borden would use her as bait and threaten to kill her and his unborn child. He was vastly outnumbered and didn't stand a chance. If he perished trying to save her, she didn't want to live. She was already slated for execution on the gallows. It made no sense for Connor to forfeit his life as well.

Please leave, and dinna make the attempt to save me. I can face my fate and go to my death willingly, but only if I know you live.

Chapter 20

Connor watched the English garrison ride down the road and out of sight. Why Borden would send half of his men out on patrol, leaving only a handful to guard Cailin, boggled his mind. This had to be a trap. However, if he was going to make a move, he had to do it now.

Convinced this might be his only fighting chance of freeing Cailin, he crept closer to the clearing and surveyed the camp. Two men guarded the horses, while several others sat around the fire. A lieutenant stood a few feet away from them talking to a man dressed in a plaid he knew all too well. He cursed at the sight of Blake MacDougall. "The traitorous bastard," he growled beneath his breath.

Borden stood on the opposite end of the field, close to Cailin. Too close. Had he harmed her in any way? Had he bedded her? The thought of him touching her made his blood boil. When the sword pressed against Cailin's belly caught his eye, Connor drew on every once of self-control he could muster, tamping down the urge to rush into the camp, and run Borden through. But with her bound to a tree and at the blackguard's mercy, he had to plan his strategy carefully.

"I know you're out there!" Borden shouted. "I grow tired of this little game of cat and mouse. I'm sure the lady would like me to untie her from this tree. It would be a shame to kill her where she stands."

Connor's hand closed over the hilt of his own sword. Anger rivaled fear for her safety, and his heart pounded against his ribs.

"Show yourself now, and I may even consider freeing the wench and letting her bastard live. The choice is yours.

Face me like a man and the two of us will have at it. A fight to the death. Winner gets the chit." Borden waved his sword in the air, and then placed the blade against her belly. "Make me wait any longer, and the babe is the first to die."

Connor stepped into the clearing with his weapon drawn. "I accept your challenge, but first, let her go." He refrained from looking at Cailin, knowing if he did, he'd lose his focus, along with revealing his weakness. Instead, he glanced beyond Borden and into the woods. He cursed when he spied three archers strategically perched in the trees, their weapons aimed at his chest. Before he could speak, an arrow whizzed by him. He managed to dodge a second, but the third caught him squarely in the left shoulder. He dropped like a stone to his knees.

"No!" Cailin shouted.

He turned his head to hide the grimace of pain and grasped for the arrow. With teeth clenched, he yanked the shaft free, and then covered the wound with his hand. Blood oozed between his fingers, soaking the front of his tunic. Seconds later, English soldiers surrounded him, their swords drawn.

"Watch her. Run her through if she so much as breathes the wrong way," Borden told George, before focusing his attention on Connor.

"You didn't think I'd let you stroll in here and take the girl, did you? I've waited three years to have her, and won't be put off this time." Borden laughed and strutted across the clearing to where Connor knelt in the dirt.

"I honored my end of the bargain. Let Cailin go," Connor challenged.

Grabbing a fist full of his hair, Borden snapped Connor's head back. "I have chased that little witch halfway across Scotland. She murdered my brother, and the king will reward me handsomely when I bring her to back to England to stand trial."

"I killed your brother, not Cailin. He attacked her and tried to rape her. I would repeat the act in a heartbeat if given the chance. That pondscum deserved to die."

"How chivalrous," Borden mocked. "Too bad a witness swears the lady did the killing. She will hang for the deed."

"He lies to cover his own guilt. Your so-called witness was waiting his turn to tup her when I intervened. Cailin escaped in the scuffle and was nowhere near the riverbank when your brother died. I killed him in self-defense, but I'm sure that holds no credence with the king. If there is any honor in your lecherous soul, punish me for his death and let her go."

Borden stalked with purpose toward Cailin. He moved behind the tree, cut the ropes that bound her, and then dragged her into his embrace. Despite her attempt to fight him off, he captured her lips in a brutal kiss, then spun her around to face Connor. He held her back against his chest, his hand resting over her belly, his blade at her throat. "Nothing you say will change my mind. She will stand trial, and she will be hanged."

Despite his weakness from lost blood and the pain radiating across his chest, Connor climbed to his feet. "All those present stand as witness to my confession! If you allow her to be tried for a crime she dinna commit, you are condemning an innocent woman, and therefore guilty of her murder in the eyes of the Almighty."

"Kill him, Morrison. But before you do, I want him to know that his woman will warm my bed tonight and every night until I see her hanged. Your bastard will not live to take a breath."

"A Mhor-fhaiche!" Connor shouted the Fraser war cry. "All my hope is in God!" The Fraser clan motto quickly followed as he lunged forward. Two soldiers tackled him before he could advance and two more dragged him to his knees. But it took all four men to hold him still.

"Kill him now!" Borden demanded.

Morrison nodded, positioned himself in front of Connor and raised his foil, but Lieutenant Williams grabbed his arm.

"I'll do it." Williams drew his sword and without hesitation, drove it into Connor.

Excruciating pain shot through his body, and he couldn't breathe. He turned to look at Cailin, wanted her to know how much he loved her and had, from the day they met, but couldn't speak. He didn't have to. Their eyes locked as if they were the last two people in Scotland. Something in the way she looked at him gave him solace, letting him know she understood what he wished he could say. Judging by the scowl on Borden's face, he saw it, too, and dragged her away.

"Connor!"

He heard her call out his name before everything around him faded to black.

Cailin pressed her forehead against the door, the fingers of one hand splayed across the cold oaken surface, the other resting over her swollen belly. After the grueling ride from Scotland to England, she was amazed that the babe survived. Then again, he was from strong, stubborn stock, and he'd kicked relentlessly, day and night, to remind her of that fact. "If only I could see you safely born and raise you to know of your father's bravery."

When Connor stood before Borden, and had offered his life for hers, she saw devotion in his eyes. He didn't need to speak the words she longed to hear. If able, she would have run to him, thanked him for the gift of his child, and begged him to wait for her at Heaven's gate. Her heart sank like a stone in a lock, and she fought the urge to scream in anguish.

She pounded her fist on the door. "Please, you cannot

mean to keep me locked up in this dreadful place forever." When the latch lifted and the heavy door opened, she stepped back out of the way. Had someone heard her plea?

"You'll stay where you are until his lordship decides otherwise." A guard she had never seen before strode across the room. He carried a trencher and a mug of ale. After placing it on a small wooden table in the corner of the room, he turned to face her.

"How long do they mean to keep me locked up?"

"Don't be fretting your pretty head, you'll be out of here soon enough. I have it on good authority that your trial is set to take place on the morrow. King Edward sent word that he is tied up with other matters and instructed Lord Borden to go ahead without him. If things go the way his lordship predicts, this place will seem like a palace compared to the dungeons."

She drew the tattered scrap of plaid about her shoulders, glanced around the small, musty, dark room, and shivered. This was a far cry from a palace. Except for the pallet of moldy straw on the floor and a small table, the room she'd occupied was empty. A single arrow loop provided the sole source of light, her only link to the outside world. A brassier sat in one corner of the room, but there was neither wood nor peat to take away the dampness and chill.

When she'd first arrived, she found her surroundings of little interest. Immersed in her grief and mourning the loss of her beloved Connor, she didn't care if she lived or died. But as the days passed and the fog of despair slowly lifted, she'd become more aware of her predicament, and fear for her unborn child took precedence.

Once a day, a guard entered the room with a tray of food and something to drink. Otherwise, she'd spoken to no one. A blessing in disguise if one really thought about it. As long as Borden kept his distance, he'd not make good on his threat to bed her. The thought of his hands upon her, of him taking intimate liberties, made her stomach roil. Pain and sorrow gripped her heart. The only man's bed she wanted to grace was Connor's, and he was lost to her forever.

"Best you eat. After the trial, there's no telling when, or if, they'll feed you again." Without saying another word, the guard left the room as hastily as he'd entered.

She pushed the food around the trencher and curled up her nose in disgust. The wooden platter contained the same fare every day—cold porridge, a slice of dry bannock, and a small wedge of cheese. She opted for a sip of ale instead.

The babe rolled and kicked—a babe that would not live to carry on his father's legacy. *Connor.* Memories of the man she loved and their brief time together flooded her mind. At night, his face haunted her dreams. During the day, she relived the events leading up to his death more times than she could bear to count. If the sentry's predictions held true, she and the babe would soon join him in Heaven.

The sound of hammering broke her train of thought. When she stood on her tiptoes and peered out the small arrow loop, a chill ran down her spine. The men busied themselves by building a gallows meant for her.

At sunrise the next day, two guards escorted her to the great hall of Carlisle Castle, where the four-man tribunal waited. She bit down on her lower lip to keep it from trembling. With the sudden weakness in her legs, would they be able to hold her upright? Her pulse raced, her head spun, and dizziness threatened to claim her, but she somehow managed to stand her ground. She was frightened and alone, yet she was determined to face the men who judged her with dignity and pride.

"Lady Cailin Macmillan, you stand accused of murder and treason against the crown. How do you plead?" William

Ormsby, King Edward's Chief Justicair, leaned back in his chair and tapped his finger on his jaw, awaiting her answer.

"This trial is a mockery of justice. I'm innocent of the charges, and demand you release me at once." Her hands protectively covered her belly, and she looked at each member of the tribunal in turn.

The hall erupted with shouts and comments regarding her deplorable conduct. It was rare, and frowned upon, for a woman to speak her mind in public. For Cailin to make demands of the King's appointed men was unheard of.

Borden waited for the din of disapproval to fade before facing the tribunal. "This impudent woman lies to save her own life, and that of the bastard she carries. There was a witness to the crime. Thomas will provide the testimony necessary to prove beyond a shadow of a doubt that the lady is guilty as charged."

When a knight stepped forward, Cailin immediately recognized him as the man, who along with Borden's brother, had tried to rape her. It would be her word against his. "My lords, I am with child, and appeal to your sense of decency—"

"The babe is the bastard of Scottish rabble and conceived in sin." Borden cut in. "Her betrothal was not sanctioned by the crown and is therefore invalid. She is no better than a common tramp. Surely you would not take the word of this gutter-swill over that of a brave knight in King Edward's army?"

"If I am gutter-swill, sir, why did you wish to soil yourself, and your reputation, by taking me to your bed? I had barely seen fifteen summers the first time you tried to force yourself upon me. The second time you initiated such desire, I was heavy with my husband's child. I am not a whore, but a woman targeted by a man who must bed bairns to satisfy his needs. As for your brother, he was a lecherous man who tried to violate me against my will, but I dinna kill him," she declared in direct challenge to Borden's claims. "As for the legitimacy of my betrothal, I am properly handfasted according to Scottish law. The betrothal sanctioned by Robert the Bruce, King of Scotland."

A collective gasp, along with murmurs, rumbled throughout the room in response to her declaration.

Ormsby slammed his fist on the dais. "Silence, or I will clear the hall. You, m'lady, will not speak again unless you are asked to, and only if you show the utmost respect for the tribunal."

A self-aggrandizing grin crossed Borden's face as he continued. "The crown does not recognize Robert the Bruce's claim to the Scottish throne. Not only does she pledge fealty to an outlaw and an enemy of England, but has committed a most heinous crime. She bewitched my brother in order to seduce him, and then when she tired of him, she murdered him in cold blood." He turned his head and addressed Thomas. "Do I not speak the truth?"

Thomas nodded. "That's exactly what happened. Poor Harold did not have a chance. Begged for his life he did."

"You lie. I'm innocent," Cailin protested.

"Silence! I'll not warn you again," Ormsby chided, and then frowned at Borden. "Your witness will have his chance to speak when he's called upon by the tribunal to do so, and not before. Do I make myself clear?"

"My apologies, my lord." Borden bowed before Ormsby. "If she was innocent, then tell me why she ran away? Have her explain why I had to chase her across Scotland, then drag her back to England to stand trial. She is a witch, my lords, and a threat to mankind. She must be punished."

"Witchcraft you say." Ormsby stroked his bearded chin and took a moment to consider the charges. "Are you a witch?" he asked bluntly.

"Nay, I am not, my lord. These accusations are a ploy to discredit me and to justify the terrible way I've been treated."

"The way you have been treated is not the issue. According to English law, Lord Borden is well within his rights to bed you if he wishes. Your refusal alone warrants an execution. However, this tribunal was called to determine if you committed murder." Ormsby looked at Borden. "Have you proof of witchcraft, something to substantiate your claim?"

Borden nodded. "I ask that Thomas be permitted to tell the tribunal what happened."

Ormsby motioned with a sweep of his arm for Thomas to step forward. "Tell us what you saw."

"Harry and me were just sitting by the stream, minding our own business, when all of a sudden, out of the water walks a siren. Her sheer gown was wet and clung to her like skin, her hair of fire flying wild about her shoulders. One look from those emerald eyes and Harry was bewitched. She taunted, teased, and he accepted what she had to offer. He couldn't help himself, being under her spell, and all." Thomas hesitated and dragged his hand across his brow, catching the drops of perspiration forming there.

"Go on," Borden ordered.

"Suddenly, she pushed him away, and accused him of propositioning her against her will. She threatened to summon the fires of Hell and cursed him to a life of pain. Harry begged her pardon and backed off, but she did not accept his apology. Instead, she mumbled an incantation. The wind began to blow with a fury and bolts of lightning shot across the sky. She raised her hand in the air and a dagger materialized. Before he could react, she snatched the blade and plunged it into his belly, gutting him like a fish. Poor Harry didn't know what happened. He lay on the ground, moaning and writhing in pain while she stood over him, laughing."

Gasps of shock and the drone of voices filled the

courtroom for the third time. "Witch! Burn the witch!" a man shouted from the crowd.

"She's guilty of witchcraft and must be punished," a woman chimed in.

"Silence," Ormsby ordered, then turned his attention to Thomas. "What were you doing when this slip of a girl attacked your friend? By the look of her, a strong wind would topple her over."

"W—why, she had me under her spell, too, my lord," he answered nervously. "I was paralyzed and couldn't move a muscle. The next thing I knew, I was tied to a tree with a knot on the back of my head the size of a melon. Lord Borden can attest to that. He saw the lump."

He is lying, why can't they see that? Cailin could not believe the way Thomas had twisted the events of that day. Judging by the way the tribunal members were looking at her, they were buying his story.

Ormsby cocked his head. "Can you confirm what he says, Lord Borden?"

"I can, my lord. We found Thomas tied to a tree and the lump on his head was as he described. Harold's lifeless body lay on the riverbank. There is no way a lady of her size could subdue two of England's finest warriors without the use of magic and treachery. She is a witch and carries the spawn of Satan in her belly."

"Was the lady present when you arrived at the scene of the murder, Lord Borden?"

"No, she had already run off, but Thomas was able to identify her."

"I see." Ormsby scrubbed his hand cross his chin, then turned to face Cailin. "What say you, my lady? These are serious charges."

"He lies. I was attacked, and they sought to violate me. They would have succeeded if not for—" She stopped before implicating Connor in the deed. He was not alive to defend himself, and she'd not have his name dragged through the mud. Nor would she see him labeled a murderer when he was in fact her hero. If she thought they would spare her child, she might consider heralding his heroic deed and pleading his case, but something in her gut told her no matter what she said, she'd already been tried and convicted. The tribunal meant to make an example of her.

"They'd have succeeded in ravaging you if not for whom? Was there an accomplice involved in the murder? Speak his name, and we may show you leniency." Ormsby pressed her for answers. "If you are found guilty of witchcraft in addition to murder, the punishment will be more severe. Purification by pain and death by fire are what you face if you continue to defy this court."

Leniency? If this whole situation hadn't been so tragic, she'd have laughed aloud. The only mercy she'd be shown was perhaps a quick death by hanging rather than torture. Cailin lowered her eyes and slowly shook her head. "Nay, there was no one else involved."

After a brief consultation with the others sitting in judgment, Ormsby announced their decision. "Lady Cailin Macmillan, we have no choice but to find you guilty. If you confess your sins and admit to using sorcery, we will hang you outright. If you continue to deny your guilt, you will be tried as a witch, and I can assure you the punishment will fit the crime."

"I am innocent," Cailin muttered softly.

"I will give you one last chance to declare your guilt and purge yourself of your sins. Do not make me force a confession." Ormsby moved to where Cailin stood, stopping a few inches away. He leaned in close and spoke so only she could hear. "Come, my lady, surely you would rather have your life end quickly. I have no desire to see you tortured, then burned alive. Confess your sins, admit to using witchcraft, and I will ask the tribunal for mercy. Edward has demanded you pay for the murder of his soldier with your life, but there is no need for you to die in agony. Think about your child."

Cailin remained silent. She was thinking about her child and refused to confess to crimes she did not commit. She would go to her grave knowing she had not crumbled under the persecution of the English bureaucracy and tyranny. King Edward could go to Hell. Borden, and all those who judged her unfairly, could join him. If she were a witch, she'd condemn them to burn for all eternity.

An angry scowl crossed Ormsby's face. "Since you refuse to confess your sins, you leave us no choice but to see you purged of them. On the morrow, the first part of your sentence will be carried out in the form of a public flogging. One week hence, if you still refuse to confess your sins, you will hang by the neck until you are dead, your eviscerated body burned, and your ashes scattered to the wind. May God have mercy on your soul."

Thunderstruck by the sentence, she wobbled on her feet, but refused to beg for mercy.

"Lord Borden. See the prisoner back to her chamber in the tower. I leave on the morrow for Edinburgh and trust you to handle things accordingly. Carry out her sentence, and to the letter. Edward will not take it kindly if you mess up again," Ormsby informed him bluntly.

Borden stepped forward and bowed. "I will see to it personally, my lord." As the members of the tribunal left the courtroom, an evil scowl crossed his face. Turning on his heels and with a snap of his fingers, he summoned two guards from the group of soldiers standing by the door. "Lewis, Smith, take her to the dungeon."

"The dungeon, my lord?" Lewis asked. "But Lord Ormsby said to take her to her chamber."

"You heard me. If you wish to question my orders, perhaps you'd care to join her." Borden handed Smith a key. "She is to be kept in the iron cage until further notice."

The guards led her out of the courtroom. She offered no resistance. There didn't seem to be any point to it. She was greatly outnumbered, and no one lifted a hand to help her or offered up a kind word in her defense. She would not grovel, and she would not be dragged from the hall kicking and screaming. With her chin held high, she kept pace with her jailers and did not say a word.

On the way to the dungeon, villagers lined the path, shouting obscenities, and calling for her execution. Ignoring the cruel words and the sting of the rotten fruit, vegetables, and eggs they tossed, she held her head high.

The guards escorted her to the back of the castle, stopping at the entrance to a dark tunnel. Lewis held her by the arm while Smith lit a torch. Her senses were immediately assaulted by the stench of human excrement, mold, and death. Cailin stared down a steep, narrow staircase. "You cannot mean to take me into that horrible place."

"I'm sorry, my lady, but this is to be your home until your execution is carried out." Lewis placed his hand on the small of her back and urged her to move forward.

Cailin stiffened her spine, asked the Almighty for strength, and stepped through the gateway to Hell.

The leather thongs binding her to the hitching post cut off the circulation to her wrists. Struggling only made them tighter. She drew in a ragged breath, steeling herself for the first part of her sentence—a flogging meant to purge her of her sins and to make her beg for mercy. Exhausted from lack of sleep and weakened by the absence of food and drinkable water, she lowered her head, resting it on her arms. Even though the sun had yet to rise above the horizon, curious onlookers filled the bailey.

The cheers and shouts of the villagers when Borden

descended the stairs of the castle made her stomach sink. She shivered in the cold morning air, her teeth chattering. When she exhaled, she could see her own breath. Frost covered the ground, bushes, and castle walls. The guards had removed her gown before bringing her from the dungeon. She wore only her kirtle and was exposed to the elements, and for all to see.

"You seem to have drawn quite a crowd, my lady," Borden said as he crossed the bailey, stopping only a few feet away. "Nothing starts the day off like a public flogging, don't you think, John?" He turned to face the man that accompanied him and slapped him on the back.

She glanced up at a tall burly man dressed in black and brandishing a whip. Fear gripped her heart and she closed her eyes, hoping that when she opened them again this would all be a horrible nightmare. She counted to ten and slowly raised her lashes, but they were still there.

"Let it be known that Lady Cailin Macmillan has been tried and found guilty of murder, treason, and witchcraft. As part of her sentence, the tribunal ordered a minimum of twenty lashes. Should she confess her sins and beg for mercy, the flogging will cease. If she does not repent, the full sentence will be carried out." Borden turned to the man in black. "Begin the punishment."

Silence fell over the crowd—her own breathing and the thunder of her heart the only sounds she could hear. She sucked in a ragged breath and prayed for the strength to endure the pain and humiliation, prayed she would not break down and beg for mercy.

The sudden displacement of air and crack of the whip caused her to jump. She ground her teeth when the sting of leather connected with her flesh, refusing to call out or surrender to the pain. The second and third strokes of the whip bit with equal intensity, and her world began to spin. Lost in a dark abyss, she did not feel the rest of the beating.

She didn't feel her body slump to the ground when the guards released from the hitching post. She wasn't aware that they'd returned her to the dungeon.

A soft pitiful moan left her lips, and her eyes fluttered open. Immersed in total darkness, she wondered if she had slept the day away—a blessing, given the fiery pain radiating across her back. Cailin shifted her position, but with her hands and feet bound she could not get comfortable. She lay on the cold damp floor, thankful the guards had the decency to put on her gown. The babe? Fear washed over her as she waited, and prayed, for him to move.

It seemed like forever until a tiny foot pressed against her ribs, a kick, and then another, stronger than the first. She heaved a sigh of relief. For now, the babe remained unharmed. She tried again to shift her position, but pain and exhaustion won out, and she closed her eyes.

Chapter 21

A well-placed blow to the back of the head rendered the guard unconscious. Connor glanced nervously over his shoulder, surprised that there was only one man watching over the prisoners. Obviously, Borden did not expect another rescue attempt. Then again, everyone believed he was dead, and he would have been had his brothers and Cameron not come along when they did. Despite his grave injuries, he had refused to die, not while Cailin needed him. By the grace of God, her execution had been delayed long enough to give him time to recover.

He grabbed the ring of keys that hung on a chain around the guard's neck, and fumbled with the lock until he heard it click. The oak door opened with a loud groan. As he stepped inside, the putrid stench of urine, feces, mold, and rotting flesh assaulted his senses. His stomach heaved. Choking back the urge to vomit, he moved with stealth into the center of cold, dank dungeon. Except for the occasional squeal of rats as they battled for scraps of food, an eerie silence shrouded the room.

I swear by all that is holy, if Borden has seen fit to keep Cailin in this hellhole, I will castrate the bugger.

He narrowed his eyes, straining to see into darkness. Thin ribbons of sunlight filtered through the bars of the lone casement window, revealing sights best left in the shadows. In his worst nightmare, he couldn't have conjured up a more deplorable place.

In one corner stood a large wooden rack, used to stretch and break a man until he confessed his sins, or died in agony. On a table in the other corner of the room were thumbscrews, knives, a barbed whip, and other assorted instruments of torture. There were stocks in which to administer beatings and a spiked iron cage hung from the rafters. Chains and shackles lined the walls—some of which still held the rotting remains of those who had succumbed to Borden's sadistic persecution.

A soft whimper broke the unearthly silence. Connor's head snapped in the direction of the sound and an iron cage. His throat tightened and his heart clenched when he saw someone curled in a fetal position on the stone floor. As he drew near and his eyes adjusted to the dim lighting, reality hit him like a blow to the gut. It was Cailin.

Frantically, he searched for something with which to gain access to her. He glanced down at the ring of keys clutched in his hand and tried each one until the lock gave way and the rusty door swung open. He crawled into the cage, knelt beside her, and spoke her name. She did not reply.

While it was difficult to assess her injuries in the dim light, he could see that her feet were bare and she wore nothing more than a flimsy gown. When he drew his dirk from its sheath and cut through the leather straps binding her wrists and ankles, she curled up in a ball, whimpering in pain.

Connor's hand trembled as he gently stroked it down her back. She recoiled from his touch and the soft plaintiff moan that left her lips tore his heart in two. "Och, lass, what have those bastards done to you?" His gut churned with worry. "Can you hear me, *liuadhe*?"

Cailin's lashes fluttered, and her heavy lidded eyes slowly opened. "A-aye, Connor. Your voice is as sweet to my ears as that of an angel. Have I already died and gone to Heaven?" Her voice was hoarse, barely above a whisper. "Nay, this cannot be Heaven. I'm so cold and thirsty..."

He quickly scanned the room for something to quench her thirst. A bucket of stagnant water sat a few feet from the cage. Even if she had been desperate enough to drink the vial liquid, the ladle was out of reach. Snatching the wineskin from his side, he raised her head, and brought the flask to her lips. She drank greedily. "Sip it slowly. If you drink too fast, it will make you ill." He carefully lowered her head until it lay on his lap. "Rest a minute, and then I'll give you a wee bit more."

"Connor," she muttered softly.

"I'm here, my love. Dinna try to speak. You must save your strength."

"This cannot be real." A frown creased her brow as she looked up at him. "Lieutenant Williams ran you through with his sword, and the arrow pierced your chest. I saw you die."

"Aye, they wounded me, but I am very much alive. Longshanks's needs to train his officers better than he has. The blow was enough to stop me, but not enough to kill me. Besides, I refused to die, knowing they held you captive." Tears rolled down his cheek. In his entire life, he could never remember crying. Not even at his father's funeral. "I would have come for you sooner, but it took time for me to recover enough strength to sit a horse. For that, I am truly sorry."

With a shaky hand, she touched his damp cheek. "On the morrow, they will hang me. Weep not, for I welcome the thought of death if it means joining you in Heaven. My only regret is that I've let you down."

"Shh, you have no reason to apologize." He brushed the hair from her forehead with a sweep of his hand. "And you could never let me down."

"You trusted me with your bairn, and on the morrow, he dies with me. He will not live to carry on your legacy, hear the stories of your bravery, or know the wonderful man who was his sire."

"The bairn?" Connor slid his hand over rounded belly. "You're still with child? How could this be, after all you've suffered?"

"Aye. Your bairn grows in my womb." Her eyes drifted shut and she drew in a ragged breath. Her entire body trembled.

"Cailin, look at me."

"Nay. When I close my eyes, I see you come out of the darkness, out of my dreams. You take me in your arms, and I feel safe, and warm. It is a wonderful dream, and I dinna want to wake up."

He brushed his hand over her fevered brow. "I'm here, *liuadhe*. How can I convince you that I am flesh and blood? That I am not a dream?"

"On the morrow, they will hang me, and we will be together."

He placed his finger over her lips to silence her. "Nay. You will not die on the morrow. I'll get you out of here and take you home to my castle near Inverness, where you'll heal, and we'll live out the rest of our days in peace and happiness. You're going to live to see our bairn born. I promise. Bryce and Alasdair wait outside the castle walls, and will aid us in our escape."

"You *haiver* so, m'lord." Her voice was but a whisper. "Even if you were to get me out of here, I do not have the strength to walk or sit a horse. I would only slow you down. Please, leave me here to face my fate."

"My life would be empty and meaningless without you." Gently he lifted her and cradled her in his arms.

"You're a *thrawn* man, Connor Fraser." Her head dropped against his chest, and she fell silent.

"You are the stubborn one, my love, and saints be praised you are. What you have endured would have destroyed the bravest warrior."

He carried Cailin across the room, paused at the door, and peered into the hallway. The guard lay motionless in a heap on the floor. So far, no one had come to relieve him of his duty. They were too busy preparing the gallows and celebrating the upcoming hanging. It never ceased to amaze him how the English reveled in the torture and death of another.

Alasdair stood at the top of the stairs, awaiting his brother's return. "Hurry, Connor, we must be away. The guard will be changing soon." He kept his voice low and motioned with a sweep of his arm.

"Where is Bryce?" Connor climbed the stone staircase with her protectively cradled in his arms.

"He waits with the horses in the copse of trees beyond the postern gate." He held his arms out in his brother's direction. "Give me the lass. You are still weak from your injuries."

"Nay, I'll carry her. She weighs no more than a feather. I swear the bastards have not fed her in weeks." He shifted Cailin's limp body in his arms and followed his brother through a doorway leading to a narrow path behind the castle wall.

"Connor, Alasdair, make haste." Bryce sat atop his horse and motioned for the two men to join him. His eyes immediately fell on Cailin, his expression grim. He quickly crossed himself. "Is she dead?"

"Nay, but she's injured and as weak as a newly born colt." He brushed her forehead with a kiss, shifted her in his arms, and prepared to hand her over to his brother. "I want you to see her safely away. Alasdair and I will stay behind and confront anyone who dares to follow."

Bryce waved his brother off. "You're still recovering from your injuries. It makes more sense for Alasdair and I to remain behind. Cailin is your betrothed, and she carries your bairn. You should be the one to see to the lass."

Connor shook his head. "Nay. I need you to do this for me, brother. She was arrested because I failed to protect her. It is my responsibility to see that no one gives chase. You'll not sway me on this."

Bryce quickly slid from the saddle and led Thor forward. "We dinna have time to argue. Cailin is in need of a healer, and you're still too weak to fight."

Alasdair lumbered toward them. "Bryce is right. If I want to get out of this alive, I need a strong man at my back. Now, mount the damned horse. Your stubbornness is putting us all in danger."

Cailin opened her eyes and raised her head. "Please, Connor, I want to stay with you."

Tears dampened her ashen cheeks and he heard the tremor of fear in her voice. His heart clenched when she grimaced in pain. "Dinna *fash* yourself, *liuadhe.* I'll see you safe." Her eyes closed and her head dropped back, resting in the crook of his arm.

Connor looked up at his brothers. "I'll cross the border into Scotland and take her to Buccleuch. Michael Scott will offer us shelter."

"It's about time you came to your senses. Give me the lass." Alasdair held Cailin while Connor mounted Thor, and then placed her in his arms.

"Be careful brothers, and watch each other's back."

"We will, and God speed." With that, Bryce slapped Thor's rump, and the horse lunged forward.

Chapter 22

They traveled through the night and arrived at the Scott's stronghold mid-morning. As they approached the castle gate, a guard stepped into their path with his broadsword raised.

"Halt, and state your business," the sentry growled.

"My name is Connor Fraser. I wish to speak to Laird Scott." He looked down at Cailin, and then back at the guards. "Please, the lady needs a healer."

"It could be a trick, Seamus." Another guard joined the first and grabbed Thor's reins. "What ails the lass?"

"The English held her prisoner at Carlisle Castle. She suffered greatly at their hands. We seek sanctuary. Laird Scott and I are old friends." He shifted Cailin in his arms. "She burns with fever and will die if her injuries are not tended."

Seamus moved closer. "She doesn't look well. I dinna believe this to be a trick. Come, we'll take you to Laird Scott. But before we do, you must give me your blade, and any other weapons you carry."

Connor handed over his sword, pulled a dirk from the sheath at his waist, along with the one hidden in his boot. Under normal circumstances, he would never surrender his weapons, but Cailin needed help, and he'd lay down his own life for hers if necessary. He would not let her down again.

"Hold! Seamus, who are these people, and what do they want?" Atop the castle parapet stood a tall man, cloaked in black.

"He said his name is Connor Fraser and claims he knows you. The lass needs a healer." Seamus pointed at Cailin. "Should I send them away, m'lord?"

"Raise the portcullis and bring them to me at once," Michael Scott demanded, before disappearing into the shadows.

Seamus escorted them over the narrow wooden bridge and into the bailey, where the presence of strangers drew a great deal of interest. But the sea of curious faces sobered and the drone of whispers ceased when Laird Scott descended the castle steps.

"There's naught to see here. Be about your business, lest you wish to see the inside of the dungeon." Laird Scott crossed his arms over his chest, and waited for the crowd to disperse.

"I appreciate your help, Michael."

"It's been a long time, my friend. I'm glad you came to me for help." He bowed his head and crossed himself. "I was very sorry to hear about your cousin, Simon. Scotland suffered a great loss when he was captured at Kirkenclif and executed by Longshanks." His eyes narrowed when he looked at Cailin. "What happened to the lass?"

"She was charged with a murder she dinna commit, and the English held her at Carlisle Castle pending execution. My brothers and I rescued her before they had the chance."

"Where are your brothers now?"

"Alasdair and Bryce stayed behind to stop anyone that might try to follow. They'll join us once it is safe to do so."

Scott turned abruptly and addressed his two guards. "Seamus, the lady is to be taken to the chamber atop the North Tower. Unless I tell you otherwise, no one but you and Brodie are to know of her identity. If anyone asks, they are two weary travelers in need of lodging. Do you understand?" He waited for the two men to nod in agreement before he continued. "Brodie, find Fallon and tell her to bring her healing herbs and potions. Best you send for Father Francis as well."

"The fewer people who know of your identity the

better. Give her to me." Carefully taking Cailin into his arms, Michael waited for Connor to dismount before handing her back to him.

"Husband, what is it?" A petite, dark-haired woman descended the stairs and joined the group of men.

"This is my wife, Lauren."

Connor nodded. "Lady Scott."

Lauren stepped closer and immediately ran her hand over Cailin's brow. "Husband, the lass needs a healer."

"I've sent for Fallon. Connor is an old friend, and I've offered them refuge in the North Tower. Will you show them the way?"

"I'll see to it immediately." Lauren gathered her skirts and hurried into the castle. Connor followed.

They crossed the great hall, then climbed to the top of a steep, winding staircase. Lady Scott paused at the end of a dark hallway and slid a key into the lock of a large oak door. "This solar once belonged to my husband's mother." She grabbed a torch from a sconce on the wall, pushed the door open, and stepped inside. "The chamber will serve well as a sickroom."

The room was cold and dark, but Seamus entered on their heels and started a fire. He lit several tallow candles, placed two on the mantle of the hearth and one on a table beside the bed. "If you need anything else, m'lady, just call. I'll be standing guard at the foot of the stairs."

"Has Brodie gone to fetch Fallon?"

"Aye, he has."

"Good. If I need anything, I'll let you know. Be off with you now, and send Fallon up as soon as she arrives." Lady Scott dismissed him with a wave of her hand. Once Seamus had left the room, she turned to faced Connor. "Best we get her settled."

He carried Cailin across the room and gently placed her on the bed. "I'm grateful for your kindness, m'lady."

Lady Scott joined him beside the bed. "The lass is very weak and her breathing is labored." She pressed a hand to Cailin's flushed cheek. "Her fever is high. How did she come by her injuries?"

Her husband had not elaborated, but Connor felt she had a right to know they housed fugitives. He explained the circumstances leading up to Cailin's arrest and the details of her rescue. "The English will come after us. I'll understand if you wish to turn us out rather than risking Longshanks' wrath."

"We have no intention of turning you away. You are welcome to stay as long as necessary."

"Thank you, m'lady. You're most kind." He moved to the other side of the bed. "She's with child. I'm not even certain the extent of her injuries. After we rescued her from the dungeon, there was no time to seek a healer. I treated the wounds I could see, but I know there must be more than meets the eye."

A soft rap on the door interrupted their conversation. "Aye, who is it?" Lady Scott called out.

"Fallon. Brodie said you're in need of my healing skills."

"That we are, and none too soon." Lady Scott rushed across the chamber and threw open the door.

A striking young woman with hair as black as coal, flawless porcelain skin, and eyes the color of sapphires stepped into the room.

"Did Brodie explain what happened?" Lady Scott asked as she escorted Fallon toward the bed.

"Aye. He explained everything."

"Please see what you can do for her." Lady Scott placed her hand on Connor's shoulder. "Come with me and let Fallon tend to her."

"I'll not leave." He crossed his arms over his chest and looked at Fallon. "Can you help her?"

After a quick assessment of Cailin's condition, Fallon shook her head and clucked her tongue. "I'll do my utmost to make her comfortable and will see to her injuries, but I can make no promises."

"What of the babe?" Connor asked.

She placed her hand over the swell of Cailin's belly and closed her eyes. "The babe has a strong spirit. If the mother lives, the bairn has a good chance. Only time will tell."

With a sweep of her hand, Fallon motioned toward the door. "I'll do what I can to save both mother and bairn. Now, be off with you, and let me to do my work."

Connor moved closer to the bed. "Cailin is my betrothed, and it is my duty to stand by her side."

"Your dedication is admirable, but she is in good hands. You trusted us enough to bring her here, now you must trust us with her care." Lady Scott grasped his arm. "Fallon will let us know of her condition once she has treated her injuries."

"She is very young. Are you sure she knows what to do?" he asked Lady Scott.

"She may be ten and nine summers, but her mother taught her well. I trust her judgment. Fallon has also been blessed with the gift."

"The gift?"

"*Taibhsearachd*. She has the gift of second sight. Her mother had it, as did her grandmother and great-grandmother before that."

Connor arched a brow. "I dinna set store in such things. Her ability as a healer is what matters." He found it hard to hide his skepticism.

"I'd trust her with my life. Come, we'll join my husband in the great hall and await word of Lady Cailin's condition." She placed her hand on Connor's forearm, but he refused to move.

"I'll step aside and allow the healer to work, but I'll not

leave the room. I have no intention of letting Cailin out of my sight."

"Fine. You can stay if you promise not to interfere with my treatments," Fallon conceded.

"You have my word." Connor reluctantly moved to the far side of the room and sat in a large wooden chair.

Fallon added willow bark, coriander, rosemary, comfrey, and henbane to a large pot of boiling water. "The tea will aid in the replenishment of fluids. The herbs I have selected will help to combat the fever, pain, and infection." After stirring the bubbling concoction several times, she moved to a small table beside the hearth. In a crockery bowl, she ground cloves, saffron, and fox cote into a fine powder. "In a poultice, these herbs reduce swelling and are effective against wound infections."

"C—Connor," Cailin muttered softly. Her head rolled from side to side and she arched her back, moaning in pain.

Connor sprang to his feet and took a step toward the bed, but stopped when Fallon held up her hand in protest. "You promised not to interfere."

He grumbled under his breath and fisted his hands at his sides, fighting the urge to rush to Cailin's side. Guilt tugged at the pit of his stomach.

Had I stayed with her, instead of going off to battle with the Bruce, Cailin would not have suffered at Borden's hand.

Cailin moaned again, and it took every ounce of inner strength for Connor to stand his ground.

"Easy lass, you're safe, and your man is here. You must rest, save your strength." Fallon dipped a linen rag into a bowl of cool water, mint, and willow bark. After ringing out the cloth, she laid it across Cailin's fevered brow. "If you've any hope of surviving, we must get the fever to break. First, I need to remove this wretched gown."

Cailin whimpered when Fallon rolled her to her side. "I know this hurts, but it must be done." She used a dirk to slit the tattered garment up the back, then removed the layers of filthy fabric, exposing Cailin's back. "Holy Mother of God, what did those English bastards do to you?"

Connor moved forward, gasping when he saw the angry welts and gashes lacing her back. "I had no idea she'd been flogged. If I'd known, I'd have found Borden, cut off his ballocks, and rammed them down his throat."

"And you'd both be dead." Fallon shook her head. "This is not the first time she has felt the lash." Her hand lightly traced several raised ridges of flesh, scattered amidst the new wounds.

"I noticed the scars the first night we spent together, but she refused to talk about what happened, and I dinna push the issue. From what I know of her childhood, there is no doubt in my mind that her father is responsible. If I could have one minute alone with him, he'd rue the day he ever laid a hand to her."

"You can not change the past." Fallon pointed with authority at the chair. "Sit down, or I will have Seamus and Brodie remove you from the chamber."

Connor reluctantly obeyed, straining to watch Fallon heal his beloved Cailin.

After carefully cleaning the wounds, Fallon applied a thick layer of herbal ointment. "There. I'm done torturing you for now." She wiped her hands on her apron, replaced Cailin's soiled clothing with a clean night rail, then covered her wraith-thin body with lightweight plaid.

Getting Cailin to drink the healing liquid proved to be a challenge. Fallon carefully slid a spoon between her dry, chapped lips. "You need to drink, lass," she encouraged softly, but most of the tea trickled down Cailin's chin.

After another unsuccessful attempt, Fallon placed the

bowl on a table beside the bed. "Rest now. I'll try again later. All we can do now is pray that you have the strength to fight, and a strong will to live."

Chapter 23

Cailin whimpered, and this time Connor refused to be naysayed. He quickly crossed the chamber, but stopped at the foot of the bed. The flush of fever tinted her gaunt cheeks and she lay deathly still. Her shallow breathing was scarcely noticeable. If not for the occasional soft moan, one would believe her already gone.

Icy fingers of despair squeezed his chest until he couldn't breathe. Connor moved to her side and fell to his knees. Clutching her hand, he lifted it to his lips. "I'm sorry I wasn't there to protect you," he muttered against her knuckles.

He loved Cailin, but until this moment, he hadn't realized how much. It didn't really matter when or how it happened, he loved her with every fiber of his being. Right now, he'd willingly stand naked on the parapet and declare his feelings to the entire world if he thought it would make a difference. If he could change places with her and take away the pain, he would. If he could erase the horrible memories of the last few months and give her back her youthful innocence, he'd do it in a heartbeat. However, he was painfully aware that in that same heartbeat, the Almighty could snatch her from this earth, and there wasn't a damned thing he could do to stop it.

He wasn't a religious man. The brutal murder of his mother and youngest brother had put his faith to the test. The death of his father and oldest brother, Keith, squelched what little had remained. No, he was not a religious man, yet he bowed his head and prayed. He begged the Almighty to spare his betrothed, and their unborn child, and if by some miracle she lived, he swore a silent oath to spend the rest of his days protecting her.

She was the bravest woman he had ever known, a warrior in her own right. Perhaps it was not on a battlefield, but she'd stood up for what she believed in, faced Borden's wrath, and English tyranny with grace and dignity. Her father had condemned her as a child for her wild spirit and temerity, but today Connor praised her for it. Not only did he love her, he respected and admired her.

"Tha gaol agam ort...I love you!" he whispered against the back of her hand, but she did not stir. In desperation, he leaned over and repeatedly kissed her lips and cheeks, but there was no response. Tears welled in his eyes as he sank to the floor, her hand clutched to his heart. "*Tha mi duilich*...I'm so sorry. Please dinna leave me, *leannan*."

He heard Fallon cross the room, but his gaze remained on Cailin. "Borden's men will surely give chase, and I must get her as far away from the border as possible. I dinna want to put Laird Scott or his clan at risk. If she survives, how long will it be before she can travel?"

"That is a question I cannot answer. Laird Scott is a man of his word and a fierce warrior. He offered you sanctuary and would never surrender the lady without a fight. I'm certain that you are welcome to stay as long as necessary. As to when she will be strong enough to travel, she must first make it through this night."

He nodded, pulled a chair up beside the bed, and sat down. It wasn't long before his head dropped back and he drifted off. The sound of her calling out in her delirium woke him and brought Fallon rushing to the bedside.

He leaned forward and ran his hand across her brow. "What is it, *leannan?*" He tried to understand what she said, but it made no sense to him. "The fever burns hotter than before." He looked up at Fallon and shook his head.

"P—please, papa, I'm sorry. Dinna lock me in the pit.

I'm afraid of the dark." Cailin sobbed. "I won't disobey you again." Her head rolled from side to side as she thrashed beneath the covers. "Please dinna hit me again."

His heart twisted in his chest.

"She must be reliving a punishment from her childhood. When a person is ill, their mind conjures up all sorts of memories," Fallon said softly. "From the sounds of it, her father must be a terrible man."

"She told me her father never forgave her for being first born and blamed her for the death of her mother and twin brother. From what I gather, he had no use for a daughter, and there was no love lost between them.

Cailin cried out again.

Connor leaned in close and whispered in her ear. "Everything will be all right, *mo gaol*, I'm here, and no one will ever hurt you again." He placed a cooling cloth on her brow and glanced up at Fallon. Fallon frowned. "So far, nothing I have tried seems to work. I could try purging or bloodletting, but to be honest, I believe those rituals do more harm than good. I feel the same way about leeches. While they are often helpful in treating a bruise, they are good for little else."

"After the battle of Dumfries, one of the wounded burned with a fever that would not break. The healer immersed him in water from the stream and saved his life. While not the usual practice, it might help."

"We could try. I have oft struggled with the age-old tradition of keeping the room so hot one cannot breathe, of smothering fevered flesh with furs and plaid when more heat is the last thing they needed." She smoothed her hand over the blanket on Cailin's bed. "In the past, my ideas were considered heretical. Some even accused me of trying to kill the person, not heal them."

"Her time grows short. Do what you can to save her."

"If you are in agreement, I'll ask Brodie and Seamus

to bring up the laird's tub, and fill it with temped water. Mayhap, if I add yarrow, willow bark, and comfrey, it will also help to ease the pain and fight the infection." She picked up a bowl of steaming liquid and handed it to him. "I made a tea containing many of the same herbs, but I've not had much luck getting her to drink it. Mayhap you could try."

He curled his nose up in distain at pungent smelling amber liquid and held it at arm's length.

"The benefits far outweigh the unpleasant odor." She smiled and moved toward the door. Before leaving the chamber, she turned and looked at him. "I'll give you some time alone with your lady and arrange for the tub. If she wakes, see that she drinks as much as she can stomach. She needs the fluids, and the herbs will help to ease the pain."

Connor settled into the chair beside the bed. He plucked another rag from the bowl of cold water and placed it on her fevered brow. "I'm here, *liuadhe*," he muttered softly, but she did not respond.

Fallon returned a short time later. On her directions, Seamus and Brodie brought a large wooden tub into the chamber and filled it with warm water before taking their leave. After adding an assortment of herbs, she turned to Connor. "Bring her to me. We'll immerse her in the tub and pray the fever will break."

He carefully slid one arm beneath Cailin's knees, the other behind her back. She moaned when he lifted her, but did not come fully wake. He carried her across the room and eased her into the warm water, night rail and all.

Cailin opened her eyes at the shock of being submerged, but closed them again before he could even speak her name.

After what seemed like forever, Fallon told him to lift her from the tub. She waited by the bed, where she'd laid out a dry night rail, healing salves, and a basket of linen dressings. "Wrap her in the toweling I left beside the tub and bring her to me. I'll tend to her wounds, then help her into some dry clothes."

Once Cailin was back in bed, he tugged his wet shirt over his head and tossed it on the floor. His trews followed.

Afforded an unexpected view of his bare backside, Fallon gasped. "What do you think you're doing?"

He grinned at her embarrassment and slipped beneath the blankets. "I'm lying with my lady." He gently eased Cailin to her side so she lay nestled in the curve of his arm, with her cheek and hand resting on his chest.

"You cannot possibly think to bed her?"

"I dinna plan to tup her. I only mean to lay by her side. I could not prevent this terrible thing from happening, but I will hold her now, and keep her safe. If the Almighty sees fit to take her this night, he will have to pluck her from my arms. If she lives, my face will be the first thing she sees when she awakens."

Cailin opened her eyes and blinked several times, uncertain if she was dreaming, or delirious from fever. Her fingers curled in the soft dark chest hair on which her hand rested. Connor's broad chest gently rose and fell with even breaths, and his heart beat rhythmically beneath her open palm. The familiar scent of male, musk, and spices, unique to the man she loved, filled her senses. She wasn't dreaming or dead. He was alive, and holding her in his arms. Her heart soared, and she wanted to spring from the bed and shout with joy. But she couldn't muster the strength to raise her head. The slightest movement caused the room to spin. Nausea rocked her stomach, and the pain radiating across her back served as a vivid reminder of the flogging she'd suffered.

"Cailin?" Connor's thick, dark lashes lifted from his cheeks and their eyes met. "Thank the Almighty, the fever has broken. How do you feel?"

He held her so tightly she could hardly breathe and repeatedly feathered kissed across her brow, cheeks, and the tip of her nose. "I feel like I've been trampled by horses and dragged for miles."

"That doesn't surprise me, given what you've been through." He carefully shifted his weight and rolled to his side. They lay face to face. He caressed her belly with his hand and smiled. "Our babe is strong. Throughout the night, I felt him kicking and moving about. How do you ever get any sleep?"

Her hand covered his. "I would gladly stay awake the entire nine moons, as long as the babe is safe and healthy. "It pleases you?" Her eyes searched his.

"The babe?"

She nodded.

"Aye, *liuadhe,* more than words can express. I'm sorry that I was not there when you needed me."

She raised her fingers to his lips. "You are not to blame for what happened. I'm so thankful you're here now. When I saw Williams run you through, I was certain you were dead."

"I should have been. If I dinna know better, I'd say he missed his mark on purpose. The arrow I took in the shoulder did more damage than the sword."

A thought flashed through her mind. Had the soldier's poor aim been intentional? Had she actually managed to reach the man's heart? Perhaps not all of the English were the scoundrels and blackguards she believed them to be. She closed her eyes, shook her head, and banished the thought. After what she'd seen of English justice, and mercy, Williams was an exception at best.

The door opened and a woman entered the chamber carrying a wooden tray. She crossed the room, stopping at the foot of the bed. "Don't you look as bright as a new coin this morning?"

"Who is she?" Cailin whispered.

"Her name is Fallon. Thanks to her healing skill, you are alive."

"You flatter me, m'lord. While I would like to take the credit, the lass's strong will to live played a big role in her survival." She smiled at Cailin. "I'm glad to see you're feeling better. You had us all worried."

"I'm sorry to have caused so much trouble. Where are we?"

"You're at Buccleuch, the castle of Laird Michael Scott. They brought you here three days ago." Fallon placed the tray on the table beside the bed.

"We are in Scotland?" She sighed in relief. Her father had mentioned the powerful border family, but she had never met any of them until today.

"Aye, *liuadhe*. Michael Scott is a childhood friend. When I was a lad, Simon brought me with him when he went to buy horses from Michael's father. He had the finest destriers in the Borderlands. When we rescued you from Carlisle Castle, it seemed a logical place to seek refuge."

The grief in his eyes at the mention of his cousin's name was unmistakable, and her heart went out to him. "I'm very sorry about Simon. I know how much he meant to you and your brothers," she said softly. "Mary was devastated. Have you seen her? Please tell me she is safe and well."

"Eventually all men die, but Simon gave his life for a cause dear to his heart. A man can only hope to leave this world with such honor." Connor tried to clear his throat before he continued, but his voice thickened with emotion. "Mary is safe at Oliver Castle with her mother."

"Saints be praised." She crossed herself and bowed her head.

Fallon moved toward the bed, her hands planted firmly on her hips. "I may have been weak last night when I allowed you to stay here, m'lord, but I have come to my senses today. I'll see you up and dressed, so I can tend to the lass's dressings. Then she needs to rest." Fallon tugged at the plaid blanket, leaving him exposed. "Get up before I take a switch to your arse." She cocked her head and grinned. "And bonny arse it is."

"Woman, you try my patience." He leapt from the bed, grabbed the blanket from her hands, and wrapped it around his waist. He reached for his trews. "Were you never taught that a man should only be seen naked by a woman he wishes to bed?"

"You showed no shame last night." Fallon chuckled. "I'm here to tend to my patient and do not want you underfoot. Whether you're dressed or not makes no difference to me, but I want you out of here. As clan healer, you're not the first man I've seen without his clothes."

Cailin covered her mouth, stifling a grin. "Best you do as she says. I have a feeling she is not one who takes kindly to being crossed." As he stood beside the bed with the plaid clutched in his fist and draped around his hips, Cailin couldn't help admiring his magnificent body. If she had the strength and wasn't in so much pain, she'd have insisted he stay and Fallon be the one to leave.

He grumbled beneath his breath and slid his legs into his trews. "I'll leave the bed, but not the room." He grabbed his shirt and slid it over his head.

Fallon stood her ground. "You'll go down to the great hall and break your fast with the laird and his lady wife. If you've a mind to be helpful, ask the cook to send up some broth." She turned to Cailin. "I was not expecting you to be awake. Mayhap you would like a wee bit to eat."

"I'll not leave her." He stood with his feet braced slightly apart and his arms folded over his chest.

"I'll be fine, Connor. Please go and break your fast. I'm sure Fallon will call you if there's a need."

"I will. Now be gone with you." Fallon pointed to the door.

"I can see I'm outnumbered on this. I'll go, but I'll be back." Before he left, he lifted Cailin's hand and pressed a kiss to the back of it.

Ignoring the fact that the door slammed behind him, Fallon opened several small linen sacks and poured their contents into a wooden bowl. She added some water and stirred the mixture. "He's a good man, and he loves you very much."

Cailin lowered her eyes. "He has never said the words." She shifted in the bed trying to get comfortable, but movement caused the pain to worsen and her head began to spin.

Fallon patted Cailin on the shoulder. "Trust me when I say he loves you. Some people just have a hard time finding the words. Your man carries a heavy burden on his shoulders for one so young. He must learn to let go of the past and look to the future."

"Aye, he is a fine man and will make a wonderful father."

"You must also learn to forget the past."

"I don't know what you mean."

"You've carried your own share of pain for a very long time. You must let go of the disappointment and loss you suffered as a child. What happened to you at the hands of your father and again with the English are terrible injustices, but physical injuries heal with time. I know that a wounded heart does not heal as easily, but you must try. You'll soon be a mother and with a good man like Connor by your side, the future is bright."

How did she know all of this? There was something about Fallon that Cailin couldn't put her finger. She rested her hand on her belly. "Is the babe going to be all right?"

"You are both lucky to be alive. Like his mother, the babe is a fighter. I have every reason to believe he will be fine. Provided you rest and dinna do anything too strenuous."

She returned her attention to the bowl of herbs. "Used as a poultice, these will help to fight infection. It doesn't smell very nice, but it works well." She lay several strips of linen on the tray and spread the pungent mixture over them.

Cailin closed her eyes and bit her lower lip. The pain and nausea had returned with a vengeance.

Fallon pressed her hand to Cailin's forehead and frowned. "Your face is flushed, and I worry your fever might return."

"I am fine. A little tired is all. When will I be well enough to travel? It can't be wise for us to tarry in one spot for too long. Borden will surely be searching for me."

"You're safe and have no need to worry. Laird Scott will protect you as long as necessary. Once I have dressed your wounds, you'll need to rest." Fallon placed the tray of dressings on the bed. "I'm afraid this is not going to be pleasant. I'll try to be gentle."

Cailin ground her teeth and closed her eyes as Fallon lifted the edge of a dressing and eased it from her back.

Once the task was completed, Fallon gathered up her supplies and covered Cailin with a fur pelt. "You need to try and get some sleep."

Fallon was right; she needed to rest. If not for her own sake, for the babe.

But how can I rest? Borden will not give up easily. This very moment he could be lurking outside the castle walls, plotting how to capture me and exact his revenge.

She shuddered at the thought. Her presence at Buccleuch put her in peril, but also endangered everyone who lived within its castle walls. When Connor returned, she would try to convince him to leave as soon as possible. The more distance put between them and their nemesis, the better.

Chapter 24

In the week that followed, Cailin regained her strength. Connor agreed that the longer they remained at Buccleuch, the greater the risk of being discovered. While he appreciated the sanctuary offered by his friends, aiding fugitives was a treasonable offense, and he did not want to put them in danger. After discussing their options with his brother, the decision was made to return to Beauly before winter set in and heavy snow made traveling impossible.

"I wish I could convince you to wait until after the babe is born." Lady Scott frowned. "I dinna think it a good idea for you to travel so close to your laying in."

"While we're grateful for the offer, we've already overstayed our welcome and must be on our way. If we leave now, we can be home before the worst winter weather sets in."

"You are welcome to stay as long as necessary. I dinna like the idea of you traveling at this time of the year with a woman who is breeding." Michael Scott pointed to a cluster of dark clouds on the horizon. "You never know when things will change."

"Our presence at Buccleuch has put your clan in danger. I dinna want to be responsible bringing Longshanks's wrath down upon your heads." Connor slid his arm around Cailin's waist and drew her against his side.

"Nonsense. Buccleuch is well fortified. My husband's army numbers close to three hundred men and more are available from neighboring clans should the need arise." Lady Scott glanced up at her husband and sighed, a look of longing in her eyes. "I was actually looking forward to having a wee one in the Castle again. Our bairns are growing so fast, and I miss having a babe around."

"Dinna be getting any ideas, woman," Scott replied curtly, but his attempt to appear gruff fooled no one.

"Are you ready to go?" Bryce asked as he joined the group. "I've prepared everything you requested. The horses are saddled, and the men are anxious to mount."

"Men?" Connor glanced across the bailey. Six men with heavy horses waited by the cart.

"Since you insist on leaving, I'm sending some of my finest warriors to accompany you," Michael replied.

"Again, I'm grateful." Connor grasped his friend's forearm and gave it a shake.

Bryce stepped forward. "I'll drive the cart for the first part of the journey, and mayhap Alasdair can spell me after a few hours."

"Cart?" Cailin asked. Her brow rose in question, and she glanced from one brother to the other.

"Aye, for you to ride in," Bryce replied.

"We will be traveling over some rough terrain, and I want you and the babe to be comfortable." He slid his hand over her belly and smiled. "Humor me in this."

Cailin covered his hand and sighed. "As you wish." She didn't want to be coddled, but she had to admit, his attention and concern for her and their unborn child caused her heart to soar.

Michael stepped forward and patted Connor's shoulder. "I hate to see you go, but if you must, it's best you be on your way. If the weather holds, you can travel a good distance before nightfall."

Connor grasped his friend's forearm, giving it another hardy shake. "Thank you for everything you've done for us."

Lady Scott hugged Cailin. "Take care of yourself and the wee one. Send us a missive when the babe arrives."

"Mayhap you could visit in the spring," Cailin

suggested.

"That sounds wonderful." Lauren smiled.

Connor clasped Cailin's elbow. "Come, we've said our goodbyes and must leave."

Bryce tied Lucifer to the back of the cart and climbed into the driver's seat. As he waited for the others to mount their horses, he glanced around the bailey. "Have you seen Fallon this morning?" he asked Lady Scott. "I thought she might come to see us off."

"Nay, she has gone to help with a birthing. The last time Fiona gave birth, she labored for almost two days. Knowing her husband, he likely panicked with her first contraction and summoned Fallon far too early. Once there, she will not leave until the babe is born."

Bryce nodded. "When she returns, tell her I said goodbye."

"I'll do that." Lady Scott grinned. "I'm sure if you are in the area again, Fallon will be most please if you stopped in for a visit."

"It sounds like Fallon has caught your eye." Alasdair laughed and slapped Bryce on the back.

Bryce grumbled under his breath, but offered no response.

Cailin smiled at Connor. "Your brother dinna deny his feelings for Fallon. Do you think he has fallen for her? Mayhap we should invite her to come for a visit as well."

Connor pinched the bridge of his nose and shook his head. "My brother is a grown man and doesn't need a matchmaker." He lifted Cailin into the cart, handed her a fur pelt, and drew a plaid curtain across the rear opening.

Two hours into the journey, they entered a small clearing. The horses slowed to a walk, and Connor called to his men. "We'll rest here."

"So soon? We've not been on the road for long. At this rate of travel, we will reach Beauly by mid-summer,"

Alasdair grumbled.

"I said, we'll stop here." Connor's eyes flashed in Bryce's direction. "And what have you to say about my decision, brother?"

The wood groaned as Bryce shifted his weight on the seat of the cart. "I dinna say a word. I know better."

Cailin sat up when Connor drew back the curtain. "Alasdair is right. It will take forever to reach Beauly at this rate." She giggled when the babe tumbled and kicked, as if in agreement.

"Are you warm enough?" Connor asked.

"Between the straw and the furs, there is scarcely enough room for me in the cart." She laughed. "Since you insist on stopping, mayhap you could help me down. I might as well tend to my needs." Strong hands lifted her from the cart. Once her feet touched the ground, she pressed her hand to the small of her back and twisted from side to side. A bothersome ache had settled low in her spine, but she'd not admit that to her husband. "Yonder grove of trees looks to be suitable."

"Not without me to accompany you." He took her elbow and escorted her across the clearing. But as they reached the tree line, he stopped abruptly and turned his head in the direction of the horses.

"What's wrong?" Cailin craned her neck in an attempt to see what had caught his attention, but saw nothing.

He brought his finger to his lips. His eyes scanned the nearby forest and surrounding area, and he listened intently.

"Connor, what is it? You are making me nervous," she whispered.

Alasdair lumbered toward them. "There is nothing amiss, but an overactive imagination. You fret like an old woman, brother."

"Who's keeping watch?" Connor snapped.

"I've posted one of the Scott warriors at every possible entrance to the clearing. Things are secure." He pointed to the sentries standing guard around the perimeter of the forest.

"You're overreacting, husband. Now if you two will give me some privacy, I must attend to my needs." She moved toward a thicket at the edge of the clearing and ducked behind the bracken while Connor stood watch a few feet away.

After completing the task, she rejoined her husband and his brother. "Mayhap, we can travel three hours before we stop again," she said in jest.

Bryce joined the trio. "If I dinna know better, I would swear you were an old married couple."

"You know not—" Connor began a quick retort, but stopped mid-sentence when a flock of startled pheasants took flight. He spun around, facing the horses. Thor raised his head, his eyes wild and his nostrils flared.

"Do you think it might be a deer?" Bryce asked.

"Mayhap a fox or a boar?" Alasdair added.

"I dinna know what it is, but I have a gut feeling we're not alone. Bryce, see Cailin to the cart, and make ready to depart. If anything happens, dinna leave her side."

"I'll guard her with my life." Bryce held out his hand.

"Take her to the cart, now!" Connor placed her hand in that of his brother, turned abruptly, and ran toward the edge of the forest.

"Best we make haste and do as he says." They hurried across the clearing, but as Bryce was about to lift her into the cart, all Hell broke loose. English soldiers burst from the forest on all sides, engaging the Scott warriors. The odds were two against one. Connor and Alasdair rushed to their aid.

Her heart raced with fear, but Cailin dug in her heels and refused to get into the cart. "We can't leave without them. Connor and Alasdair need our help."

Ignoring her protest, Bryce lifted her from the ground and placed her on the bed of straw. "Lie down and hold on." He climbed into the driver's seat. After a sharp crack of the reins, the cart lurched forward.

When the sound of clashing metal and men shouting faded into the distance, Bryce slowed the cart to a crawl and turned to face her. "This should be far enough. Are you all right?"

"I'm fine, and we are well out of harm's way. Please leave me here and see if you can assist Connor and Alasdair."

"I promised Connor to see you safe."

"You've kept your promised. Please go back and see if there isn't something you can do to help." Determined to remain strong, she fisted her hands in her skirt and fought back tears.

"I won't leave you unattended," he replied adamantly.

"Will you see my child born without a father? I beg of you, please help them."

"Connor is right. You're a *thrawn* woman." He raked his fingers through his hair. "Stay here and dinna leave the cart. I'll go back and see how things fare. But, I won't risk your safety. If there is nothing I can do, I'll return and we'll leave immediately. Do you understand?"

Cailin nodded. "Aye. Please hurry."

Bryce pulled the dirk from the sheath at his side and handed it to her. Her fingers wrapped around the hilt as she stared down at the weapon in her hand.

"Use it if necessary, and aim to kill." He untied Lucifer from the back of the cart, threw his leg over the horse's back, and pulled himself into the saddle. "Dinna leave this place. I'll be back and, God willing, Connor and Alasdair will be with me."

As she watched Bryce ride out of sight, Cailin drew her cloak around her shoulders and begged the Almighty to spare her husband and his brothers.

"I didn't think finding you would be this easy."

Her prayers were interrupted by the sound of a familiar male voice.

Borden stood behind the cart, blocking her only means of escape. "I'm surprised the fools left you unprotected. This will be like taking sweets from a bairn." He laughed and moved forward. "You've led me on a merry chase, but it is time to pay for your sins."

"Why won't you leave us in peace? Surely you have better things to do than to traipse across Scotland looking for an innocent woman."

"*Tsk, tsk, tsk.*" Borden shook his head and clucked his tongue, his expression menacing. "I can't believe you are still claiming your innocence."

"You know very well I was falsely accused of your brother's murder."

"We have been through this before. There was a witness to your crime, and the tribunal's sentence of execution stands."

"The so-called trial was a mockery of justice." She faced her nemesis with her chin held high. "You pursue this because I wounded your pride by denying your advances."

"No one humiliates me and gets away with it!" He absently stroked the scar on his cheek. "I have waited a long time to settle the score. Do you think I would forget your insult so easily, or that you did this to my face? I will see justice served...my justice."

"How did you find us?"

"I have my sources, but if you must know, a peddler came to me a weeks ago with news that he thought might reap him a hefty reward. He told me that while he was selling his wares at Buccleuch, he'd heard rumors that Michael Scott had visitors staying with him, including a woman heavy with child. I sent spies to check out his story. My suspicions confirmed, I was on my way to arrest you when I learned you had already left the village and were heading north." He leered at her and tried to grab her leg. "Get out, or I will drag you out. You've already caused me enough trouble."

"Nay, I refuse to go with you." She defiantly drew her knees up and scooted out of his reach. "When Connor returns, he'll—"

"I can assure you, we are very much alone. At this moment, my men are making short work of your lover and his pathetic band of Scottish rabble. They are no match for my soldiers. In fact, he might already be dead."

"I dinna believe that to be true. Connor will come, and if you dare lay a hand to me, you'll live to regret it."

This time when he reached into the cart, Borden caught her around the ankle and pulled her toward him.

She screamed and fumbled for the dirk, but dropped it in the straw. Frantically kicking out, she tried to fight back, but to no avail. She clutched at the walls of the cart and held on, but was no match for his brute strength. Splinters pierced her palms as they slid along the wooden planks. Why didn't Connor or Bryce come when she called for help? Could Borden be right, were they dead? She screamed again. No one came.

Borden wrapped one arm around her protruding belly, covered her mouth with the other hand, and dragged her from the cart. He held her against his chest, her feet dangling in the air, but she'd not give up without a fight. Cailin bit down hard, her teeth sinking into flesh. She tasted blood.

He yowled in pain, released his grip, and let her fall to the ground. "Bitch!" he snarled as he examined his hand. "You will pay dearly for this." Without warning, he kicked out at her.

She turned in time to protect her stomach, but the blow hit her squarely in the back. She saw stars and gasped for air—the wind knocked from her lungs.

"Get up!" Borden grabbed her by the upper arm and

pulled her to her feet. "There is nowhere to run, and no one will help you."

"Where are you taking me?" She bit back a sob.

"I am taking you back to England. There, you'll be executed in accordance with the sentence handed out by the tribunal, and I'll redeem myself with the crown." A lascivious grin tugged at his lips. "You'll hang, but not until I have settled our old score. I intend to see myself fully sated before you die."

He tightened the bruising grip on her arm and pulled her across the small clearing. She dragged her feet, offering as much resistance as she could muster. Her mind raced. She had to do something. In a last ditch effort, she tried to bite his arm, but he retaliated with a backhanded slap that sent her tumbling to the ground.

"You got away with that once, but you'll not do it again." Borden pulled a dagger from its sheath and waved it in front of her face. He took a menacing step in her direction. "Mayhap we should finish this here and now."

"As long as there's a breath left in my body, you'll not harm her or the babe." Connor stepped out of the woods and blocked the path. Despite the rage he felt when he saw the dirk in Borden's hand, he managed to keep his anger in check. Cailin's life depended on it.

Borden glared at him, his lips drawn back in an evil grin. "Your death can easily be arranged."

Using Borden's momentary distraction, Cailin tried to crawl away, but he grabbed her by the hair and snapped her head back. "Where might you be going?"

Connor gave a low curse when the blackguard pulled her to her feet and twisted her arm behind her back. With Borden holding her like a shield, he could not risk the bastard harming her or his unborn babe.

A quick survey of the area revealed a steep cliff overlooking the river on one side of the path and a rocky ravine on the other. Connor took a step forward with his sword drawn, blocking Borden's only viable means of escape.

"Halt where you are, or I'll slit her throat." Borden pressed the blade against Cailin's neck.

"Release her now. Most of your men are dead, and those that were able have run off. You have nothing to gain by killing Cailin."

"You're bluffing, and I have no intention of setting her free. Lay down your sword, and move aside."

Connor took another step in their direction. "Only a spineless coward hides behind the skirts of a woman. Harm one hair on her head, and I'll reach down your throat and pull your heart out with my bare hands. That is if you have a heart."

"I said, don't come any closer." Borden shuffled backward, his heels resting on the edge of the cliff. "I'll toss her over if you don't back off!"

Connor's heart pounded wildly and his chest tightened. He could scarcely draw a breath. They stood so close to the edge that a strong gust of wind could send them both plummeting to their deaths on the rocky crags below.

A single tear rolled down Cailin's cheek, and a thin red line appeared across her neck, blood tricking across the blade.

Connor stopped his advance. "If you need a hostage, take me instead. If you desire blood, take mine." He lowered his sword and held his arms out to the sides in an open plea. "There is no honor in killing a defenseless woman."

"What does the son of a Scottish whore know about honor? I will be doing the world a favor if I kill the witch and the devil's spawn she carries. I rue the day she crossed my path. I was a rich man, a lord in high standing with the king and his minions. When I present her to Edward, I'll regain his favor, and he'll drop all notions of taking my title, my land, and Carlisle Castle. I have nothing to lose, and everything to gain."

"Let her go. You have no hope of escaping."

Borden laughed. "I'll let her go when Hell freezes and I am crowned King of England." Teetering on the edge of the cliff, he quickly glanced over his shoulder.

Connor sucked in a sharp breath. He had to do something and had to do it fast.

"She is responsible for my brother's death, and I demand restitution. Poor Harold had only seen thirty summers and was in his prime. He—"

"You know I killed your brother. The swine tried to rape her, and I was not about to let that happen."

"You lie to protect her!" Borden's eyes flashed with anger. "Regardless of whether she wielded the dirk or not, she is the reason Harold is dead."

"The lass committed no crime. I'm the one you have issue with."

"Ah, but you're wrong. If what you claim is true, then I have issue with both of you. Because of that, her death will be more poignant than ever. The tribunal has spoken, and she will be executed for my brother's murder. And you will die knowing her life was forfeited because of your deed." Borden threw back his head and laughed.

"If you don't want to see her broken body on the rocks below, I'd suggest you toss your weapon over the cliff and let us pass."

"You are in no position to issue orders," Connor replied.

"Neither are you," Borden snarled.

"Connor, please do as Lord Borden asks. I dinna want to die."

It wasn't like Cailin to show fear or to surrender, yet

her voice trembled when she spoke. Her eyes widened as she stared beyond him.

"I'd listen to the lady if I were you."

The sneer on Borden's face made Connor's blood boil. It took every ounce of self-control not to tear him apart with his bare hands.

"Connor, please, think of the babe." Cailin clutched at her belly, and her knees buckled.

Borden's eye widened as he frantically clutched the arrow protruding from his neck. He met Connor's gaze, then disappeared with a wild cry over the edge of the cliff.

Connor dropped his sword and lunged forward. His finger wrapped around Cailin's arm as she crumpled to the ground. He hauled her into his arms, cradling her against his chest. He glanced over his shoulder when Bryce stepped into the path with a bow in hand. "Good aim, brother."

"It was a lucky shot." He peered over the cliff, then nodded at his brother. "He'll never do anything to harm her again."

Connor looked down at Cailin, huddled in his arms. Her entire body trembled, and she buried her face against his chest. "You're safe, *liuadhe*." He closed his eyes and swallowed hard past the lump in his throat. The reality of how close he'd come to losing her hit him like a blow to the chest. He couldn't hold her tight enough, afraid if he let go, she'd vanish.

Cailin peered up at him with tear-filled eyes. "I was certain he'd kill me. That was until I saw Bryce hiding in the forest."

Connor rocked her in his arms. "He will never harm you again."

"Aye, but I am still wanted for murder. Now that Borden is dead, the truth dies with him. Longshanks will send someone else in his stead."

"No one will ever take you from me again. We will find

a way to clear your name, but in the meantime, we need to get you somewhere safe and warm." Connor lifted her in his arms and carried her toward the cart.

"Beauly is at least a five-day ride, and Buccleuch two hours. We will go back, so Fallon can see to you and the babe." He jumped onto the driver's seat and picked up the reins.

"What about Thor, and the wounded?" Bryce asked.

"You can bring Thor. How many wounded?" He'd been so worried about Cailin, he hadn't given any thought to the outcome of the battle.

"We lost Douglas, and John took an arrow to the shoulder. There are seven dead English soldiers and three wounded prisoners. The rest ran off."

"Alasdair?"

"He's fine."

"Tie the prisoners to a tree, and leave two men to guard them. See to John's injuries, and then bring him back to Buccleuch. I will ask Michael to send a garrison to gather the dead."

Chapter 25

Three months later, Fraser Castle.

Well-wishers filled the hall, and with the stage set, all Connor needed was his bride.

Bryce came up from behind and slid his hand over his brother's shoulder. "You look like you have seen St. Stephen's ghost."

Connor shifted his weight from one foot to the other and glanced toward the stairs. "What if she turns me down? After everything she has been through, I wouldn't blame her if she wants to end the handfast when the year is over."

"Then she'd finally be showing some sense. If she's smart, she'll run the other way while there is still time." Alasdair joined his brothers and let out a loud belly-laugh.

"Dinna pay him any mind. He's a buffoon and knows not what he says." Bryce glared at his oldest brother, then returned his attention to Connor. "The lass loves you, and you love her. She carries your babe, and nothing is going to change her mind about marrying you."

"I jest, brother." Alasdair reached into his sporran, and pulled out a small velvet sack. He grabbed Connor's wrist, dumped the content of the pouch into his brother's hand, and closed his fist around the ring and pendant. "A gift for your bride."

"These were our mother's." Connor gasped with surprise. "I forgot that you carried them with you for luck."

"She'd want Cailin to have them," Alasdair replied.

In keeping with tradition, their father gave his mother's

prized possessions to their oldest brother, Keith, the day after her funeral and bid he give them to his future wife. But with Keith's untimely death at Berwick on the Tweed, they were then passed down to Alasdair. Of great sentimental value, he'd carried them as a talisman, a good luck charm ever since.

"Thank you. She'll love them." Connor sputtered, choked by his brother's gesture. Cailin had never known her mother and after giving birth to five sons, his own mother had longed for a daughter over which she could fuss. He opened his hand and studied the ring, a delicate band of Celtic knots surrounding a thistle. The matching gold pendant held an emerald as green as Cailin's eyes. "Mother would have adored her, and the babe she carries."

"Mother would have spoiled them both. Since I never plan to marry and you are the clan chief, it only seems fitting they should go to your bride." Alasdair turned his head, wiping his hand across his eyes.

"You say that now. Wait until some beauty comes along and leaves you breathless. You'll be singing a different tune then," Bryce interjected.

Alasdair faced his youngest brother and grinned. "Are you trying to tell us something? Have you been bitten by the same bug as Connor? Mayhap seeing Fallon again has given you ideas."

"You're spouting nonsense as usual." Bryce glared at his brothers.

Alasdair gave Connor a knowing glance. "I told you he's smitten."

"Dinna be rushing, my lady, you've plenty of time. Just a few more steps and we'll be in the great hall." The lilting sound of Fallon's voice echoed down the stairs, interrupting the banter between the three brothers.

A hush fell over the room when Lady Scott rushed into the hall and brought her finger to lips—a signal for all to hold their tongues. "They are on their way down, and I'm sure Cailin has no idea what you're about." She looked at Connor and smiled.

"I am so glad you came for a visit, Fallon. Mayhap you can convince Laird and Lady Scott to stay until after my babe is born."

"Lady Scott told her husband she is not about to leave until she holds your wee one in her arms."

"I appreciate your help. At Connor's insistence, I have spent a good deal of time in bed these last few weeks. I'm afraid my legs are a wee bit shaky."

"It is to be expected when you are this far along. Take your time. There is no need to hurry," Fallon cautioned.

When Connor heard the conversation between the two women, he fought the urge to rush up the stairs and carry Cailin down the rest of the way. But to do so would spoil the surprise. If he could be patient a moment longer, she would be at his side, where she belonged. They'd exchange vows, then settle in for the largest *ceildh* the castle had ever seen.

When Fallon and Cailin reached the bottom of the stairs, and rounded the corner, a cheer burst from the crowd. Both women jumped. Cailin clutched at her chest and drew in a sharp gulp of air. "What is all of this?"

Connor stepped forward and took her hand. "Your wedding, *mo gaol*. If you'll have me."

"About time it is, too," Alasdair bellowed. "The wee lassie is near to bursting with your babe, and if you wait any longer, she will not be able to walk to the dais." A stab of Bryce's elbow directed at his ribs silenced him.

Cailin slid her hand over her swollen belly and smiled. "He speaks the truth. I've grown as large as a croft." She looked at the clergyman standing near the laird's table and her brow furrowed. "How can we marry without the reading of the banns? I have no dowry, and—"

Connor placed two fingers over her lips, silencing her.

"There is nothing to worry about. A priest can forego the reading of banns if there is just cause." His grin broadened as he stroked her belly. "Dinna be concerned about a dowry. I already have more wealth and own more land than I need. Having you by my side is reward enough. My life will be enriched beyond my wildest dreams." He dropped to one knee. "You are the most beautiful creature on the face of the earth, and you've held me spellbound since the day we met." He lifted her hand and pressed the back of it to his lips. "Before the Almighty and these witnesses, I ask you, Lady Cailin, of the Clan Macmillan, will you have me for your husband?"

"Aye, nothing would make me happier," she answered on a breathy sigh.

Michael Scott joined the couple at the foot of the stairs. "Come, the priest waits to perform the nuptials." He stepped aside, motioning with the sweep of his arm toward the dais where the clergyman waited.

"*Tha mise Connor Fraser, a-nis 'gad ghabhail-sa Cailin Macmillan gus an dean—*" He began his vows, but hesitated when he saw the tears rolling down her cheeks. "Are you not happy, *mo gaol*?"

She sniffled and raised her chin. "I'm very happy. Joy summons my tears, not sadness. My heart is about to burst with it. Since I was a wee lass, I've dreamed about this day, but never thought it would happen. I never dared to believe."

"Believe, *liuadhe*," Connor replied in a soothing voice. He tucked two fingers beneath her chin and brushed her lips with his own.

The priest coughed and cleared his throat. "Shall we continue?"

"Aye." He nodded and began his vows again. "I Connor Fraser, take you, Cailin Macmillan, to be my wife. I will honor you and protect you, until death sees fit to part us." His eyes searched hers as he waited for a reply—one she offered with equal sincerity and enthusiasm.

Caught up in the moment, Cailin put all of the fear, pain, and suffering of the last few months out of her mind, concentrating on her wedding vows, on her handsome husband, and their future as man and wife. He still hadn't told her that he loved her, but when Connor slipped the ring on her finger and draped the pendant around her neck, her heart leapt with such joy, she thought it would shatter with happiness. She stared at the ring and clutched the pendant with her free hand. "They're beautiful. Where did you get them?"

"They belonged to my mother, and to my father's mother before that. They've been in the Fraser family for more than two hundred summers. After our mother died, it was Da's wish that they be given to next Lady Fraser and passed on to the generations to come. It would please them both to know you wear them."

Tears rolled down her cheeks. "No one has ever given me such a wonderful gift. I will cherish them for as long as I live."

"Then it is way past due." He pressed his lips to her forehead, then to the ring on her hand. "Cailin, you are my heart and soul. I will protect and provide for you and our children all the days of my life."

With their vows said and the ceremony completed, he dipped his head and kissed his bride. Cheers and whistles filled the air when he slid his arm beneath her legs and lifted her. "Lady Fraser, it will be my pleasure to see you to the dais and later to our chamber." He didn't need to elaborate. The wolfish grin on his face said it all.

The heat of a blush rose in her cheeks. "You forget, husband, that I'm about bursting with your bairn. I hardly think you'll find me attractive or an alluring partner in your bed."

"On the contrary, wife, I have never been more aroused or enticed by a woman. Seeing you swollen with my babe fires a lust I can hardly contain." He dropped his head and kissed her soundly.

"That can wait until later." Michael laughed and patted Connor on the shoulder. "May I be the first to congratulate you on your nuptials Lady Fraser?" He took Cailin's hand, bowed, then looked at Connor with a raised brow. "To you, my friend, I wish happiness and many more babes."

"Thank you, Laird Scott." Still tucked securely in her husband's arms, Cailin rested her head on his chest. "You could put me down and let me walk."

"You will do as you're told, wife, and I will put you down when I'm ready." He carried her to the dais, set her on a chair, and sat in the one to her left.

Laird and Lady Scott joined them, as did Bryce and Alasdair. Michael remained standing and raised his tankard in the air. "May the best you've ever seen be the worst you've ever seen. May you always walk on the sunny side with much love and few cares. May you stay hale and hardy until you're old enough to die. And may you both be in Heaven before the devil knows you're gone. Long may your chimney smoke, and may the Almighty bless your home with more bairns than you can count. May—"

Lady Scott touched her husband's arm. "Enough said, my lord. If you keep haivering, they'll be old and grey, their bairn grown to a man before the toast is done."

He cleared his throat, and looked at the bride and groom. "Err...umm, as always, my wife has a point." Laird Scott concluded his speech, and then downed the contents of his tankard in one gulp.

Cheers erupted again throughout the hall, and every tankard was lifted in good wishes. In response, Connor rose to his feet and picked up his mug of ale. "I would like to thank Laird and Lady Scott for all they have done for us. We will be eternally grateful. Not only for the lodging you provided, but for your friendship." He raised his tankard in the air. "Please join me in a toast to good friends and to Scotland."

"*A Fraser*!" The crowd joined him in the clan war cry.

Connor took Cailin's hand and led her to the center of the hall. "May I have this dance, Lady Fraser? It is tradition for the bride and groom to—"

"I dinna think this is a good time to dance." She doubled over in pain. "My birth-water has broken and the babe comes."

"A birthing room is no place for a man. Leave us to do our work." Fallon blocked the door, refusing to let Connor in.

"I was present when the babe was created, and I'll be damned if you'll forbid me to be there when he's born. We've been through too much, and come too far. No one will keep me from her side. Now get out of my way, and let me go to my wife." He grasped Fallon's shoulders, moved her aside, and stepped into the chamber.

Lady Scott placed her hand on Connor's forearm. "Fallon is right. This is no place for a man. She could labor for hours, mayhap days."

"Then there's all the more reason for me to be at her side. You'll not sway me in this. I mean to stay. You have managed to keep me out for two hours, and bid me walk around the perimeter of the castle more times than I can count, but I will not be put off any longer." Ignoring the women's protest, he stormed across the chamber, but paused at the foot of the bed.

His heart clenched, and he balled his fists at his side. She was so small and frail, her body and night rail soaked with perspiration. Cailin thrashed about in delirium, moaning and mumbling his name. Unable to bear the sight of her suffering, he turned to Fallon. "Is there nothing you can do to ease her torment?" His voice was thick with emotion.

"Unfortunately, the pain is part of the birthing process. We must wait and let the Almighty decide her fate, and that of the babe." Fallon joined him beside the bed. "We put a knife under her mattress to cut the pain, and you've encircled the castle as we requested. I've prepared a tea of willow bark and comfrey, but she is too weak to drink it."

Connor sat on the edge of the bed. He lifted Cailin enough to slip in behind her and gathered her in his arms. "Give me the cup." He raised it to her lips and spoke softly. "You must drink this. It will ease your pain."

"Connor," she said in a raspy whisper.

"Aye, *liuadhe*, I'm here. You can do this. My son wishes to be born." He brought the cup to her lips.

After drinking her fill, her head dropped back against his chest. Tears welled in her eyes, and she released a soft sob.

"I know it hurts. If I could take the pain away or bear it for you, I would." He swept his fingers across her cheek, catching the tears as they fell.

"It is not the pain."

"Then tell me what has you so upset."

"You have your heart set on a son."

"Aye. All men wish for sons, but why should that distress you?"

"What if the babe is a lass?"

"A lass?" He paused to think about what she asked. She'd referred to the babe as a boy for so long, he'd started to do the same. He gazed into her eyes and smiled. "Then I would be the happiest man in all of Scotland. I would love to have a wee lassie to pamper and spoil—especially if she looks anything like her mother." He felt the air rush from her lungs as she released a sigh.

"You will not be disappointed if the babe is a lass?" She sniffled and peered up at him, her eyes wide and questioning.

"I'd love and cherish a daughter, as I do her mother." He pressed a kiss to her lips.

"You love me?"

"Aye, I love you more than my life. I thought you knew that."

Cailin closed her eyes and a smile crossed her lips. "I love you, too, Connor, with all my heart." Another contraction caused her back to arch and her belly to clench. She gripped his hand, and together they waited for the arrival of their child.

Late the next day, Connor paced the floor, his brow creased with worry. "Why hasn't she woken up? Five hours have passed since she gave birth." He turned to face Fallon, a small bundle wrapped in plaid nestled in his arms.

"She'll wake when ready," Fallon assured him. "She had a very rough go of it and needs to rest."

"What if she doesn't wake up?" Connor found it hard to hide the tension and worry in his voice.

"Dinna *fash,* Connor," Cailin muttered, her voice barely above a whisper. Her lashes fluttered against her ashen cheeks, then she slowly opened her eyes.

"I'm here, *mo gaol*...we're here." He sat on the bed beside her, just as the babe started to cry.

"The babe is hungry," Fallon announced with a smile.

"My babe." Cailin reached for the bundle her husband carried.

"Our son is a hale and hardy lad," Connor announced proudly. He placed the babe in her arms, then kissed her brow.

"A boy? We have a son?" Tears rolled down Cailin's

cheeks.

"Aye, and I'd like to name him Andrew Simon, after my father and cousin. I hope you approve."

"I think it is a wonderful name." She folded back the plaid, examining their son. He was the image of his father. After counting his fingers and toes, she looked up at Fallon. "He is so small. Are you certain he's all right?"

Fallon placed her hand on Cailin's shoulder and gave it a comforting squeeze. "He may be small now, but he'll grow quickly. I'm guessing that he'll be as tall as his da, and just as handsome. But let's hope he does not grow up to be as stubborn as the rest of the Fraser men."

Andrew let out a loud cry, as if in protest, and Connor laughed. "My son is hungry, a true Fraser." He held out his arms. "Give the lad to me. Fallon has arranged for a woman from the village to feed and care for him."

"Nay. I dinna want a nursemaid for my son." She clutched the babe against her breast.

Connor frowned, and stroked his hand across the lad's silken hair. "It is common place for the wife of a laird to have a wet-nurse tend her bairns. You need to rest and regain your strength."

"I wish to nurse my own babe. He will know my voice, my touch, my scent, and my love. When he cries, I will be the one who comforts him. I dinna have that with my mother, and our bairn will not suckle the teat of a stranger." Cailin slid her night rail off her shoulder and brought the babe to breast. He latched on right away.

"He takes after his da," Connor boasted.

"Men!" both women said in unison.

A knock at the door caught everyone's attention. "Who is it?" Fallon called out.

The door opened. "Can an uncle come in and offer his congratulations?" Bryce strolled across the room and stopped at the foot of the bed. "I'd also like to borrow my brother for a while, if that is all right with you, m'lady. Alasdair has opened a jug of our finest whisky and wishes to offer a toast to the wee laddie."

Cailin held the babe to breast, his blanket of plaid providing for her privacy. "Go. Once Andrew is fed, I plan to take a nap."

"I'll only be gone a short while, and then I'll join you." Connor leaned down and kissed her passionately.

"Don't you think it is a bit early to start working on another babe? Mayhap you should wait a while." Bryce's boisterous laugh echoed in the chamber.

"On the contrary. I'm hoping for a daughter next spring," Connor announced and stole another brief kiss. "What say you, wife?"

"I think it sounds wonderful." She lifted the babe to her shoulder and patted his back.

Fallon steered Bryce toward the door. "Let's leave them be. They might like a minute alone before you steal Connor away. I'll not take any arguments," she said firmly, and pushed him out of the room. "If you need anything, we'll be out in the hall." With that said, she closed the door behind her.

Connor slid his arm around Cailin's shoulders and pulled her against his chest. He placed a kiss atop Andrew's head of raven curls. The babe crinkled his nose and his dark brows knit together in a frown. When he wrapped his tiny fingers around his father's thumb, any doubt Connor had left about family, love, and commitment dissolved instantly. Cailin and Andrew were his life and his future. He planned to spend the rest of his days protecting them...loving them.

"Are you happy, wife?"

"Aye, husband. I am the happiest woman in Scotland. I never dreamed I would marry a man who loved me as much as I loved him. I never thought I would have a babe and a place to call home." She took his hand and brought it to her cheek. "I have all those things and more. My life is complete."

"And mine, *liuadhe*." He glanced down at Andrew. "The lad has blue eyes."

"All babes have blue eyes. I hope when he is grown, they'll be a beautiful brown like his father's. I fell in love with them the first time we met." Cailin gently touched her husband's cheek.

"On that same day, I fell madly in love with his mother."

Follow Bryce's story in HIGHLAND QUEST.

No longer content to live in the shadow of his older brothers and determined to continue his clan's support in the battle for Scotland's independence, Bryce Fraser rejoins the cause. But his quest to seek his destiny is thwarted by an unexpected reunion with Fallon, a beguiling woman he vowed to forget, and a confrontation with his nemesis, a traitorous man he swore an oath to kill. When Fallon's attempt to warn him of an impending attack puts them both in danger, Bryce is forced to make a choice between his duty and his heart.

CPSIA information can be obtained at www.ICGtesting.com
Printed in the USA
LVOW071920130712

290015LV00004B/1/P